P9-DEM-678

Praise for

ON TURPENTINE LANE

·‑⊱⊰‑·

"Light and tight, *On Turpentine Lane* is constructed with an almost scary mastery . . . The story folds out and back in as neatly as an origami flower, and Faith recounts it all with a raised eyebrow and plenty of cheek . . . A neat bourbon swapped for the usual rom-com grenadine." — *New York Times Book Review*

"The cleverly tangled plot — along with some snappy dialogue and a wry, likeable heroine — makes Lipman's latest a diverting delight." — *People*

"When there's already too much darkness in the world and a cheering respite is in order, we can all be glad for Elinor Lipman's *On Turpentine Lane,* a romantic comedy with just enough sly wit to keep it from turning sugary . . . We can trust that like her foremothers Jane Austen and Laurie Colwin, Lipman will find a way to make the world right for her heroine. Would that she could do so for the rest of us!" — *O, The Oprah Magazine*

"The novel's fast, funny dialogue keeps things light. Yes, that's the Lipman way: alerting us to cultural wrongs even while entertaining us with her cultural zingers . . . Lipman has taken lessons from our great chroniclers of the quotidian, from Geoffrey Chaucer to Jane Austen. The result, in *On Turpentine Lane,* provides a light but serious antidote to what ails us all these days." — *Washington Post*

"Genuine, deft, and witty, Lipman's *On Turpentine Lane* doesn't skewer American contemporary life as much as roast it . . . Lipman's neat plot twists and smart repartee propel the novel, but it is its sharp social observations and far-ranging curiosity that elevate it beyond the traditional romantic comedy into a work of real heft and charm."   — *National Book Review*

"[Lipman] has a way of crafting books so utterly charming that you want to set up residence inside them. And yet, in a seemingly effortless balance, she's never saccharine, but writes in a wry, warm, we're-all-friends-here-so-let's-have-a-drink tone . . . Like all of Lipman's books, *On Turpentine Lane* quickly becomes a friend."   — *Seattle Times*

"A new Elinor Lipman novel is always a cause for celebration . . . *On Turpentine Lane* is another pitch-perfect, delightful romantic comedy."   — *Pop Sugar*

"Tartly observational wit and a deep understanding of all-too-human foibles."   — *Buffalo News*

"Swift and smart."   — *Lowell Sun*

"With a witty cast of characters and her usual delightful dialogue and insightful observations of human behavior, Lipman captures the complications of modern love." — *Publishers Weekly*

"Lipman . . . is known for her dialogue, so snappy, funny, and real . . . [*On Turpentine Lane*] is warm, clever, and a lot of fun."   — *Kirkus Reviews*

"As loyal Lipman readers have come to expect, there are messages of hope, resilience, and discovery tucked behind the frothy rom-com scenes Lipman draws oh so well."   — *Booklist*

"Delightful! I read it in one day — truly a peak reading experience. Every page was packed with wonders."
— Maria Semple, author of *Today Will Be Different*, *Where'd You Go, Bernadette?*, and others

Praise for
ELINOR LIPMAN
·᠁᠁·

"I have not read an American writer who can do what Elinor Lipman does: take a poignant situation and transform it, in a moment of instant recognition, into something as wryly perfect as a *New Yorker* cartoon."   — Anita Shreve

"An author who was born with an autoimmune system already primed against clichés and an ear for dialogue sharper than an electronic listening system."   — *Times* (London)

"Up there at the top is where this enchanting, infinitely witty yet serious, exceptionally intelligent, wholly original, and Austen-like stylist belongs."   — Fay Weldon, *Washington Post*

"One of the last urbane romantics."
— Julia Glass, *Chicago Tribune*

"A full-fledged talent, a witty, compassionate chronicler of modern sensibility . . . Contemporary as Lipman is in her choice of setting and language, she is also a refreshingly old-fashioned writer who sets up on our expectations and then, by golly, delivers."   — *Boston Globe*

BOOKS BY ELINOR LIPMAN

Into Love and Out Again

Then She Found Me

The Way Men Act

Isabel's Bed

The Inn at Lake Devine

The Ladies' Man

The Dearly Departed

The Pursuit of Alice Thrift

My Latest Grievance

The Family Man

Tweet Land of Liberty: Irreverent Rhymes
from the Political Circus

The View from Penthouse B

I Can't Complain: (All Too) Personal Essays

On Turpentine Lane

ON TURPENTINE LANE

Elinor Lipman

Mariner Books
Houghton Mifflin Harcourt
BOSTON   NEW YORK

First Mariner Books edition 2018
Copyright © 2017 by Elinor Lipman
Q&A with Author © 2018 by Elinor Lipman

All rights reserved

For information about permission to reproduce selections
from this book, write to trade.permissions@hmhco.com or to
Permissions, Houghton Mifflin Harcourt Publishing Company,
3 Park Avenue, 19th Floor, New York, New York 10016.

hmhco.com

Library of Congress Cataloging-in-Publication Data
Names: Lipman, Elinor, author.
Title: On Turpentine Lane / Elinor Lipman.
Description: Boston : Houghton Mifflin Harcourt, 2017.
Identifiers: LCCN 2016002265 (print) | LCCN 2016006171 (ebook) |
ISBN 9780544808249 (hardcover) | ISBN 9780544808270 (ebook) |
ISBN 9781328745583 (pbk.)
Subjects: LCSH: Man-woman relationships—Fiction. | BISAC: FICTION /
General. | FICTION / Contemporary Women. | FICTION / Humorous. |
FICTION / Jewish. | GSAFD: Humorous fiction. | Love stories.
Classification: LCC PS3562.I577 O5 2017 (print) | LCC PS3562.I577 (ebook) |
DDC 813/.54—dc23
LC record available at http://lccn.loc.gov/2016002265

Book design by Kelly Dubeau Smydra

Printed in the United States of America
DOC 10 9 8 7 6 5 4 3 2 1

The author is grateful for permission for the use of "In This Short Life" from
The Poems of Emily Dickinson: Variorum Edition, edited by Ralph W. Franklin,
Cambridge, Mass.: The Belknap Press of Harvard University Press, copyright
© 1998 by the President and Fellows of Harvard College. Copyright © 1951,
1955 by the President and Fellows of Harvard College. Copyright © 1979, 1983
by the President and Fellows of Harvard College. Copyright © 1914, 1918,
1919, 1924, 1929, 1930, 1932, 1935, 1937, 1942 by Martha Dickinson Bianchi.
Copyright © 1952, 1957, 1958, 1963, 1965 by Mary L. Hampson.

For Jonathan

1

What Possessed Me?

I F I HADN'T BEEN NAÏVE and recklessly trusting, would I ever have purchased number 10 Turpentine Lane, a chronic headache masquerading as a charming bungalow? "Best value in town," said the ad, which was true, if judging by the price tag alone. I paid almost nothing by today's standards, attributing the bargain to my mother's hunch that the previous owner had succumbed while in residence. Not so off-putting, I rationalized; don't most people die at home? On moving day my next-door neighbor brought me a welcome loaf of banana bread along with the truth about my seller. *A suicide attempt . . . sleeping pills . . . she'd saved them up till she had enough, poor thing. And who could blame her?* "Strong as an ox," she added. "But a whole bottle?" She tapped the side of her head.

"Brain damage?" I asked. "Brain *dead?*"

"Her daughter had to make that awful decision long distance."

I'd negotiated and settled with that very daughter. Sadder and spookier than I bargained for? A little. But now I know it was an act more logical than tragic — what a sensible ninety-year-old felon might consider the simplest way out.

I first viewed the property through rose-colored glasses on a sunny October day. There was a brick path leading to the front door, a trellis supporting what might have been August's wisteria, and a gnarled tree that hinted at future fruit. Inside I saw gumwood that hadn't been ruined by paint and a soapstone sink that a decorator might install in a Soho loft. The linoleum beneath my feet made me want to look up the year linoleum was invented.

The real estate agent, who said she'd gone to high school with my brother, had been Tammy Flannagan then, was now divorced. How was Joel? Divorced, too, she'd heard.

"He's fine," I said, somewhat distracted by the carved pineapple on top of the newel post, yet another harbinger of domestic tranquility.

There was hardly anything to see on the second floor, just a bathroom from another century, and two square, darkly wallpapered bedrooms facing each other, one with a view of the street, the other overlooking the miniature backyard. The bathroom had a claw-foot tub, its porcelain yellowed and its plug desiccated. The small sink had separate hot and cold faucets, which, Tammy insisted, were back in style.

I asked which one had been the master bedroom.

"Does it matter? They're equal in square footage," said Tammy.

"It might matter to someone who'd rather sleep in a room where nobody died."

She pointed silently to the back room, then directed my gaze to a hatch in the hall ceiling. "When you open that, there's a ladder you can pull down."

"Then what?"

"The attic."

"Have you seen it?"

"Me personally? No. Someone from my office did, of course. I've been told it's empty and dry. Want to see the cellar?"

I knew cellars were important — their foundations, water heaters, boilers, pipes, mousetraps — so I said, "Sure."

"May need updating," said Tammy, "but everything's in good working order. This is a little doll house. I'd buy it myself if I wasn't already in contract for a condo."

I thought I should add, hoping to sound nonchalant about the property, "I'm engaged to be married. This would be fine for a single person, but I really need a bigger place."

She helped herself to my ringless left hand, then dropped it without comment. I said, "We're not a very traditional couple."

"Congratulations anyway," said Tammy. "Do you want to make an appointment to come back with him? Or her."

"A man, Stuart. He's away."

"On business?"

His absence was hard to explain and harder to make sense of, so I just said yes.

Whether it was the impulse to change the subject or sound less like the real estate novice that I was, I said, "I couldn't even think of moving forward without an inspection."

But I'd already made up my mind. "A little doll house" sounded exactly right to me. Two bedrooms would be plenty, and I preferred baths to showers. There was a gas stove, green milk-glass mugs hanging from cup hooks, a one-car garage, leaded glass in the china closet, and a price that seemed too good to be true. So on that day, like someone who bought and sold properties with abandon, whose profession was flipping houses, I offered two-thirds of the asking price.

Tammy said, "Well, honestly, I don't even think I can take that offer to the seller."

I reminded her that this was a one-bath cottage, surely uninsulated, with an antique boiler and a postage stamp of a backyard. I'd have to start from scratch. "The wallpaper must be from the 1950s," I scolded, at the same time thinking, *I love that viny wallpaper.*

Tammy looked up at the ceiling fixture, a white globe that was not unhandsome, and said, "I suppose I have to present your offer. Expect a counteroffer if she's not too insulted to make one."

"Every inch of this place needs updating. It's my final offer. And it's not like I'm in love with the place," I lied.

It took one phone call, a counteroffer that I spurned, a fax, a signature, a return fax, and a relatively small check. On the other side was a lawyer representing the uninterested daughter five time zones away.

My counsel added to the purchase and sale agreement a sentence that struck me as curious: that if the lending bank refused to close for any reason — unrelated to my finances — I could back out.

"Is this standard?" I asked.

"Boilerplate," she answered.

Simple. I signed it.

2

·ⓒ⪖⪗ⓥ·

A Different Man

THE AFOREMENTIONED FIANCÉ was out of town for an indefinite period because he was walking across the continental United States. His purported goal was not necessarily the Pacific Ocean, but finding his own path in life. It wasn't just his mission statement but how he talked, on the road or off, raising consciousness, searching for awesomeness in the everyday.

People often looked perplexed when I tried to explain Stuart's expedition or what I saw in him. There was a time during the period I call Stuart 1.0 when his Instagrams almost exclusively chronicled our dates and were followed by a festival of hashtags expressing affection and devotion. There was a thoughtfulness that I saw as a predictor of husbandly attentiveness; there was a full-time job with the Massachusetts Department of Transitional Assistance that paid for the tickets and trinkets he hid rather adorably around my apartment.

As for the arena I'll delicately call "relations" — had I been dealing with amateurs before him?

But he changed — and "overnight" isn't an exaggeration. He started using words such as *potentiality* and *wholeness* after an emergency appendectomy. During his recovery, he quizzed anyone in scrubs until a nurse confirmed, "Yes, it could have ruptured; yes, people can die from that." He emerged from his hospital stay a different man. It wasn't organic or neurological, but social, a rebirth inspired by the free soul in the next bed whose worldview sounded good to Stuart, postsurgically, supine, and dangerously close to turning forty.

I gave it some time — accepting the new, softer, vegetarian Stuart 2.0. When friends heard about his walk and asked me if he was a nonconformist or a nut, I told them that this was just a new lifelong goal, to find himself by crossing the country on foot, a sabbatical of sorts after his agency had closed its doors.

I agreed to be one of his sponsors in the form of a jointly held credit card, which he vowed to use sparingly if at all. His quest sounded sincere: his embrace of everything and everybody, whether it was scenery or wildlife, or the people who offered him a couch, an indoor shower, a sandwich. I was skeptical that his lightweight cause would attract the goodwill and hospitality needed. But sure enough, thanks to coverage by local TV stations, big-hearted families stopped their cars to ask what they could do. I knew when he'd failed to find free lodging, because those were the days he blogged about constellations or the howling of coyotes, which meant he'd slept in his pup tent under the stars.

He wore a sign that said IN SEARCH OF STORIES on one side and, when flipped, FREE HUGS in Spanish and English. At last count, he'd slept in three unlocked churches, one synagogue, one mosque, a few shelters, and several fraternity houses. Because he believed it's dangerous to text while walking, he checked in less frequently than I liked. We talked several times a week unless his battery was dead or he'd had too much to drink, which happened while staying with frat boys, current or emeritus. When challenged about what was looking to me like debauchery, he said what *he'd* look like to his hosts was judgmental if he didn't partake. And wasn't the whole journey about "walking two moons in another man's moccasins?" I was thirty-two. I wasn't getting any younger. I said yes, I suppose so.

After four months on the road, he'd gotten only as far as Ohio. Have I mentioned that his mom was now married to her ex-sister-in-law, that his forsaken dad and uncle were remarried to women who founded a weavers' collective, making Stuart the only child of three hippie families? When he first proposed this cross-country walk, I said, "Why don't we drive across the U.S.? It can be our honeymoon."

"Oh, really?" he said. "Maybe we can stop by Niagara Falls and Disney World in our RV."

I should have recognized by his tone that he was being facetious, that suggesting a road trip by car not only bore little resemblance to the fulfillment he was seeking but also exposed me as a comfort-seeking, conventional vacationer who had the word *honeymoon* in her vocabulary.

Whereas his various parents put a good face on it, as I tried to do, my mother was openly cynical. She enjoyed asking, "Where's Peter Pan this week? Meeting some nice potheads he'll never see again?" I'm sure it would've been fine if Stuart had been a doctor or a banker, but since he was merely, of late, a self-styled philosopher who proposed without a little velvet box, she worried that he was using me. At the time, I thought that couldn't be further from the truth, that Stuart wasn't interested in material things, only love, moral support, and occasional infusions of cash to complete his journey.

No one, including me, was thrilled that he was twice divorced from the same woman, but I did make the argument that men who get all the way to forty without commitments are the true Lost Boys of this world.

I commented regularly under Stuart's blog entries, signing every one "Faith." His gratitude seemed excessive, always thanking me for logging on and going public with my commitment to his cause. It made me wonder if he'd forgotten that Faith was my first name.

3

Stewardship

I HAD MOVED BACK to Everton, Massachusetts, from Brooklyn to take what appeared to be a stress-free job at my alma mater. My duties continue to be these: if you make a donation to Everton Country Day, especially if it funds a scholarship or endows a chair or names a prize after a loved one, I handwrite the thank-you note that describes all the good your money is doing.

Stewardship, as my position is called, is three-fourths of a whole job, with the remaining quarter understood to be beating the bushes for the annual fund. All of that makes my presence required at alumni cocktail parties and reunions, which I admit played a role in my accepting the job due to a social dry spell. In fact, Stuart and I met at an Everton function, not the most felicitous first encounter. I stopped him at the door because he was not on the guest list and was wearing a T-shirt depicting a silk-screened tuxedo, whereupon he defended it as a perfectly reasonable interpretation of "black tie optional." When I realized he was the plus-one of a Silver Circle benefactor, the category designating gifts between $5,000 and $9,999, I apologized profusely.

Since joining the team, I've shared an office with Nicholas Franconi, whose bailiwick is Major Gifts. He was more senior on the job than I by six months; he himself was something of what we in Development call a "get" because he used to raise money for Phillips Exeter Academy. When anyone asked why the change, he'd say, "I did it for love," then add, with a smile, "for Everton Country Day."

In what Nick liked to call "Stuartship," I taped a map of the U.S. on our office wall, like the ones in old movies, on which families followed their sons on the front. My pins, of course, represented Stuart's progress. Soon I was sorry I ever started it because a sliver of an inch equaled hundreds of miles, and with Stuart on foot, nothing changed very fast.

Nick made a joke every time I stuck another pushpin into the map. "Voodoo?" he asked. Or "One small step for a man, a giant leap for . . . remind me?" I didn't mean to laugh, shouldn't have found it endlessly amusing, might even have taken offense on Stuart's behalf, but I'd been having more and more trouble defining the what and why of the alleged mission. Because of Nick's job, arm-twisting for major gifts, I once asked him if he thought Stuart could find a corporate sponsor.

"Nothing's impossible," he answered. Then, after several minutes, all innocence: "Bill and Melinda Gates would surely be interested in such a meaningful pilgrimage."

It struck me as something my mother would say, except that Nick's quip was accompanied by a wry smile. Abandoning that line of inquiry, I asked how his live-in girlfriend's work was going, perhaps a little ungenerous of me since I knew Brooke was underemployed. Between full-time jobs, after having been a manager for two defunct boutiques, she sells high-end handbags on eBay, none of which I'd bought. They're all oversize, decorated with hardware; many are fringed in a cowgirl manner or are "unconstructed," according to the listing.

Nick admitted the goods didn't reflect her taste, either, but retailing was all about knowing what sells, what goes in the window, and proper signage. At that point, after three months in Development, I hadn't met Brooke. He didn't bring her to what he considered work functions, just the way I couldn't bring the absent Stuart. Nick's screen saver was a family photo of the two of them with a dog who's since run away, all three wearing sunglasses. Both Brooke and the dog had layered honey-colored hair. She looked pretty — fit and flexible, arms bare and tanned. The humans are grinning, and quite adorably Tramp is baring his gums in what looks like a matching smile.

One of the reasons Nick was drawn to Brooke was her pragmatism, he once mentioned. I asked for a definition.

"She's a bottom-line kind of gal. She likes her creature comforts and is willing to work for them."

Was that a good thing? I knew what he was implying: that employment was an important attribute in a partner or future spouse. Was he sending me a message that there was something he'd missed about Stuart that recommended him for the Gold, Silver, or Bronze Circle of my affection?

It would be the very thing *I* was missing: the original Stuart, the formerly attentive, employed, unphilosophical, sexually solicitous fiancé I used to know.

4

Inspection

WAS I SUPPOSED to have noticed the curled roof shingles, the severed ropes in half of the window pulleys, the pilot lights requiring personal igniting, the bird's nest in the chimney, the asbestos insulating the pipes? It took an inspector, a friend of my brother's — as was everyone in Everton to some degree — who shook his head sadly with each new prod from his inventory of inspection tools.

"Deal breaker?" I asked, watching him click a light switch on and off to no avail.

"Not my call," he said. "I just write a report. People buy all kinds of places. But you might want to check what your P and S says about the inspection."

"What would I want it to say?"

"That you have an out."

Had my original visit been too hasty? Too starry-eyed? I called my lawyer from the front porch and got her paralegal, who said she'd look up the purchase and sale agreement. "Good news," I heard after a musical interlude. "You have our default inspection clause."

"Which means what?"

"That you don't have to go through with it."

"What if I want to?"

"Everything's negotiable."

"Don't do anything yet," I instructed.

I went back inside, called to Joel's friend — a softball teammate, it turned out —"Wally? How's it going?"

His answer, not more than a grunt, sounded farther away than just one floor. Mystery solved: the ladder that led to the crawl space was now dominating the hallway between the bedrooms. "You're brave," I yelled up to him from the bottom rung.

"Not in the least," he answered.

"Is there a light?"

"Flashlight. Mine."

"Can you stand up?"

"Almost."

"They told me it was dry and empty. Is it?"

"Dry enough. Clean. Pretty empty. Some stuff."

A snapshot at that moment would have captured me with a dreamy smile, antiques floating in my mind's eye. A steamer trunk? A dressmaker's form? A trove of love letters? A Flexible Flyer? "Anything good?" I called.

"A whatchamacallit — a cradle."

"Is it a nice one? I mean, an antique?"

"People expect me to know stuff like that. I don't."

I figured, at best, hand carved and charming. At worst, I'd put it out on the curb with a sign that said FREE.

Sometimes things work out because it's in the stars or because a smart real estate lawyer picks up her phone. In my case, the break came from the deceased seller's distant daughter, who must've seen a future filled with more dud inspections and thought Faith Frankel might be 10 Turpentine Lane's only hope.

My lawyer called me at work, and gushed, "Are you sitting down?" Before I could answer, she said, "The seller is paying for all the fixes. For the roofing, the asbestos removal, the stuck windows. She didn't budge on the stove's pilot lights, but that was an easy gimme. What else? Doesn't matter. She's taking care of just about everything we asked for."

I said, "I didn't expect this! I thought you'd talk me out of the deal."

"I first tried to knock another fifteen grand off the purchase price, and this was her counteroffer! Who wants to have to hire all those people and coordinate the repairs?"

"Did you accept?"

"Not without running it by you. I'm going to ask that we choose the contractor so you don't get some unlicensed handyman."

"When will all this happen?"

"The work? ASAP. Before you take possession. I mean, you can move in before every little thing is fixed, but what's the rush? You don't want to be there with asbestos being excavated and a racket on the roof."

"But it's officially mine now?"

"If you still want it, and all the contingencies are met . . . absolutely."

"Yes, I want it. Tell them my answer is yes to the repairs. It's off the market, right?"

"Definitely. Besides . . . no, never mind. It's nothing. We're fine."

I knew her unspoken words were *No one else had given this house a second look, let alone made an offer.*

I didn't care. Even if it was the mangy one-eyed shelter dog of real estate listings. To me that made it all the more lovable.

Both Joel and my mother came for the walk-through the day before we closed. Tammy the agent was present, but I led the tour, pointing out my favorite features. The newel post! The leaded glass in the china cabinet — a *corner* china cabinet. The pantry. Who gets a pantry anymore? A clothesline in the basement! Hardwood floors in the bedrooms.

"Not sure if pine is considered hardwood," Joel volunteered, then opened the nearest window — still stubborn despite new ropes and pulleys.

"Does it smell a little musty in here?" my mother asked.

I pointed out that cold air would fix that; let's open another window and get some cross ventilation.

"Has Stuart seen it?" my mother asked. And to Tammy, employing a tone I recognized purely as a way to dispense with her spinster daughter's social status, "Stuart is Faith's fiancé."

I pretended to be studying the unexciting view of the driveway from the parlor window until I came up with "Not an issue. Stuart gave me power of attorney."

"That sounds right," said Joel.

"Who did you say was the previous owner?" my mother asked Tammy.

"A Mrs. Lavoie."

"Widowed?"

"I should think so — she was at least ninety!" I said.

"Children?"

"One. In Hawaii."

"Nieces or nephews? No one close by?"

"Ma! What's with the third degree?"

"If it's the title you're worried about," said Tammy, "everything's in order. No one but Mrs. Lavoie's family owned this house. Her in-laws came here as newlyweds, and apparently she and her husband took it over when the parents died."

"Did they die *here* by any chance?" my mother asked.

Tammy said, "That I don't know."

"Do you know what year it was built?" asked my mother.

I was too annoyed to do anything but sputter, "It was 1906, okay? Would you like to count the rings on the trees in the backyard?"

"Don't be so sensitive," said my mother. "You know I'm interested in genealogy."

"Since when?" asked Joel.

"As I've said so many times, it's a little doll house, don't you think?" Tammy cooed.

"And it does have what one might call personality," said my mother. "Have I said that yet? Nearly charming. I can see the appeal . . . for you."

Joel laughed. I'd taken a half day off for this walk-through and signing, and soon these five and a half rooms would be officially mine. Wait till my New York friends heard that I'd bought a whole house with two bedrooms, an eat-in kitchen, a parlor, a claw-foot tub, a backyard, and a garage for the price of a studio in Queens. As soon as the house was spruced up, I'd invite everyone to Everton for a housewarming. So far, no one knew that Stuart had proposed. Though I'd pictured a squealing dinner in a Dumbo café, with the sudden appearance of pink champagne, I'd hold on to that announcement. It's the kind of news you want to tell your friends in person.

5

The Secret Life of Henry Frankel

H OW DID MY FATHER feel about Stuart? Unfortunately, or maybe fortunately, they'd never met because my allegedly happily married father and mother had lived apart since Dad retired, just as Stuart was heading sort of west. For many months no one adequately explained why Dad had moved out, except for the wishy-washy reassurances that this was not an official separation. He dined with my mother a few times a month, and with Joel and me about half that. Once we learned of his semimonthly visits with Mom, Joel jumped right in and asked if their sleepovers were conjugal.

"I told you. He pays the bills and mows the lawn, just like always."

Joel asked me in private, "Do you think Dad moved out so he could fool around?"

I said, "Ask him."

When we did see our dad, it was in Boston, at restaurants. We talked in generalities — about my work, about Stuart's progress, about towing and plowing, which was Joel's latest business ven-

ture. In retrospect, I see that we assumed that life in his little
Gainsborough Street studio was too sad to ask about — just TV,
the Sox, the Patriots, beer, and General Tso's chicken too many
times per week.

I began calling the situation "The Secret Life of Henry Frankel," which I'd reference even in front of my mother. Finally,
several months into the allegedly friendly separation, she said,
"He's made himself very clear. He wanted to paint, and he
needed a studio."

I said, "You're just telling us now? Since when did Dad want
to paint?"

"Since . . . I don't know. It was his big retirement plan: paint
every day, all day. The place is a mess, but he doesn't mind squalor. I mean, it's artistic squalor. With oil paint, there's no easy
cleanup."

"You've been there?"

"I helped him choose it. Correction: he allowed me to come
along when he was being shown some garrets."

Joel said, "Well! Don't Faith and I have the most evolved
parents! I guess we shouldn't have been worried about you
and blaming Dad and, let's be honest, thinking he had a girlfriend —"

"Or a boyfriend," I added.

We were at my mother's kitchen table, drinking sherry from
cordial glasses, the only alcohol on hand. "He says it's all about
painting," she said. "I have a spouse who's married to his art."

"And how are you doing with this?" I asked.

"I'm adjusting. It might be a phase he's going through. Remember when he threw himself into golf? I was a golf widow for
two straight summers. Now he doesn't even go to the driving
range."

Joel said, "All of a sudden the father I've known for thirty-four years is a painter?"

"Do you know what abstract expressionism is? I believe that's the term he used."

Joel asked me — or did I ask him? — "Is it possible for two adult children *not* to know that their father is an abstract expressionist?"

"How could you have known? I don't think *he* even knew," our mother said.

"Have you seen his work?" I asked.

"Pictures of it. He e-mails me a photo when he finishes one." Less than eagerly, she asked, "Would you want to see some?"

Joel said, "I'm not sure."

I said, "I would."

As soon as she left the room, he whispered, "They could be shit."

She returned holding snapshots, three by fives, one in each hand. "I get these made up from his e-mails," she said. "They do that at CVS while you wait."

She gave one to each of us. Mine was a photo of an easel, on which sat a small unframed canvas depicting a gold square sitting on top of an orange square with a horizontal crimson stripe between them. Joel and I swapped; the other was orange on top of purple with a turquoise stripe between. I said, "I like these. They look happy."

"Why wouldn't they? Happy painter, happy paint."

Joel emitted something like a *hmmmff*.

"Is this public knowledge?" I asked. "That he paints? Can I tell him we saw these?"

Our mother asked, "How about this: I'll tell Norman Rockwell that I showed you two pictures from his Orange Suite, and you really liked them. Is that an accurate statement — that you like them?"

I said yes. Joel took another look, and said, "Okay, me, too."

I asked her when the artist was next coming to dinner.

She squinted in the direction of the wall calendar, each month showcasing another dairy product from the local creamery. "I invited him for Friday, for beef Stroganoff, but he hasn't confirmed."

"If it's on, could we come, too?"

"I can't on Friday. I have a date," said Joel.

Of course, that triggered the instant engagement of my mother's and, to an only slighter degree, mine.

"Is it someone new?" she asked.

"It's always someone new," I said.

I texted Stuart about the discovery: **Mystery solved. Dad left bec he wants 2 paint. oil on canvas, abstract, mom OK w it so way better than I thought. Miss u.**

I didn't like using the abbreviations of a twelve-year-old, but Stuart believed it was stuffy to spell things out if you could get by with less, just like in life. He texted back the next morning, **Was this 4 me?**

6

Pointers

WHEN IT CAME to Joel's social life, sometimes my mother and I could hover. Especially me, since I was subletting a one-bedroom apartment two floors above his until I took possession of my bungalow. He'd been married at thirty and divorced a year later, the innocent party, which I say not out of blind loyalty but as fact. He had the bad luck to fall for an adultery-prone woman named Brenda, whom the rest of the family considered unworthy.

I'd love him to meet someone deserving of his big unlucky heart. He isn't the most conventionally attractive or fittest guy in the world, but for those who notice, his face wears his goodness quite handsomely.

Growing up only eighteen months apart, our solicitousness is a two-way street. The same night I told him about what I called our engagement and what Stuart characterized as "our promise," Joel asked for the play-by-play. "Set the stage for me," he said, taking a first sip from his dessert, a chocolate martini. "It's research, in case I meet someone. All pointers welcome."

I tasted his drink then ordered one of my own. "It happened the night before he left on his quest. We were having takeout from Peaceable Nation at my place, and we'd had a bottle of wine. And he quite literally asked for my hand. 'Right? Left?' I asked. First he snapped off a piece of the fringe from the scarf he was wearing — red cotton, made in India — then took my left hand and tied the thread around the fourth finger.

"*I* said, 'Is this what I think it is?'

"'It's a placeholder.'

"'For . . .'

"'For when I'm back.'

"'And then . . .'

"'We'll be together, under one roof.' He patted my hand. 'Good fit? Not too tight?'

"I said, 'It's perfect. A metaphor.' I wanted to ask whether the 'under one roof' meant as husband and wife, or just roommates. But I didn't want to spoil the moment. Instead, I asked, 'Would it be okay if I replaced it with something a little sturdier?'

"He told me that was his intention, of course; that's what he meant by 'placeholder.' He said the red was no accident, that it had major symbolic heft in many religions and cultures.

"I asked, 'And when you're back, were you thinking we'd live here or at your place?' He said he was subletting his apartment during his hegira, and the lessee had signed on for six months, renewable verbally or by text in six-month intervals up to eighteen months."

I didn't tell Joel the rest, that we'd made farewell love in a new position that Stuart said he'd learned from kabbalah teachings, and in the morning, his departure documented with photos destined for Facebook and Instagram, he set out more or less west. I'd made him three cheese sandwiches and three peanut butter and honey ones on pita bread. He said he'd eat dropped fruit that he'd source from orchards along the way, so just an apple and a banana to start with.

After he left, I looked up *hegira*. I don't think he knew that its dictionary definition was "a journey, especially when undertaken to escape from a dangerous or undesirable situation." Over the next few weeks, I switched from red thread to string to yarn and back to string when the wool made my finger itch. The infirmary's nurse questioned my needing hydrocortisone cream when I could simply remove the irritant. I called Stuart and told him of my dilemma.

I must have woken him. "Red thread?" he repeated, his voice a little thick. "Remind me."

7

Halloween

I'D STAYED HOME, giving out generous amounts of candy to the mere half-dozen trick-or-treaters in the apartment complex. Between visitors, I was reading Stuart's Facebook posts, noticing he was looking thinner, which didn't worry me since he was walking the equivalent of a half marathon every day. His tan was deepening despite his safari hat, his SPF precautions, and the fact that it was late October. Though I made a point of "liking" all of his Facebook pictures, many I actually hated. He seemed to be running into old girlfriends and every female classmate from social work school; one might even have deduced that his route was not a spontaneous meander but a romantic scavenger hunt. I didn't want to make an issue of his socializing with women he once dated, but each post unsettled me. I reminded myself that he chose me, committed himself to me; that I was the one with the red string around my finger. And only those closest to him — his parents and I — had our credit cards in his wallet.

I didn't want to be seen as a jealous partner, and it was hard to argue with "Am I not supposed to see/talk to/have a drink with interesting and accomplished women just because I'm not dating them anymore?"

I didn't quibble with the "accomplished" because he would judge me a snob. Stuart claimed to be unimpressed by fame or degrees or job titles, especially if the latter fell into categories he considered conventional. He once said that if he had to be on a desert island with only one person and the choices were a doctor or a nurse, he'd pick the latter. Or between a college professor and a kindergarten teacher? A football player or a cheerleader? In every case, he favored the less-lettered alternative.

Our engagement hadn't gone public. Once I asked why, among all the signs he held up in photos, one never says LOVE YOU, FAITH! Or even just HI, FAITH? He said it was because the signs were a team-building tool. He had a public persona, and — as with actors and celebrities — being *perceived* as unattached helps with socializing, which may lead to cash contributions, a necessary evil along his journey.

I tried his cell. He said he couldn't talk — he was with hair and makeup at a cable TV station in Terre Haute.

"While you're there, charge your phone so when you call me back —"

"Babe, gotta go. Seriously."

He did call back after the interview, but not immediately; in fact, he woke me up. His greeting was "I hit the jackpot! The TV station is putting me up at a Hilton Garden Inn! I'm calling from the tub!"

I said something I'd never said to him, or to anyone over the phone, ever, maybe now from some altered sleep state, "Are you naked?"

I was expecting his answer to be at least a little encouraging. Such as "Why do you ask?" or "What are *you* wearing?" But all he said was "I'm in the tub, dummy. Of course I'm naked."

I said, "Oh. Just trying to get a picture."

Another guy might have said, "Really? Want a picture? I can do that." But what I heard was "I think I was pretty good tonight. The reporter was giving me the usual tests about my motive, about what I was trying to accomplish, and I told her I was in the business of seeking kindness. That it wasn't just for myself, but what I'd discovered was that the dispensers of kindness or generosity or a thumb's-up from behind the wheel or support in the form of cash came away feeling better about themselves. And she said, 'So you're giving forward?' which was really a great takeaway. I said, 'Exactly.'"

I said, "Stuart? I'm in bed. I wish you were here."

"Me, too, babe."

"I've never had phone sex, but I can guess that one person in bed and another one in the bathtub would be a good start."

I heard the slurp of the drain. "I can't go there, babe. It's been a really long day, and you wouldn't believe how clean sheets and HBO appeal to me. And you know, of course, that the government constantly monitors cell phone conversations. There's no such thing as privacy anymore."

I said, "I have nothing to hide. And wouldn't it be just some noises we made? I don't think I'd be using actual words."

He said, "I have another call. Gotta take this! It's the producer from tonight!"

"Call me back —"

Maybe the station had gotten good feedback and possibly contributions. I left my bed and went to my laptop. His last blog entry had been posted at what he described as "twilight."

I'm seeing kids on the streets of Terre Haute in masks and costumes & here are the messages I'm taking away: violence, gender bias, racism, missogyny, war, sexpot, Hollywood, commercial, commercial, commercial, so I started thinking of this 1 thing and couldn't get it out of my head . . . where are those little boxes kids carry while Trick or Treating, where you ask for money for Unicef instead of candy? If your reading this and its not too late — ask your kids if they really need candy or do they realize that some children have never tasted one single piece of candy in their whole war torn life? Plus they have TB, malaria and worse.

Peace,
Stuart

Not feeling terribly indulgent, I commented, "You can't just send kids out asking for money without the official UNICEF box. BTW, they get candy, too. What kid is going to ask for JUST money?"

Naturally, I was having trouble falling back to sleep. It was 11:45, too late to call one of the girlfriends I'd been neglecting since meeting Stuart, so I texted Joel, who'd had an all-important date — all-important because it was his first online venture — membership having been my birthday gift to him. **How was tonight?** I wrote.

I had to wait until morning for the return call, which I mistakenly took for a good sign. "No go" was his greeting.

"Okay. Tell me everything."

"I get to the restaurant, and she's sitting at the bar dressed like an Indian maiden —"

"You're joking."

"It was her Halloween getup, supposedly on her way to a party afterward. I walked over, and said, 'Nice to see you, Pocahontas. I'm John Smith.'"

"Good line."

"Maybe. If she'd gotten it. But she had no clue that I was talking Jamestown. She thought it was my name even though my e-mails were all signed 'Joel.'"

"Then what?"

"I told her I was just making a little Virginia Colony joke. John Smith was an actual person, and supposedly Pocahontas saved his life. I could tell she was embarrassed so I said, 'Well, I could've been another total stranger named John Smith. No harm done.' I sat down, ordered a martini."

"Then?"

"She asked what I did. I said I have my own business. 'Such as?' I said, 'Plowing and towing.' That did it. She had to go to her Halloween party about ninety seconds after that."

"And you think that was it — your job?"

"I know it was. She actually said, 'I'm a teacher with a master's degree. I hope you understand, but I don't see myself with a truck driver.'"

"Then I hate her," I said.

"Thank you. I will, too."

"But don't give up. Keep answering those winks, or smiles, or whatever they're called."

"I will if you will," he said.

I asked him what that meant.

"Test the waters. See what's out there. What's the harm, with Stuart out of the picture?"

Maybe I didn't correct that as fast as I should have; maybe I'd had the same thought myself but in a distinctly hypothetical way. "He's only out of *town*. We're engaged —"

First I heard an impatient huff, followed by a killjoy "Sometimes I wonder."

I asked him how long he'd been having doubts about Stuart and me ending up together.

"You don't want to know," he answered. "The real question is are *you* having doubts?"

I could hardly admit that I'd suggested phone sex and had been spurned, so I told him that he was catching me when I was a little sick of seeing my fiancé with his arm around a different woman every day.

"Have you told him to cut that out?"

"He knows."

"But he posts that shit anyway?" Before I could answer, Joel asked, "What would happen if you cooled it? I mean would Stuart say no way? Or would he say, 'Babe, I didn't want to be the one, but . . .'"

"How do you know he calls me babe?"

"Surprise, surprise."

"Do you think he'd be glad if I broke it off?"

"Jesus! Don't ask me that."

"I suppose, even if I was having doubts, there's plenty of time to make a decision. He's only in Indiana."

"Which may say it all . . ."

"Like what?"

"Like he's in no big rush to get to the Pacific Ocean, i.e., to reverse direction, get on a plane, and fly back to his fiancée."

Had I not entertained the same thought? But who can judge how long it should take to hike from Massachusetts to Indiana? I said, "Everyone has doubts, right? In every relationship?"

"Did you send him photos of the house?"

"Not exactly."

"Does he know you bought a house?"

I told him I was waiting to see if I was approved for the mortgage. No point in getting Stuart all excited and then having to
break the news —

"Is he a *child?* You have to protect him from news like 'I got
turned down for the mortgage. How'd you like to throw some
money into the pot?'"

That's when I admitted I didn't *want* Stuart throwing money
into the pot.

"Because he *has* no money? Or because you don't want to own
a house with him?"

"I can swing it myself" was the nonanswer I mumbled.

"Good. Dad would probably cosign if that helped. If he ever
called anyone back. All the banks in town know him."

I tried Stuart's phone and got his long annoying voice-mail
message that provided his website address and philosophy of
life. "It's Faith Frankel," I said after the beep. "Would you mind
calling me back someday?"

8

Excellent Friends

I DIDN'T KNOW BEFOREHAND why we'd all been summoned
to the long mahogany conference table at eight a.m. — not
just my officemate, Nick, but the school's CFO; its headmaster, Philip "Dick" Dickinson; the school attorney, Amanda
somebody, dressed in exceedingly corporate, asexual pant-
suited fashion; and Reginald "Reggie" O'Sullivan, the unde-
serving head of Development.

In a nutshell: an alum I'd been sending thank-you notes to
for as long as I'd been head of Stewardship, had, right before his
death, reminded his not-totally-with-it/about-to-be-widowed
wife that he wished to grant the gift we'd been discussing.

Great! Except the widow dug out my business card and lovely
thank-yous, all of which she'd saved, and wrote a check for
$100,000 made out to the very nice woman who'd been danc-
ing attention on them: me. Pay to the order of Faith Frankel,
without a mention of Everton Country Day except for the ac-
companying note that said, *Payne wanted to fund those things we
talked about.*

And here was the evidence, the damning check. Did they really have to encase Exhibit A in plastic and handle it with latex gloves?

When it registered finally that I was suspected of steering donations into my own pocket, I said, "I never saw this check! Mrs. Hepworth — she's like ninety years old — obviously just made the check out to her contact person."

"What did she mean by 'the things we talked about'?" asked the headmaster, another ex-jock whose hand had once grazed my backside in a way that could be argued was accidental.

"To reshape the swimming pool . . . and to renovate the locker rooms," I explained. "Mr. Hepworth had swam . . . swum for the school." Now I was rattling. "A championship one! He was captain the year they beat some college team."

"Yale," said Nick quietly, looking red-faced, looking as if he'd been forced at gunpoint to attend.

I said, "I don't understand why you'd think that a check made out to me — a check I never cashed, never even saw, puts me under suspicion."

Reggie said, not kindly, "This is a major gift, Faith. This isn't stewardship, per se, where you're having tea with some nice people who put their name on a debate club trophy. This was planting a seed, and watering it, and cultivating it until it grew into a major gift."

Nick said, with a sneer, quietly, "Exhaust a metaphor, why don't you."

I said, "Oh, then excuse me for doing such a good job and getting a huge donation instead of a token one."

"You'll probably want to engage a lawyer," I heard one of them say.

"Does the accused need a lawyer if it's a kangaroo court?"

Nick asked. Then: "Did anyone call Mrs. Hepworth and ask her what her intentions were?"

"Of course," snapped the lawyer. "And her answer was not what I'd consider exculpatory."

"Why? What did she say? What could she possibly have said that didn't straighten this out?" I cried.

The lawyer said, "Most unfortunately, Mrs. Hepworth is under the impression that her husband wanted the money to go to you."

I said, "Well, she must be senile. Or *he* was. Because I never ever, *ever* —" At which point I broke down and managed only a string of soggy protest syllables.

Nick asked if I needed a tissue or water.

"She's fine," snapped the lawyer.

The headmaster said, "Another name came up. Which seems to have played a major role in Payne Hepworth's largesse."

"What name?"

"A man named Stuart. Did you tell the Hepworths about his foundation?"

"Foundation?" I repeated. I looked at Nick, who was shaking his head in a way that seemed both depressed and furious.

"Mrs. Hepworth said that Sandy — she called her late husband Sandy — was very taken with the story of the man walking across the country for some noble cause —"

I said, "No! I never told them that."

"But this Stuart is your fiancé, correct?" said the lawyer. "And he raises money for his charity?"

"This is crazy! I told them about Stuart walking across the country, but Mr. Hepworth must've mixed it up — he was, like, a hundred years old — with a real charity."

The headmaster said, "Mrs. Hepworth said that the money

was meant for you and for the young man who was walking across the United States. That was her understanding."

"Did I cash this check?" I demanded. "Did I ever *see* this check? And if I'd seen it or if it had been addressed to me — *was* it addressed to me? — I would never have guessed in a million years that it was actually to me, let alone Stuart. Who is no charity, believe me."

Nick said, "May I speak?"

One or two nodded begrudgingly.

"This is fucking crazy! Some old, probably demented guy gets all mixed up about what Faith is asking him to donate to, and he writes a check, and the wife is no swifter, and it's Faith's fault? It could've happened to anyone given the geezers we solicit donations from."

When his speech was greeted with only silence, Nick asked, "What else? Am I missing something here?"

"Mrs. Hepworth believes she was following her husband's instructions," the headmaster began.

"Wanna bet?" said Nick.

"Well, be that as it may, she won't rewrite the check."

I said, "She doesn't have to. I'll endorse it and put it straight into the capital fund."

"On the sly? Listed as 'anonymous' in the list of donors? No plaque outside the natatorium?" said the headmaster.

"I can't believe you're blaming me! I've been visiting them for a year, with one goal — that he remembers Everton in his will. And he'd get to designate where the money would go, into the pool. Of course we talked. They fed me tomato sandwiches. I drove them to home swim meets. I went to his funeral."

Reggie asked, "Since when are major gifts your bailiwick?"

I said, "Development is my bailiwick! I write letters to thank people for their generosity and describe all the good their gift is doing. And sometimes I visit them because they don't have children and they don't get many visitors. And sometimes I become friends with them —"

The lawyer who knew me not at all said, "It's your word against the widow's."

"How does that sentence make any sense?" asked Nick.

I said, "And the check was mailed here. To the school! I never touched it! I never saw it —"

"Luckily, the envelope was addressed in such a shaky hand that it's a miracle it ever reached the —"

"Was it even addressed to me?"

"Of course it was," said the headmaster. "But by a stroke of luck, your department secretary opened it before it got to you."

I might've asked, *Why the hell is Sheila opening my private correspondence?* but it wasn't the offense I needed to litigate at this juncture.

The lawyer said, "May we get back to the role of this Stuart?" With that, she reached for a manila folder and pulled out a photograph of the map of the continental United States, with one red pushpin designating his progress. "This would indicate otherwise," she said.

Nick said, "Just because she was charting his progress doesn't mean she was supporting this half-assed . . . I don't even know what to call it."

"Hegira," I heard myself whisper.

"Ha-what?" Reggie asked.

"Look it up," said Nick.

"It's a journey to a happier place," I sniffled. "It comes from Mohammed's flight from Mecca . . . to escape persecution."

"Mohammed?" snapped the lawyer, making a note without taking her accusatory eyes off me. "Are you a practitioner of the Muslim faith?"

I didn't want to offend any Muslims who might be in the room, but I did say, "I'm not a Muslim."

"What is Stuart's last name?" the lawyer asked.

"Levine."

She wrote that down, too.

"He's Jewish."

Nick said, "Isn't it against the law for an employer to ask someone his or her religion?"

Reggie said, "I ask people that all the time, conversationally." He grinned like the idiot he was, adding proudly, "People don't have to ask an O'Sullivan that."

"You think this is funny?" Nick snapped.

I whimpered, "I'm getting a lawyer, and I'm suing you back."

"For what?" asked Reggie.

"For this. For traumatizing me . . . for accusing me of a terrible thing and giving me a heart attack."

Nick jumped in again. "I repeat. Is this a kangaroo court? Because some dotty old couple writes a check clearly meant as a donation to Everton Country Day to a Development person, who, to them, personified ECD. Who did *not* cash this check. Who did not even know about it!"

"And if I had seen it, I'd have danced around the office and asked that we get a bottle of champagne because the Hepworths just made a gigantic major gift." I returned to the logical solution — "Give me the check. I'll endorse it over to the school!"

"That is not something Mrs. Hepworth is allowing," said the CFO.

"She won't know! She'll just know that her check got cashed. I don't want her stupid money!"

"It's a delicate situation," said the headmaster, drawing who-knows-what doodles on the edges of his folded Everton *Echo*.

"Apparently not when it comes to my feelings," I said. "To my . . . reputation. To my pride and . . . and —"

"And impugning her character," said Nick.

Character thoroughly impugned, it was then that I tried to make a dignified departure even with my navy blue Everton canvas bag slipping off one shoulder and my pocketbook left behind so I had to come back for it, silencing them mid–accusatory sentence. It was at this time that they said, "Sit down, Faith. We're not finished."

"I need to make a phone call," I said, not knowing yet to whom. Did I have a lawyer at the ready? I did not. And I needed a specialist, someone who exonerated people who'd been wrongly accused of pocketing nonprofit funds they didn't know they'd raised.

My cell phone was both ringing and vibrating. I fished it out of my purse, thinking it might be just the right savior at the right moment. It was not. It was Stuart.

I answered with a quick "Can't talk. I'm in the middle of a crisis."

He said, "Babe, don't stress about stuff. About you and me. And I got a solar phone charger at a RadioShack!"

"I can't talk."

"Who was calling?" the lawyer had the nerve to ask.

I was exhausted and must have looked that way because Nick now stood up, and said, "C'mon, Faith. It's way past time to leave."

I turned at the door, and said, my voice shaky once again, "I graduated from this school. My parents were able to pay the full freight. So what I do all day long is try to get kids scholarships. You should be ashamed of yourselves for accusing me of stealing a hundred grand from a widow who mistook me for a charity."

"I'm plenty offended, too," Nick added.

"And *he* came here from Exeter," I said. "Where they probably know what to do with a check made out to an innocent bystander."

Nick actually laughed. Did it lighten the mood in the room? Not one watt.

9

Why Take It Out on Me?

I DID NOTHING BUT SIT at my desk and stare at the stupid map of the United States. Across the room, Nick squirmed and muttered, taking phone calls but making none. After I'd stared at the wall for what he must have deemed far too long, he asked, "How about we rip it down?"

I said no, we shouldn't. It would make me look like I was packing up to leave.

"I meant what I said in there. We need to get you a lawyer."

I said, "Isn't that what a guilty party does? Like when the trashy mother says her children were kidnapped, and before you know it, she's a person of interest and hires a famous defense attorney when they find the bodies?"

"Whoa. I'm not talking about a defense attorney. I mean someone who'll protect you from further harassment. And makes them pay for pain and suffering."

I wanted to say, *You were so wonderful in there, the only one who stood up for me,* but a bout of choked-up gratitude made it impossible for me to get the words out.

"When you left the meeting for about five seconds, they asked me whose side I was on," Nick said.

"Did you have time to answer?"

"No. But it wasn't even a question. It was a warning shot across the bow."

"Don't get fired on my account," I said.

"Might be too late for that . . ." He smiled. "We'll start our own school. Can I be the headmaster?"

I was too weepy to say anything but "Yes, you can."

"Right next door. We'll call it Better and Cheaper Than Everton Country Day. That'll show 'em."

There was a knock on our door, and without waiting for permission to enter, Reggie materialized. "Hey, guys," he said.

Yes, he was the head of our department, but we enjoyed treating him like a fool. And never more than this morning. His outsize self-esteem was the result of having been a quarterback for Everton Country Day — "QB1" was how he signed notes to alums in graduating classes anywhere near his own.

"What do *you* want?" Nick asked.

Reggie held his hands up in an insincere gesture of surrender. "Just wanted to say something to Faith."

"Such as?"

"It wasn't my idea, this business about the check."

"Business?" I repeated. "*Business? How about witch hunt?* How about *crucifixion?*"

Reggie had the nerve to perch himself on the corner of my desk and shake my Empire State Building snow globe. "I know in my gut that you'd never steal money from the school —"

"Wait! In your gut, you know that? Like you have to look deep into your soul to find me innocent? How about just on the face of it?"

Maybe this wasn't the right response; maybe I was supposed

to be showing gratitude for his ham-handed sympathy, because he stood up, and said, "Just trying to show some team spirit here, Faith. Sorry you can't hear it."

"Wait," said Nick. "You can't blame her for saying any of that. In the meeting you sounded very happy to be at the prosecution table."

"And I have a question for you," I said. "Who did Sheila give the check to when she opened the letter from Mrs. Hepworth?"

"Oh. I guess . . . moi."

"And instead of breezing in here, and saying, 'Whoa, a huge check just came in. Congrats. A hundred grand! Now just one minor housekeeping detail. The donor made it out to you, so you'll have to endorse it over to the school. But well done!'"

"I guess I could've," said Reggie.

"I could've handled this myself — called Mrs. Hepworth and thanked her for the donation to the school. And she might've said, 'The school?' and I'd have said, 'Of course! That's my cause. That's my charity. That's my —'"

"Fucking life's work!" Nick supplied.

"Thank you. Then I'd say, 'The pool will be such a tribute to Sandy. I mean, we could hold the next Junior Olympics here! And the lockers will be in the school colors and so beautiful.'"

Nick asked Reggie, "So you got the check and you went running to whom?"

"I didn't go running to anyone. I walked it over to Moose's office —"

"Moose being?" said Nick.

"Mustafa Mahmoud, in Finance," I told him.

"I gave it to the secretary over there," said Reggie.

"Please tell me it wasn't Mindy Rooney," I said.

"Who else would it be?" asked Reggie.

"Why is that significant?" asked Nick.

"She hates me," I said. "Truly. I don't even know why. Well, maybe I do."

"Why?" asked Nick.

"You tell him," I said to Reggie.

When he didn't, I explained, "You had a fling with her, remember?"

"And if I did?"

"Then it ended, and soon after that, I got hired. That's all it took for Mindy to be — you'll excuse the expression — jealous."

Grinning, Reggie said, "She was a cheerleader when I was QB1."

I said, "Yeah, like twenty-odd years ago. Maybe it's time to stop calling yourself that."

Nick asked, "That's it? Misplaced jealousy?"

I told him that Mindy once applied to be Reggie's assistant. No go. And then she applied for this job, the one I got. Again, no go.

Reggie said, shrugging, "She wasn't my first choice, anyway. And HR woulda gone ape shit if they found out."

"Found out what?" asked Nick.

"That Mindy and I hooked up."

Reggie gave his shirt an unnecessary tuck into his chinos. "It's over, trust me." He smiled, man to man. "Make 'em and break 'em, right?"

"Ya, right," Nick said. "Especially smart with a coworker."

"It wasn't always against the rules," said Reggie.

Nick was twisting the cap off a bottle of Excedrin, then swallowing two pills in a gulp. "Even if you dumped Mindy, why is she taking it out on Faith?" he asked.

"Because she's a crazy bitch!" Reggie said. "Faith's here, head of whatchamacallit. Mindy's still sitting at the front desk over in Finance, calling parents who are in arrears on tuition."

"So do we think that Mindy marched into her boss's office, and said, 'Look what Faith Frankel thought she was getting away with'?"

"Probably."

I said to Reggie, "I know you're my boss, and I shouldn't say this, but today, this" — I made a circle, indicating the inside of our windowless office — "is a free zone, right? Given what happened this morning?"

"Sure," said Reggie.

"In that case, I truly hate you."

"Fine," he said. "I get it. My bad."

"You better fix this," said Nick. "You started it, and now you have to make it right."

"Relax," said Reggie. "We're gonna make this happen."

"Happen?" I shouted. "What's going to happen? What about me?"

"I meant the money. It'll end up in the capital fund. Even if it takes a little sweet-talking with the old lady." He smiled. "That's where I come in."

I said, "You're not getting credit for this donation."

"Hey! Take it easy! I'm not gonna bogart someone else's get. I'm just gonna take her to lunch."

"Not without me."

"You can't," he said.

"Why the hell not?" asked Nick.

Hand on the doorknob, Reggie threw back, "Why? She's on probation. I thought that was obvious."

"Probation!" I yelped.

Reggie said, "Gotta run," then left without a word of explanation, without a grimace that might have been interpreted as regret.

Probation. Like a felon. Like a freshman caught smoking behind the chapel. I asked Nick, rather calmly, considering, "Now what? Do I go home? Do I take a mental health day?"

"Do *not* leave. Don't move. I'll be right back."

"Nick," I called after him. But he didn't stop.

At times like these, even a mature adult woman tries to reach her parents. I had my cell phone in hand, about to call my mother, when I realized there was some emotional opportunism in play — a person does that sometimes, uses a bona fide crisis to reach a person who's nominally disappeared.

I left a message, the urgent kind even a hermit father with an artistic temperament can't ignore. "Dad! Call me back as soon as you get this!... Where are you? Call me. Something happened and I need advice. We're all fine — I mean, no one's hurt. It's about work! Call me!"

Did he? Not immediately. Wondering what my particular probation meant, I considered e-mailing Human Resources. Simultaneously, and possibly in shock, I waited for Nick to return, or my father to call, or for one of the heretofore friendly security guards I'd known since my student days to escort me to my car like a company loyalist suddenly, unfairly, tragically sacked.

10

What Do I Do Now?

I REACHED MY BROTHER, who was in the process of towing a car that died on an off-ramp. As swiftly as I could, I summed up my predicament. After only "They thought I was raising money for myself!" he yelled, "What the fuck!" and then to an apparent passenger, "Excuse my language but my sister just got fired."

I said, "No, I didn't! They're threatening probation," then I supplied a few more details of my dilemma.

"Did you say the check was for *a hundred grand?*"

"I actually said a hundred thousand dollars, but yes."

"I swear to God," he said. "If I didn't have a client in my truck and her SUV hooked up to the back, I'd race over there and — I don't know — make somebody apologize."

Next thing I knew, he was saying to his passenger, "You wouldn't know a good lawyer, would you?"

"For what?" I heard.

"It's my sister. She raises money for Everton Country Day and a big check came in made out to her instead of the school."

I said, "Joel! That was confidential! She could be a reporter for the *Echo* for all you know."

"I'm not," a woman's voice said. And then another muffled sentence, which Joel amplified for me. "Her brother-in-law and his wife are lawyers, both with fancy firms."

"In Everton?"

"In Boston," the woman said.

"Boston's good. Big-city lawyers. That'll scare 'em," said Joel.

Next I heard this passenger ask therapeutically, "What's her name?" — the prelude to Joel passing her his phone.

"Faith? It's Paula Gabriel. My car died coming off 495. Sorry to hear about your troubles. One question re the hot water you're in. Forgive me, but . . . did you do it?"

"Do what?"

"Arrange for the check to be made out to you? I have to ask because neither my brother-in-law nor his wife are criminal attorneys."

I sputtered, "I'm not a criminal! I worked and worked to get this donation, and the husband died and the wife — because she was grief stricken or just in a fog — wrote a check. To *me*. Because she was confused. She just copied the name from my business card!"

And then, as if we were acquaintances or even intimates, she announced, "Your brother seems upset. I don't think he should be talking about this while driving."

Joel yelled, "You're damn right I'm upset."

I asked if I was on speaker.

"It's okay," he said. "What's said in my cab, stays in my cab. Right, Paula?"

I said, "I hope so. The whole day has been a nightmare. A meeting in a fun house . . . in an insane asylum."

That last reference inspired Paula Gabriel to confide that she was a psychiatric social worker specializing in family counseling.

Though ten seconds earlier Joel had been spitting mad, he now let out a hoot of laughter.

"What's so funny?" I asked.

"This! My sister's flipping out, and whose car breaks down but a shrink's?"

"I am not flipping out and you have no discretion. None!"

I detected a change. Joel's voice was now sounding closer. "It's just me," he said.

"Good! Did you hear what she asked me? Was I *guilty?*"

"Sorry," he said.

"I have to go. I don't know why I called you."

"I'm your big brother. I beat people up for you. I bet it'll be settled without a lawyer. Are you on paid leave?"

"I don't know anything."

Paula was expounding again. Joel translated. "She's asking if you're faculty and if there's a faculty union. Because then you'd get representation."

"No, I am not. I'm not faculty, and FYI Everton faculty isn't unionized. I'm getting off."

"Look . . . sorry. It'll be okay. I'll call you tonight. Wanna do dinner?"

I said, "I guess so. Not in public, though. Come down."

"I'll bring pizza."

Paula was talking again, but I only caught "relationship."

"Did you hear that?" Joel asked. "She said she envied our relationship."

"I couldn't care *less* what she thinks."

"Roger that," said Joel.

⌒

Nick returned, looking anything but victorious. I asked where he'd been and whom he'd talked to and . . . anything good? *Anything?*

He shook his head sadly and plopped into his chair.

"Speak," I said.

"I went to see Dickenson. He was in a meeting, which I barged in on, and it was totally unrelated . . . architects . . . additions . . . so I had to back out, apologizing, looking like an idiot. Then I went looking for the chaplain. Good idea, right? Did you know he teaches two classes every morning?"

"Meaning you didn't speak to him?"

"Correct. But I thought he'd be sympathetic . . . would want to do the right thing. Ethics and all that."

"What about Reggie?"

"What *about* Reggie?"

"You left here chasing after him."

"I caught him. He's not the one who can fix the probation part of it. That's only Dickenson."

"I'm fucked."

"No, you are *not* fucked. Did you do anything about getting a lawyer?"

I told him I'd made a call, which went nowhere.

"Okay. Time for some tough love. You, miss, have to get your shit together."

"Where'd you learn that lovely expression? Phillips Exeter Academy?"

In decidedly un-Nick-like fashion — tentative and apologetic — he said, "Maybe this is the right time to tell you that I didn't leave Exeter voluntarily."

Did I just hear that Nicholas Franconi, the jewel in our crown, the man with the golden résumé, had left Exeter involuntarily?

He repeated, "Did that penetrate? I said I didn't leave Exeter voluntarily."

"Fired?" I whispered.

"They whitewashed it. If I quit on my own, they'd call it a resignation. And give me good recommendations without mentioning my Achilles' heel."

"Which was what?"

"Too embarrassing," he mumbled.

"You brought it up. You have to tell me."

"I will. But first I have to tell you that I'm cured," he said. "I've fixed the problem."

I was expecting something confessional or criminal or pharmaceutical, but his hands were over his face covering an unexpected grin. The answer that escaped between his fingers was "Time management. *Aaargh!*"

"Time management? Like late for work?"

"I kept missing planes and trains — chronically, they said — so at the other end, I'd miss meetings with potential donors, which, believe me, tends to piss off everyone. So at first it was just 'Try harder . . . buy a watch, set it ahead, set your alarm earlier, read a book on time management, for Chrissake.' And then it was *see a shrink* and pretty soon *don't put him on the road.* And finally . . . *Sayonara, asshole.*"

"Yikes," I said. "I never would've guessed that in a million years."

"I have my tricks now."

I said, "I appreciate your telling me. And not just because it startled me into forgetting my own troubles for two minutes."

"I was asked to leave. *You're* only on probation. And may I remind you, until you get it in writing, it's just hearsay."

~ ❧ ~

I was still sitting at my desk thirty minutes later, trying not to do anything rash like packing up my personal effects. Surely Nick would return, having fixed some or all of this mess. I knew Stuart would be unavailable. I tried anyway and left a message saying, "Did you grasp that something terrible happened at work? Here's a clue. I've been wrongly accused of steering money into my own pocket. With a little help from you, by the way. If interested, call me back."

Next, I sent an e-mail to myself at work to see whether I'd been snuffed out. It didn't bounce back. And there was my picture and bio still on the school's website.

Stuart texted me, **That sucks. Cant talk now wcb asap.**

Of course, being unreachable due to his exalted role in life, he couldn't talk, now or ever. It evoked a thought that was increasingly running through the part of my brain that handled logic — that maybe we weren't engaged at all. And if the red string on my finger *was* a symbol of his marital intentions, maybe I should I break it off, literally *and* figuratively.

But I did nothing, recognizing that my bad mood might be responsible for this romantic disillusionment. And also because my phone was ringing — my father calling back! Without my having to say hello, I heard, "What's wrong? What happened?"

For the umpteenth time, or so it felt, I outlined the morning's charges. He said, "Are you at school? Do you want me to come get you?"

And for the umpteenth time — or so it seemed — I asked, "Where *are* you?"

"Didn't Joel tell you? Or your mother? I was in Florida, but —"

"I've had it with your 'Florida'! Like that explains anything!"

"But I told them . . . they both know — it's business."

"What business! You're a painter. That's not a business! What's the big secret? Is there a woman down there?"

"Faithy — what's gotten into you? I mean besides being accused of embezzling?"

"You're impossible to reach! It's like you have a secret life. And my fiancé can't call me back, either, due to God knows what."

He said, "I flew home today. I was on a plane when you called. I'm back in Boston now. I'll drive to Everton tonight. We'll have a family meeting and we'll get this straightened out."

Such a simple phrase. *We'll get this straightened out.* Not that it was clear which "this" he meant, but finally I was hearing a string of syllables I believed could be true.

11

Family Caucus

MY FATHER LOOKED GOOD, better than the rest of us, with his off-season tan and what appeared to be product in his gray hair.

By dinner, I was sick of myself, very inclined to change the subject from Everton Country Day to anything else. For a few minutes, between her arrival and the ordering of pizzas, my mother was furious on my behalf. We were an ECD family to the core! Well, Joel had gone to the public high school, but still, when she thought of my lifelong attachment and paying full tuition, not to mention the PTO meetings chaired and the cakes baked — hundreds of pounds of butter over those thirteen years!

My father said, "Let's not leap to any conclusions about Faith's job. This is a tempest in a teapot. She did nothing wrong. In fact, they should be congratulating and promoting her for this major get."

"You're acting awfully calm and rational," said my mother.

"It might look that way, but believe me, I'm plenty offended.

I called my lawyer this afternoon and left a message with his secretary."

My mother said, "Not Bent MacPherson, I hope."

"Of course not. He's an ambulance chaser. And not even good at that. But my new guy handles intellectual property, which I think could be an interesting crossover."

Did Henry Frankel just say that his lawyer's specialty was intellectual property?

I didn't have to wonder for long because Joel asked, "What do you need with an intellectual property lawyer?"

Dad said, "One of my clients suggested it."

"Are you talking about insurance clients?" I asked.

My mother said, "Tell them, Henry. It's nothing to be ashamed of." And then to Joel and me, "Your father is doing some work that he thinks you'll find not quite on the up-and-up."

"It doesn't have to do with drugs, does it?" I asked.

"Of course not!"

"It's art," said my mother. "But it pays."

"For Chrissake," said Joel, who had been consulting the pizza menu more than engaging in Everton Country Day hand-wringing. "Just tell us. How bad can it be if it has to do with, I assume, paint?"

My father said, "Shall we order first?"

We passed the take-out menu around, taking too long to choose from the café's stylish pizzas baked in their much-touted new oven. Joel called in a Bianco for the ladies and one laden with all available meats for the men.

"So what gives?" Joel said, pouring from the first of the two bottles of red wine my father had brought.

We learned over the course of the next fifteen minutes that his hobby was not a hobby as much as, quite suddenly, a business. It had started out as a favor. He'd copied a famous painting, *Still Life with Onions,* for some art lovers who weren't trying to pull a fast one; they just loved Cezanne.

"That's it?" Joel asked. "You copy paintings and you get paid for that?"

"Are these forgeries?" I asked.

"No, they're copies. Each piece is clearly identified on the reverse as a reproduction."

"They're not bad," said my mother.

"And I make the client sign something that says they won't misrepresent or sell it or attempt to sell it as the original."

"Very cool," said Joel. "How'd you think of this little sideline?"

"I *personally* had to refuse some clients insurance on their second homes — Florida, the Bahamas, those kinds of places — in the hurricane belts. Which meant, for the one or two who had important paintings, no coverage. So, what do you do after you've stored them in safe, dry places, like a bank vault, or, in one case, donated them to a museum, and you don't want empty walls, and you miss your beloved Picasso? You commission a copy."

I said, "Then I don't understand what the big secret is about."

Our mother said, "Maybe your father thinks that copying famous paintings is not art in the purest sense."

"It's an honorable tradition," Dad said. "In Europe, in museums, you see students sketching and painting in front of famous works —"

"What do you get for a copy?" Joel asked.

"Depends on the size. But at this stage, starting out, two to three."

"Thousand," my mother supplied. "Not what I'd call a living."

"How long does one take you?" Joel asked.

"If I'm working full-time, day and night . . . a week, ten days. The longest was two weeks."

"Then it has to dry," said my mother.

I said, "Dad! You're giving us every reason why this is completely kosher and nothing to be embarrassed about!"

"Now tell them about the Chagalls," said our mother.

The doorbell rang: pizza delivery, followed by a wallet skirmish as to who was going to treat.

We opened the second bottle of red and finally settled, silverware dispersed and pizza served. "What *about* Chagall?" I asked.

"He personalizes them," said my mother.

My father explained. A client saw a copy he'd done of a Matisse for a restaurant pal and called him up. She asked if he could make a copy of a Chagall, but perhaps more lavender than blue — purple was their daughter's favorite color — and work her daughter's name into it, and give the angel *her* face, with her bangs but without her braces? She played the violin just like in the painting, and her bat mitzvah was in three months. Would he be willing to tweak it that much and was that enough time?

"Then one thing led to another . . . ," our mother said. "Or so I've gleaned."

"What your mother means is that my client exhibited *Blue Mitzvah* on an easel in the lobby of the synagogue before and after the service, which brought two more commissions — another bat mitzvah and an engagement."

"Angels, brides, stars, livestock," my mother said. "Everything from the four food groups."

"It's an expensive present," I said.

"It's for the ages! It'll be passed down from generation to generation, or at least that's part of the pitch," my father said. "From across the room, your friends think you have a Chagall.

And then you get closer and you see that it's about your wedding, or your grandson's bar mitzvah or bris, and that's your daughter's face on the angel."

Joel asked if these patrons had to be Jewish.

"It doesn't hurt," he said. "Excellent pizza, by the way. How's that white one?"

"Want to swap a white piece for a red one?"

Both men said sure, plenty to go around. "Maybe we should've ordered a salad," said my mother.

"Not tonight," said Joel, nodding in my direction. "We're rewarding ourselves after a hard day."

"And have we forgotten, despite what might be happening at school, that I'm buying a house?"

"Your mother already told me." My father picked up his fork and pierced another slice. "By yourself, I understand. On your own."

"It was a bargain. And my lawyer — speaking of lawyers — when I explained Stuart's walkathon, said he would be no help at all in the eyes of the bank as a cosigner, so I might as well just go for it." I couldn't help adding, "You have your studio. It's obviously not a reflection of anything . . . personal or marital."

Neither parent picked up on that theme. Finally, my father said, "It *is* working out. Well, the place is a mess. It smells like paint and turpentine and cigar smoke. I feel like a real artist. It's romantic, in a Greenwich Village or Paris-in-the-nineteen-twenties kind of way."

"Look where it's led," said my mother. "Your father is the new Chagall."

"Now tell me about the house," said my dad. "Turpentine Lane, correct? You have fire, theft, homeowners?"

"I mean to. I will. You have to see it. It's such a sweet little place. All it's missing is the picket fence."

"Of course I want to see it. It's just a matter of when."

"He's on deadline," said our mother. "Apparently working day and night."

"A fortieth-anniversary present for a Miami couple, based on Chagall's *Wedding 1918,* but I'm adding all three kids — they commissioned it — not just the one cherub hovering above the couple."

"And I think I know what Faith will be getting for a wedding present," Joel said. "I mean, whenever, whoever . . . someday."

"Or a housewarming present," my father said. "You just have to name your artist. A Van Gogh? A Magritte? A Rothko? Or I'll surprise you."

"One thing at a time," my mother said. "Let's just say, God forbid, you lost your job. Would you be able to make the mortgage payments?"

I said, "I don't want you guys to worry. What's the worst that'll happen? I get fired, I sue, I put the house on the market? Someone else will fall in love with it exactly the way I did."

All of that was met with nervous smiles. Was it my job outlook, my choice of property, my choice of fiancé, or just an unconvincing delivery? I couldn't tell.

12

·⁓⁕⁓·

The Confluence of
Bad Things

OST PEOPLE expecting imminent probation would show up at their office and stage something like a sit-in. Not me. I called in sick.

Tried you at work. You ok? my mother texted. I didn't phone her, didn't want to be engaged in a mother-daughter heart-to-heart when Stuart inevitably returned one of my calls. Each time I'd tried him, I got only his outgoing message defining his journey and informing me that his "callback metabolism was slow, so please be patient."

I texted my mother: **Needed a mental health day.**

You home? she wrote back.

Approximately fifteen minutes after I answered yes, my doorbell rang. It was she, more dressed up than usual for mid-morning, in a ruffled blouse and a pleated plaid skirt I'd never seen. Her greeting was "May I say something?" which was accompanied by a pained maternal puckered brow.

"Not if it's going to upset me."

"I hope it doesn't. It won't be about Stuart, per se."

I waited.

"Are you going to invite me in?"

I opened the door wider, revealing my oldest nightgown, a faded once-blue flannel thing that my college roommate would have recognized.

"None of my business, but that needs to go straight onto the rag heap," she said, striding past me to collect and wash last night's wineglasses. Eventually I pitched in, wiping the table halfheartedly.

She relieved me of the sponge and sat down. "I'd like to know, has Stuart called?"

"Not since yesterday."

"*When* yesterday?"

"During the horror show. I told him I was in the middle of a crisis so I couldn't talk."

There followed a not entirely restrained diatribe, allegedly about all of mankind — about attention being paid, about putting someone else's troubles before your own, about returning someone's calls. At minimum!

I said, "If you're trying to get me more upset, congratulations. You've succeeded."

"I have to ask. What are you getting back from Stuart? What does he give you besides the obvious?"

"What's the obvious?"

"A boyfriend! A partner! Someone to go out with and, I assume, sleep with."

"All of the above."

"But when?" she cried.

"All the time, in theory."

"In *theory?* What does that mean?"

"It means . . . when he's not out of state."

She closed her eyes. Her lips moved but no words came out

until she promised aloud not to say anything critical, given the confluence of bad things. "You need his support. You need the simple courtesy of —"

"Yes, I do! And I don't need your couple's therapy. I don't want to be on the defensive! I want everything to be all right at work, and I want credit for getting the stupid swimming pool upgraded."

"Has anyone called from work?" she asked.

"Maybe. I haven't answered my phone."

"Is that wise?"

"It makes sense if I'm having a breakdown."

"Which you are *not*. No one in our family has breakdowns. You're just angry and worried. And I wouldn't be surprised if you were a little heartbroken."

I said, "It's all mixed up — the anger, the disappointment. I think I have posttraumatic stress disorder, so I can't tell which percentage, if any, of the heartbreak is Stuart's fault."

"But the phone's been ringing, right?"

I said yes, the landline, quite a bit.

"And you know it's not Stuart because he always tries your cell?"

Always, except hardly ever, I didn't say aloud.

"Okay. Listen, you stay here. Someone's got to play back those messages. The school might have called. Have you had breakfast?"

I lied and said I had: oatmeal.

"Give me a few minutes. I'll report back."

What could I say? "I didn't make my bed," I called after her. "It's kind of a mess in there."

I heard the bedroom door close. Well, that made sense, protecting me in case one or all of the messages contained bad news. I dunked a tea bag in a mug of not-quite-boiled water and waited.

Was that *her* talking, or was it voice mail? I soon found out. Two charities were looking for donations, a dentist appointment reminder, and a carpet-cleaning business with an introductory offer. Thus the female voice I'd heard *was* my mother's. On behalf of Team Frankel, she was alerting my father and brother to launch Operation Save Faith.

13

Collaborators

SOON ENOUGH I LEARNED that my newly collusive parents had conceived two campaigns, like something strategized at a war college. There was the Mrs. Hepworth Saturday mission and, if needed, the headmaster assault. Would I have sanctioned either if I'd known in advance about Plan A or B? I like to think I'd have argued for nonintervention.

As for visiting the unsuspecting Mrs. Hepworth, it helped that my father had sold insurance and had once run for Everton City Council. Knocking on strangers' doors, asking for a vote or a few minutes of their uninsured time, was not something that gave my father pause.

My mother called me late Saturday afternoon as I was walking fast around Brown Slake Pond, music turned up but cell phone on alert. She began with "Good news! You may be all set."

"In what way?"

"Don't say anything until you hear the whole story. Where are you?"

When she heard "the pond," she said, "Go back to your car while I explain so you don't freeze."

I ignored that, kept walking, and ten seconds later said, "I'm in the car now, nice and warm."

"Let me begin this way. Your father's argument was a thing of beauty."

"Argument?"

"Not an argument, a presentation. He had perfect pitch, rhetorically speaking. I went with him just in case she was wary of a strange man ringing her doorbell. But it turns out, he'd once given her an appraisal on homeowner's!"

"Who? *Who* might've been wary of Dad?"

"Didn't I say that? Edith Hepworth."

I yelped, "No, you did not! Tell me you two didn't take it upon yourselves —"

"We didn't just drop in! We called first. I said I was your mother, that we raised our kids on Waverly, and my husband and I wanted to pay our respects. From there, it was a hop, skip, and a jump to the big question. Had anyone told her that you would very likely lose your job at Everton Country Day because of a little miscommunication? At first, she insisted that she had *not* . . . Faithy? You there?"

"Barely."

"You're breathing hard. Are you sure you're not still exercising?"

"I'm not exercising. I'm hyperventilating."

"It's all good. Dad said, along these lines: 'Maybe someone from your husband's beloved alma mater recently asked if you meant to write the check to Everton Country Day instead of Faith Frankel?' So at this point, she said, 'Now that you mention it . . .' Dad helped her along with 'You repeated that you wanted the money to go to Faith and her causes. Is that still the case?'

"Next thing we know, she's hurrying off to another room and came back waving her checkbook. We said, 'No, no. No need to write another check. Faith can endorse the other one over to the school.'" My mother stopped there, surely expecting me to be in the throes of deep gratitude and relief.

I said, "Did you ever think that going directly to Mrs. Hepworth would get me into more trouble?"

"We fixed it! How could a friendly visit to a neighbor get you into any trouble?"

"Because I'm in the doghouse, and it's just the kind of thing that would piss everybody off. Like I'm a baby whose parents have to fix her problems."

"I've never heard such nonsense," she said.

The next call was from my father, arriving in the time it took for my newest meltdown to boomerang from Brown Slake Pond to my mother to him, apparently in the next room.

"You have to give us more credit," he said. "Mrs. Hepworth was so happy to have callers. I don't suppose your mother told you that she promised she would *not* mention our visit when she remedied the situation?"

"Dad! Dickenson isn't going to buy that she just woke up one morning, realized her mistake, and — what? — knew what to do and who to call?"

Did I say this aloud or only think, *Am I the only one with any dignity in this family?* Either way, the next thing my father said was "I'm putting Joel on."

There was a roiling and heating inside my head, which I took to be a spike in blood pressure. "Joel's there, too?" I asked in no one's ear as the phone passed between collaborators.

"Hey," my brother said, sounding wary in a single syllable.

"You let them visit Mrs. Hepworth?"

"I wasn't consulted. They asked me to meet them there. I figured someone needed a tow. I waited in the truck. Well, for most of it."

"Then you went in?"

"You're not going to like this . . ."

"Just say it."

"Look. It's what Mom does. She asked the old lady if she had a contract with anyone to plow her driveway. She didn't know and then remembered that the kid across the street shoveled it. So of course Mom said, 'Well, from now on Frankel Towing and Plowing is taking care of all that!'"

"And you just rolled over?"

"Oh, please. The woman's like ninety. I gave her my business card and she said she'd cherish it. I kid you not, that exact word."

"You're doing it for free, you realize."

"It's no big deal. She doesn't drive, so I can do it any old time — as opposed to every other client who wants me there at the crack of dawn."

"Joel," I started, but didn't go on.

"You're not crying, are you?"

"Maybe."

"Where are you? Want me to come over?"

That made it worse. Mostly it was mortification and anxiety over Team Frankel's interference. But on the other hand, who wouldn't choke up, witnessing how much her infuriating family loved her?

14

·⁓⁓·

Still Here

STUART MIGHT AS WELL have been missing. He hadn't called me back, nor had he added a word to his blog, nor posted on Facebook, nor bared his soul on any other social medium I am acquainted with. His voice-mail box was full, so I couldn't even leave another needy, irritated message. I confided this to no one, since it would be interpreted less as MIA and more as laughably indifferent fiancé. I considered calling the police but then asked myself, *Which* police? Indiana can be a very big state.

Monday, nine-ish, I was at my desk, facing an undecorated wall. Nick noticed immediately. "You took it down?" he asked.

"Who else would've?"

"No one," he said too quickly.

"Were you thinking it could have been HR?"

"Only a fleeting thought."

I told him I hadn't heard one word, official or unofficial, about probation, which was why I was back at work. I waved three addressed envelopes containing notes already written this morning. His "well done" still sounded worried.

"I tore down the stupid map. It didn't even have roads on it, so how did I know where to stick the pin?"

He unwound a long bumpy brown scarf that I hadn't seen before and hung up his parka on our communal coatrack. "'Tore it down' sounds a little hostile."

I confessed that it *was* a little hostile.

He sat down, busied himself turning on his computer. "Hostile toward what's-his-name, the hiker?"

"Stuart."

"Something happen?"

"Only that he's not picking up and he's not calling me."

"Is that so unusual?"

"It's unusual in a crisis! I left him a message using that exact word — *crisis!*"

"And you know it's unusual because you've had other crises since he left?"

Just doubts, I thought, crises of confidence. "Not really," I said. "And I'm trying to keep a level head because there's always the possibility he's getting no bars on his phone. Or he's dead."

Nick's answer was delayed; he was working his cell phone, thumbing it with authority, frowning over whatever new compelling images it rendered.

"What?" I asked, after long enough.

"Your boyfriend's not dead. He's in Illinois."

I asked, "Are you on Facebook?"

"Instagram. He loves it."

"You follow him?"

"You don't have to follow people to see their posts. But I do now. Don't you?"

"I thought I did. He must have a new user name for the trip. I thought he'd stopped posting."

"It's 'At Fund Stuart Levine.' That's what I'm seeing."

"Do *I* want to see it?" I asked.

"Maybe you should."

I knew what that meant. Even if it was a knife to the heart, I should see the evidence for my own enlightenment. He walked the phone over to my desk.

"There are three new ones," Nick instructed. "All since yesterday."

This is what I saw: Stuart looking too happy at a bar. His companion was a man who appeared to be a Native American, with a long black braid, ethnicky headband, and oppressed frown. The next, taken an hour earlier, was minus Stuart, just the architecturally interesting Wild West saloon doors of Wiffy's Place. And minutes earlier: Stuart getting out of a compact car, saluting its occupants. This one had a caption. "Thanks for the lift, Ashley, Katelin (sp?) and Kristy!!!"

I read the three names aloud, then asked Nick, "How old can an Ashley, Katelin, and Kristy be?"

"Young. And I thought he was walking across the country, not hitchhiking."

"Sometimes, if his feet hurt, or it's bad weather, or the air quality is poor, he sticks out his thumb." I handed the phone back. "At least I know he's not dead."

"And that's good enough?"

"It wasn't good enough this weekend," I confessed.

"So he doesn't even know about this shit storm at work?"

I shook my head. I could see he was searching for a Stuart rebuke that wouldn't go too far, that wouldn't call my judgment into question. Eventually, he asked, "Do you think he reads his comments?"

Unless it's from me, I thought. "I have no idea," I said.

When Nick began typing, I asked what he was doing.

He read aloud. "Douche bag, exclamation point. Faith is worried about you. Call her for fuck's sake."

I let out a yelp of protest.

He said, "Nah. I wrote, 'Dude! Faith is worried about you. Call her!'"

"Do you think he's a douche bag?"

"Only if you do."

Writing while nursing two separate abandonment anxieties took all my powers of concentration. I managed another note. *Yaddy yaddy yah,* counterfeit enthusiasm, manufactured gratitude over measly amounts on my best notecards — the school crest engraved rather than embossed — because they were YAFTD: Young Alum First-time Donor.

My office landline and cell phone were still silent twenty minutes after Nick had asked Stuart to call me.

"I have a meeting at ten," I heard him say.

I looked up. "One that concerns me?"

He said, "It could. It's with Dickenson. But it's been on the calendar for weeks."

I hadn't yet found a way to tell Nick about my parents' mission to Mrs. Hepworth's house and the alleged fix, but now was the time. I took a sip of my tepid coffee and began with "I may be okay. Workwise, I mean."

"I *did* notice you were still slaving away on your prize-winning notes."

I was mildly distracted from my confession by his use of "prize-winning" and thanked him for the compliment.

"You were saying . . . ?"

"My parents . . . well, my brother, too . . . they took matters into their own hands by visiting and sweet-talking Mrs. Hepworth into making things right."

Eyes narrowed, thinking if not plotting, Nick asked, "Do you have her phone number?"

"I'm not calling her!"

"Not you. Me."

"To say what?"

"Wanna listen?"

I did and I didn't.

Nick said, "I'm a talent. You *should* listen."

Next thing I knew, he was hitting buttons rather breezily. And then I heard "Mrs. Hepworth! It's Nick Franconi, from Everton Country Day, a colleague of Faith Frankel's." Then he was nodding rather strenuously, clearly for my benefit, a signal that she was . . . what? Pleased? Not sounding batty?

"Nicholas Franconi," he repeated. "I'm director of Major Gifts, and I heard you gave us a whopper!"

This was not the tone I was expecting. My arms were now folded on my blotter and my inflamed face was pressed into them.

"I agree! She *is* a lovely young lady! In every way. And I understand that you met her parents." When I looked up, he winked at me.

"The reason I'm calling — and I hope I'm not disturbing you — is that Faith is hard at work this morning over in her office" — another wink — "and I'm assuming I have *you* to thank for her uninterrupted service."

More listening and nodding. Then he said, "And you had no difficulty reaching our headmaster over the weekend?" He hit speaker, and Mrs. Hepworth's wrinkly voice filled the room. I heard "He lives in that beautiful house with the portico. All I had to do was call the main number and I was put through. First I talked to his wife, and then he called me back. He was at a game. The school was playing another school, but I didn't catch its name or the sport."

Nick said, "I was at that game myself! Football! Everton won!" And with that, he mouthed *Did not.*

Mrs. Hepworth said, "He called me back after the match, all apologies. And I told him that every penny of Sandy's donation was meant to go to the school to fix the cracks in the pool and . . . those other things."

"The locker room. It was a hellhole! We're so grateful."

Mrs. Hepworth, age eighty-seven, or -eight or -nine, could be heard tittering at "hellhole" while I was nearly losing consciousness at Nick's nerve.

"I hope to meet you very soon!" he bellowed. "We'll most assuredly have a beautiful dedication when the pool is refurbished. I look forward to that, as does Faith. As does every single member of our grateful community."

"Very well," she said.

I picked up my pen to write another thank-you note. This one should be going to a Geoffrey J. Kemmerer, class of '58, for his (adverb, adjective) donation to the (fill-in-the-blank) fund. Instead, I composed sentences for Nick, now absent, gone to meet with my main accuser. I wrote that no matter what the rest of this Monday brought he might be the best, most loyal coworker I could ever ask for.

Too much, I thought, too overwrought and sentimental. I crushed this first draft into an unreadable ball and threw it away.

15

Progress

I HAD NO CHOICE. As a self-respecting, more-or-less-employed adult woman, with family members and coworkers who found Stuart, at best, lacking, I had to break up with him. I did it at eleven p.m., figuring he'd be off the road, on a bar stool, awaiting some ping that signaled attention being paid in the form of a retweet.

I texted **We're done. I'm breaking up with you. I mean it this time. Your ex-fiancée, Faith.**

Followed a second later with **PS: cut up my credit card.**

My phone rang. "Babe? What're you trying to say?"

"I just told you. We're done. Finis."

"But, babe —"

"Don't call me babe. And after this, don't call me at all."

"But, but, but . . . why?"

"As if you don't know," I cried.

"I *don't* know. If you saw the stunned look on my face —"

"I've been trying to reach you every possible way short of an all-points bulletin. For days!"

So predictably and — realizing this very late — characteristically, *he* was the injured party. "You know I can't always return calls," he whined. "My roaming charges would be ridiculous."

Not totally confident in that arena, I took the plunge anyway. "Roaming charges? Within the United States? That's total bullshit."

"It's not bullshit! You know my calling plan. I had to get the rock-bottom one."

"The issue isn't your calling plan. The issue is your total self-absorption. I left you messages of every kind. I needed to talk to you. I was nearly fired for something I didn't do. I was — there's no other word for it — in despair."

In a voice devoid of empathy, reflecting only apprehension related to his empty wallet, he repeated, "You were fired?"

"All weekend I thought I was! And where were you? Instagramming in a saloon!"

"Do you want me to come home? Because I will. I'll end this journey right now, right here, in" — a long pause while he looked for a geographical cue — "Mattoon, Illinois. I'll get on a bus and be at your door by the time you get home from work tomorrow. Or maybe the day after that."

I had not been expecting this. Nor, I realized, did I even want this. "What about your journey? Your lifelong dream?"

Given his sudden desire to give it all up for the woman he allegedly loved, I thought he might say, *My dream?* You're *my dream, Faith*, or at least something with emotional content. But what I heard was "Can you hold for a sec? I have another call."

I admit it. I held. A refilled glass of wine later, I heard, "Sorry, luv. That was potential money on the other line. By the way, I heard from someone named Nick, who wanted me to call you. Who's he again?"

"My coworker. And friend."

"*Girl*friend, it sounds like," Stuart said.

"What does that mean — 'girlfriend'?"

"Your BFF, all bent out of shape because you and I didn't speak for what, like a day? You confide in him? Have lunch together? . . . Oh, shit. Can you hold a sec?"

I yelled, "*No!*" But he'd left just the same. Pride and fury dictated that I hang up.

What had this conversation accomplished? Nothing. Was he sorry, not sorry, coming home, not coming home? An hour later, a text woke me. **All good?** he asked.

Reggie, my idiot department head, was back at work after his three-day weekend, apparently taking advantage of an early snowstorm on some southern Vermont slope.

"What are these for?" I asked, pointing to the enormous bouquet of flowers he was holding aloft.

"You know . . . the stuff. Last week . . ."

"Are they meant as an apology?"

"No!" said Reggie. "Not an apology. A thank-you."

I glanced Nick's way. His eyes were open wide, a silent plea for me to keep Reggie on the hot seat.

"And you're thanking me for what exactly?"

Reggie, looking around, asked, "We have a vase, right?"

"I believe we do. Somewhere." I turned back to my keyboard, wrists high, piano-recital graceful.

"Frankel?" I heard. I looked up. Reggie was pointing the cellophaned bouquet of Thanksgiving-hued mums at me.

"Yes?"

"Bottom line? You kicked ass — a hundred-grand donation? When does *that* not deserve a big fat *muchas gracias*?"

I asked, "That depends. Is this an *adios con muchas gracias*?"

"What do you mean?"

"She's asking if this is a cheesy golden parachute," Nick volunteered.

"No way! Can't a guy, a boss, say it with flowers? Is that sexist or something?"

I said, "You weren't at work yesterday. How do you know I'm not a goner?"

"I'm your boss, that's how. Ever hear of conference calls?"

I took the bouquet. "Thank you," I said. "Although I could've done without this whole ordeal."

"C'mon. What ordeal? It's done. Over. Forgotten."

I said, "A hundred percent?"

"A hundred percent what?" Reggie asked.

"My job is safe."

"She's asking for 'dismissed with prejudice,'" Nick supplied. "Permanently. Never to be raised again. Never showing up on a written evaluation."

"Okay. I guess so. Sure."

"Flowers are nice," Nick continued, "but if I were Faith, I'd be looking for combat pay."

"Huh?" said Reggie.

"You know exactly what I mean: a bonus, for Chrissake."

"Jeez," said Reggie. "I don't have that in my budget. Plus, we don't do bonuses. I mean, we're here to raise money for the school."

"Then how about a raise? When was the last time Faith got a bump in her salary?"

"Never," I said.

"And, I'll tell ya, buddy," said Nick, "sometimes a raise at the right juncture can nip a lawsuit in the bud."

"A lawsuit?" Reggie repeated. "For what?"

"I could see a defamation suit . . . slander —"

"Pain and suffering," I added.

Nick said, "Both my brothers are lawyers. Did I ever mention that? Franconi and Franconi, LLC." Feigning deep attention to some bogus matter on his screen — and in what he would later characterize as punching above his weight — Nick said, "Thank you, Reggie. That's all. You can go now."

With Reggie out of the room, I whispered, "Do you really think you should talk to him that way? You could get fired for insubordination."

"Oh, hush," said Nick.

"Franconi and Franconi? *Really?*"

Nick smiled. "In the Yellow Pages. In Springfield, I believe. Same spelling. Who knows? Maybe our great-grandfathers came from the same village."

I waited a while, started on a note that wrote itself due to what the school was genuinely grateful for, a used van that could hold eight kids on a field trip. Then I announced, "Stuart? My fiancé? He got your message."

"He called you?"

"Sort of. I texted about where we stood, and he called right back."

Nick swiveled away from his computer so that he was facing me. "And where *do* you stand?"

I summarized my text. "It's over. PS: cut up my credit card."

Nick said, "Wow. You did it. Via text . . . very bad social etiquette." He paused. "I might be tempted to say congratulations, but then you might say, 'Actually, he called right back and was all *I'm sorry/I love you/I wanted to call but I've been lying in a ditch.*'"

"I think I did do it. He tried to put me on hold —"

"You're kidding!"

"Twice."

"What an asshole! I never met the guy, but *Jesus!* And you

were *paying* for this midlife crisis of his. Is that what the PS meant?"

"The card was supposed to be only for emergencies."

"Good luck with that. I'd call the bank and cut him off right now."

"I already did."

We both returned to work. Nick set up two appointments with alums, and I put stamps on my morning's output.

I heard, "I'm getting myself a cup of coffee, the good stuff from the faculty lounge. Want one?"

"Sure," I said. "Thanks."

He opened the door, took a step, came back. "I'm in no position to say good riddance; I mean, no one knows what goes on in a relationship. But, God, what a douche he's been — at least from where I sit. My unsolicited personal opinion is that you're well rid of him."

Did that sound . . . No, never mind.

16

Visitors

STUART WAS STILL TEXTING me nightly, using endearments, deaf to our dissolution. I answered approximately one out of three overtures but bordering on the frigid. I hadn't told him about moving into my own home, let alone buying it, but the legal notice in the *Echo* announcing the transaction was spotted by one of his many parents.

Congratts!!! Stuart wrote the day after it appeared.

4 what?

The house? Turpentine LN? LOL.

I didn't want to dignify his LOL with a return text, but I couldn't resist. **FYI, this area was once a pine forest, from which turpentine is made. PS: there is no longer such a thing as domestic turpentine.**

He answered with his favorite hip, juvenile response: **K.**

A day later, Sunday, the doorbell emitted its century-old unmusical squawk. I pulled aside two inches of curtain and saw my parents on the porch, along with two women in sweatpants, outsize sweaters, and men's high-top sneakers, one pair black, the other red. The taller woman had a waist-length gray braid; the other, yellow hair, an inch long, straight up and stiff.

"We phoned, but you didn't answer," my mother said.

"I've been screening calls," I told them, adding a one-word explanation: "Stuart."

The punk-haired woman put her hand out. "I'm Rebecca," she said. "And this is Iona."

"Stuart's mother and stepmother," my mother explained.

I didn't panic, exactly. But what would bring so many next of kin to an ex-fiancée's door in the manner of military chaplains? "Is he okay?" I asked.

"He's great!" said Rebecca.

My mother motioned *You first* to the callers, so she could mouth *Sorry . . .* behind their ample backs.

With only a couch in the parlor, I made myself busy borrowing kitchen chairs. Stuart's mothers took seats on the sofa. Rebecca was patting the middle cushion with increased energy until I had no choice but to settle between them. "Iona and I are here to say we're inconsolable that you broke the engagement," she began.

"Anyone want tea?" asked my mother.

"What kind do you have?" asked Rebecca.

"Nothing special," I said.

"Decaffeinated?"

"Are you here to talk Faith into taking Stuart back?" my father asked.

I said, "You're welcome to stay for tea, but I am not going to marry Stuart."

"Do you actually approve of this walk across the country, as if he has something to say?" my father asked. "Like it means something; like it *counts* for something?"

"He's forty-one years old," said Rebecca. "He doesn't need our approval. We don't even have to *get* it in order to accept it."

"That's just the point," I said. "He's forty-one years old! He should've done this when he was *twenty*-one! He shouldn't be living his life on Facebook."

"Does he even have health insurance?" my father asked.

"We wouldn't know," one of them sniffed.

I said I happened to know he did *not*.

Rebecca said, "Do you have to be engaged in order to live together? Couldn't you just be companions?"

"Roommates," said Iona. "Twin souls."

I said, "We do not share souls, not even close. And why would I want a freeloading roommate?"

Even my father inhaled sharply at such unaccustomed rudeness.

But there was no sharp intake of breath from the unoffendable Rebecca. "I can tell you why. Because he's good company! He's smart. He's got a big heart. He's handsome. He believes in people —"

"What does that mean — 'believes in people'?" my father asked.

I said, "Please don't explain. I've heard it a million times. I can recite it by heart."

"Who but a lost soul walks across the country?" my mother grumbled. "A lost soul with no job and no money in the bank."

I asked Rebecca if Stuart had sent them here as relationship missionaries.

"Would that be so terrible?" asked Iona.

"Are either of you Facebook friends with him?" I asked.

The two women exchanged questioning glances before saying, "No."

"Well, you should be. Then you'd understand what put the

final nail in the coffin — his arm around every woman between here and Illinois."

"Hyperbole aside," said his mother, "even if he *is* meeting a lot of women en route, he thinks of you as his anchor."

"Anchor?" my mother said. "Or meal ticket?"

"I resent that," said Rebecca.

"We both do," said Iona.

"You know what's missing?" my father asked. "And what may have been missing all along? I haven't heard anyone mention love."

If a subtitle had materialized beneath either of their ruddy perplexed faces, it would have read: *Did you just hear what I heard? Did a male of the species just speak rather eloquently of love?*

My parents stayed after the Stuart apologists left to explain that Rebecca and Iona had simply shown up at their door, trying to enlist the sympathies of Stuart's once-future in-laws. When your father has spent most of his working life insuring people's houses, he is in the habit of looking, metaphorically speaking, under the rug. It turned out that their visit wasn't just to chaperone Rebecca and Iona, but had its own purpose. Wally the inspector had told my brother about the cradle in my attic, and Joel had casually reported its existence to my mother.

"I think it's a sign," she said.

"Nancy —," my father warned.

"Of what?"

"Of a baby! One that will be born while you're living here!"

"Don't get your hopes up, Ma."

"You could do it. We're a modern family. We'd help. And you don't need to be married to have a baby anymore. There's no stigma. It's even fashionable."

"I'm aware of that. But I'm in no position to have a baby."

"And you're romanticizing a cradle that's probably been consumed by termites," said my father.

"Were there termites in Wally's report?" my mother asked. "Because that's something an inspector looks for."

I said no, but —

"Are you thinking what I'm thinking?" my mother asked, with a happy nudge.

"I don't know what —"

"Plan B: eBay! It could be a hundred years old, a valuable antique . . . Henry?"

"Henry what?" he asked.

"Go check it out. You're good at that."

"You haven't seen it yourself?" he asked me.

"It's in the attic. I haven't ventured up there."

"Jesus. I thought a daughter of mine would have more curiosity than that."

Grumbling and outnumbered, he found the step stool required to reach the hatch door then lowered the attic ladder.

Several minutes passed without a report. We heard the creak of floorboards overhead but nothing else. Later I would marvel that he didn't cry out in any fashion but rather calmly made his way back down the attic ladder. He was holding something wrapped in a flannel receiving blanket that may at one time have been pale pink. The bundle had the heft and shape of an oversize book.

"What's this?" I asked.

"An album. A photo album . . ."

"Did you open it?" my mother asked.

He shut his eyes.

"I want a look," said my mother. And as if he wasn't standing between us: "Your father's squeamish. You know he fainted when they cut Joel's umbilical cord? I didn't let him stay for yours."

I *did* know; that was the delicate-Dad story she trotted out annually on the anniversary of either child's birth.

"Henry," she instructed. "Give it over."

I said, "Maybe he should just describe what's in there. I think it's better to hear it — just words — rather than look at pictures."

"Who said pictures?" asked my mother.

"It's a photo album," I pointed out.

"Are you going to faint?" my mother asked, then noted that this very sensitivity was probably what gave his paintings such Chagallness.

I repeated that I didn't want to see anything that would forever taint my attic, let alone every square inch of my heretofore-beloved five and a half rooms.

"I need to sit," he repeated. We followed him into my bedroom, where my parents sat side by side on the bed, and I sat on the lone chair, upholstered recently in a retro drapery fabric featuring oversize ferns of magenta and green. "That came out so nice," my mother said. "Cora does such good work."

"Nancy!"

"Tell us," I said. "We're ready."

He cleared his throat noisily, once, twice, then said — the words separated by several seconds — "What I saw here... were photographs... of what appears to be... dead babies."

My mother and I reacted differently. I let out a horrified squeal, whereas my mother asked, "How do you know they're dead and not sleeping?"

"How do I *know?* Because someone wrote the dates of the births and deaths right on the bottom of the pictures!"

"What was her name, the owner? Lavoie? You'll ask at city hall tomorrow," my mother said.

"For what?" I asked.

"For a record of these babies — birth, deaths, whatever."

"I work. I can't be off doing detective work."

"Then we will," she said. "Henry? Before you head back?"

He offered the still-wrapped-up album, first in my mother's direction, then changed course and gave it to me. The pink blanket was stiff with dust. I unwrapped it the way I imagined one would unwrap a mummy, on alert for something awful inside. The album was thick, its cover brown leather, tooled and dyed to look antique, but not crumbling the way I expected it would be. I opened it and registered the twin shocks of the subjects themselves and the fact they'd been memorialized in something as pedestrian as Polaroids. I was expecting dignified images of the long-ago dead, as if a professional photographer in a black morning coat had been called to document what once had been. But these were cheap, yellowed, faded, almost casual.

Written in ballpoint on the bottom white space: *Baby girl no. 1, born Dec. 15, '56, 9:42 a.m.* And *Baby girl no. 2, 12/15/56 9:55 a.m. Taken away 12/22.*

They were dressed in quilted snowsuits and knitted caps, the kind of thing you might dress your live baby in for the ride home from the hospital on a December day.

I said, "They were twins! They lived a week, exactly."

My mother said, "So pretty for newborns, too. Especially tiny ones like these." She closed the book. "On the bright side, we could say it was very advanced of whoever took these pictures. In those days, people didn't get to hold their babies, let alone photograph them."

"You don't find this suspicious?" my father asked.

"Who knows what's normal when it comes to dead babies," she said.

"There's nothing normal about this! These had to be taken here" — he opened the book again — "and this one on a kitchen table. This is not a wake. It's not a funeral home or a funeral. This is here! They could've been born here and never had a chance!"

I leaned in for a closer look. It was *my* kitchen counter, *my* speckled Formica. My father was right. There were no signs of ceremony or proper mourning. If we three Sherlock Holmeses were polled at that moment, at least two of us would have guessed that the next step had been burying each baby out back under my suspiciously luxuriant crabapple tree.

17

Welcome to Everton

I MAY HAVE DRIFTED OFF a few times during the night, but by morning it felt like I'd had no sleep at all. I'd tried watching two shopping channels and cable news. I never turned off my bedside lamp or my phone, which was shuffling through all the podcasts I'd been neglecting to listen to.

At breakfast, like an unwelcome houseguest, the photo album seemed to be taking up the whole kitchen. Draped over the back of a chair, its swaddling flannel was equally unappetizing. Why hadn't I sent the whole creepy package home with my parents? I made coffee, toasted a waffle, and took both into the parlor so I didn't have to dine with the evidence. I opened every shade and curtain for maximum sunlight; when I took my bath, I locked the door.

I pulled into my parking space at school almost an hour early. As ever, inadequately dressed for the cold weather, the students were rushing off to their eight o'clock classes. I found Nick already at his desk. *A whole free hour*, I thought, *for forensic ventilation over coffee*. But there was no reaction when I announced,

"You won't believe it, but yesterday, when my parents were visiting, we found photos of dead babies!"

I tried again, slightly louder. "Nick? Did you hear what I said?"

He was typing, his screen at an oblique angle, affording him more privacy than usual. "Dead babies," he repeated. "That can't be good."

"'Not good'? How about incredibly sad if not creepy? How about *didn't sleep a wink?*"

Finally, he looked up, and said rather numbly, "Me neither . . . Don't ask."

I said, "I'm very inclined to ask," then spent the next few minutes silently considering what bad news he might be shielding me from. "Do you know something I don't know about my job? Something bad?"

"It's not about you," he said. "It's personal."

Well, who doesn't know that's code for *Mind your own business?* I said nothing for a few minutes until: "You didn't go to the doctor yesterday and find out you have a terminal illness, did you?"

His phone was ringing, first his cell, and when that stopped, the office landline. He answered neither. Nor did he answer me.

It wasn't long before *my* extension was ringing. "Development, Faith Frankel," I chirped.

"Is Nick there?" a woman asked.

"Who may I say is calling?"

"Is he there?" she persisted.

I said, "This isn't his direct line, but I can give you that number."

"I have that number. Believe me, I've tried it," said the caller.

"Is this Brooke?"

"Good guess, *Faith,*" she snapped.

Where was this undeserved hostility coming from? I said, "Nick's in a meeting and probably has his phone turned off."

"I bet," she said. *Click*.

"You may have noticed that was Brooke," I told him.

Now *my* cell phone was ringing, the "Bridge over Troubled Water" ringtone I'd assigned to my mother. Before I'd even offered a greeting, she was launching into a narrative. "We're at city hall. *Outside* city hall. I would've called you from the city clerk's office, but they have signs saying no cell phone usage."

"*And?*"

"Do you have a minute?" she asked, usually the preamble to a gossipy tidbit gleaned at the supermarket.

"Just the highlights. I'm in the middle of a couple of things."

"So we get there at nine on the dot. Dad started with 'Our daughter recently passed papers on 10 Turpentine Lane.' The clerk was expressionless. She takes out a roll of stamps and starts putting them on envelopes — must've been property tax bills. So Dad tries 'We're pretty sure that the name we want to look up is Lavoie.' Finally, the clerk says, 'I knew a Lavoie on Turpentine . . . Sort of knew her. I went to high school with her daughter.'"

I said, "I bought the house from that daughter."

"What are the odds!" my mother exclaimed.

"Ma, welcome to Everton. Who *didn't* go to high school together? Is there more to it? More info?"

"Of course! I asked her how well she knew the family. She said not much. So I asked if Theresa was an only child."

Even over the phone, I could tell she was mentally congratulating herself for that bull's-eye of a question.

"And . . . ?"

"She didn't answer. But then — and I know you miss living in a gigantic impersonal city, but this is where living in a small town pays off — another customer was at the other end of the counter, and she calls over, 'The Lavoies on Turpentine?' So we say yes. And, of course, Dad and I are all ears. The woman practically spits out, 'That house should've been condemned for all the tragedies that happened there.' Can you imagine? Of course, one of us asked, 'Tragedies . . . such as?'

"The woman said, 'Her husbands died there.' I asked how. She shrugged and said, 'All I remember is that people kept their distance.' So that was when Dad and I started going through the records."

"*And?*"

"Well, we went straight for the birth date given on the Polaroids, December 15, 1956."

"And?"

"And nothing. No twin baby girls born that day. The clerk said the births could've happened in a hospital elsewhere, out of town. Or maybe they were some photos that someone else left at the house — a relative or a visitor."

"Doubt it. Did you check the death records?"

"We did — nothing! So I asked the clerk again, but I think she was getting sick of us —"

"Is there going to be a payoff to this story?" I asked.

"Not yet. But we're heading to the library to look at *Echo* microfiche. Well, *I* am. Your father is itching to get back to Boston."

"Call me if you find the actual obituaries," I said, implying, *Not interested in your chats with fellow patrons and research librarians.*

"That was my mother," I told the four walls. "She and my dad are doing a little detective work about those babies I mentioned. The dead ones."

When Nick didn't react, I started collecting my notecards,

my envelopes, my fountain pen, and my phone while huffing in offended fashion. I said I was going over to the student center. To write. To have a cappuccino. And he'd have the privacy he clearly desired.

He didn't say, *Sorry. I'm being rude. This is your office, too.* What he said was "Fine."

This was not normal, engaged, collegial Nick; this was sarcastic Nick, whom I'd only experienced alongside an annoying alum or an administrative Judas.

"And you don't have to worry," I said rather grandly, "because when I return, I'm minding my own business. I hope you're not ill. I hope no one died. But maybe you need to answer Brooke's calls." I paused at the door. "Oh, and if I find out why my house is a crime scene, I won't trouble you with that update."

Finally, I got his attention. "Seriously?" he asked. "A crime scene? As in murder?" Then he said, "Sit down. I'll explain."

18

What a Pal

I T WAS THIS: Brooke had given him an ultimatum along the lines of propose, marry, propagate.

"Out of the blue?" I asked, provoking a minor Brooke-based tirade.

"With all our conversations from day one about marriage not being in the equation?" he demanded. "And now 'Where is this going?' You can bet her girlfriends put her up to this. They're all relationship strategists. One of them — Lauren, Laura? — tried the same thing and her boyfriend caved. Game over! A magic marriage bullet!"

He further volunteered that she expected a ring, the cost of which should be equal to or greater than two months' salary. And they'd marry in a year, but sooner if the hoped-for venue was available. "Do you believe that?" he demanded. "The venue!"

I wholly believed it. "That's really important to some brides," I said.

That collective noun provoked something of a shudder. There were more questions I wanted to ask, such as why was marriage never in the equation? Was it the person or the institution itself? The question I finally asked was "When did this conversation take place?"

"All weekend."

"*Are* you getting married?"

"Jesus, no! I thought that was clear."

I said I was sorry. It couldn't be easy whether you're the breaker-upper or the breakee . . . I mean, even though I was the one who broke up with Stuart . . . oh, never mind. Sorry for being so inarticulate but I wasn't sure, given his miserable mood, whether I should be offering condolences or congratulations. And I couldn't help noticing that Brooke had been calling rather assiduously.

"Slippage," he said. "Regret is seeping in. She was sure I would get down on one knee and say, 'Yes, darling. Will you be my lawfully wedded wife?'"

Our neglected e-mails were pinging. Phone calls were going to voice mail. He gestured with an impatient wave. *Gotta answer these.*

Of course, it was that moment when Reggie entered, announcing that he'd been over in Admissions, meeting parents whose kid, a hockey star at Cathedral, twenty-five goals last season, was applying for a PG year.

"How are his grades?" I asked.

"Who cares?" Then to Nick: "I didn't know you had a trip this week. Where you off to?"

"Nowhere."

"Isn't that your suitcase in the coat closet?"

"Technically, a duffel," said Nick.

"Vacation? Because I'm supposed to know about such things."

Nick finally turned away from his keyboard. "If you must know, there's been a change in my living arrangements."

This news incited Reggie to drag a chair to Nick's desk, his enthusiasm barely contained. "No kidding! What happened?"

"Take a guess."

"She kicked you out?"

I winced; I picked up my fountain pen, pretending to be lost in sentence contemplation but secretly pleased to have Reggie take over the third degree.

"It was mutual," Nick said. And less audibly: "At least that's the party line."

"Maybe Nick doesn't want to talk about his private life, Reg," I said.

Nick, for the first time all morning, laughed. "Well, if that isn't a pile of horseshit!"

"Me?" said Reggie. "What did *I* say?"

"No. Miss Innocent. She'd love to get the 411 on this."

What to do? Laugh or take offense? I said, "Brooke could be calling me back any second. Or ringing my doorbell. It would help if I had a little more intel."

"Wanna watch the Pats at Moose's tonight?" Reggie asked him. "It's the game of the week. We could pick up Chinese."

Nick said, "I think I'll pass."

Reggie leaned over Nick's desk to give one of his shoulders a squeeze. "Any time, bro. You have a place to crash?"

Nick said, "Thanks for asking."

With a cocky salute, Reggie was gone.

"*Do* you have a place to crash?" I asked.

He said he was thinking of The Evermore — the drab school-owned guesthouse that alums booked for reunion weekends when the surrounding chains had no vacancies.

I asked if they had a weekly rate, an off-season rate, an Everton Country Day faculty and staff discount, a room not over-looking the landfill . . . ?

It was only chatter as I borrowed time to analyze the propriety of the idea that was slowly dawning. Single male and single female, colleagues by day, houseguest and hostess by night? Was that asking for unwarranted workplace gossip? But what kind of colleague wouldn't invite a homeless coworker to bunk in her spare bedroom midcrisis? Especially one who'd championed her when she was in need.

"The Evermore wouldn't be long-term, just until I find a place," he said.

I told him I was going for that cappuccino after all. Could I bring one back for him?

"Thanks. Just coffee."

I got as far as the outer office door then returned. "Listen . . . I have an extra bedroom. By which I mean you'd be very welcome to stay on Turpentine Lane until you get your bearings."

"Wow," he said. "That is extremely generous of you . . ."

"But?"

"No 'but'! I accept. And I won't be that houseguest you can't get rid of. I'm combing the real estate ads already. Really, though — what a pal."

I confessed that it wasn't entirely altruistic. I needed the company. "The dead babies I've been talking about? I haven't given you the full story because I don't know what it is. But pictures of them posed on my kitchen counters — I mean it could be nothing — but then I heard about husbands dying there. Not that I think it's haunted, but even if it's just for a few days, it'll get me over the hump . . . Silly, I know."

"Not silly at all. And we have an expression for this, even if it sounds like something Reggie would say."

I waited.

"Win-win," he said.

19

I Apologize

I'D NEGOTIATED A TWO-HOUR window between my return home and Nick's arrival, needing to wash three days of dirty dishes, scrub the tub, and, most important, furnish the room I'd been avoiding due to yet another unattractive chapter in the history of 10 Turp: the site of what might have been Mrs. Lavoie's last minutes on earth. I'd run out on my lunch hour, bought a mattress and a platform bed, and enlisted my brother to pick them up from the loading dock — or else wait five business days till their overly casual delivery service kicked in.

Since there had been no word from my mother on her microfiche search, I called her before leaving school. She said she had nothing to report and couldn't talk long now that her home number was a business line. But what she'd learned today was that newborns don't get obituaries, at least not in the Everton *Echo,* and probably not anywhere in the 1950s.

"Dad didn't go with you?"

"He was in a hurry to get back to his studio. Whoops, here's a call. It might be him. Gotta go."

I helped Joel unload the cargo and hoist it up to the second floor, then teamed up for the assembly — if reading the instructions aloud and supplying a Phillips screwdriver qualified as teamwork. He seemed to be studying me as I put linens and blankets on the new mattress, smoothing every layer in, apparently, too conscientious a fashion. "What are you all jittery about?" he asked.

I said I wasn't, that I just wanted everything to look nice — this quilt was as old as I was. If you have wallpaper this busy do you need artwork? What about Dad's old felt Everton Country Day pennant? Too corny? Did he think the room was too barren with only a bed and the scarred dresser I'd found curbside on big-item garbage day?

"Compared to what? Sleeping in his car?"

"Slight exaggeration," I said. My next task was emptying the top two bureau drawers, which I'd been using as a substitute linen closet.

"He's a guy," Joel said. "He's gonna live out of his suitcase." He checked his phone. "If we're done here, I'll pack up this rubble and take off."

"You don't want to stick around and meet Nick?"

"Can't. Sorry. Another time."

I asked if he had plans.

"You could say that."

"Is it a date?"

He took the pile of towels I was holding and walked it across the hall. "Here?" he asked at my bureau. "Or where?"

"Anywhere. Thanks. If it *is* a date, did you meet online?"

"Nope."

"Did you meet . . . just out in the world?"

"Sort of. She called me."

"That's nice, don't you think? I like hearing that a woman asked a man for a date."

"How about we drop the subject?"

Then I knew. He was meeting his ex, who'd never left Everton, who hadn't remarried, who was surely on the prowl, and no doubt was angling to get my sterling brother back. "You're not having a drink with Brenda, are you?"

I followed him back to the guest room where he was collecting assorted packaging debris. "Trash bags?" he asked. "As for Brenda, not a chance."

I said I'd be right back with the bags. I got only as far as the top step when I backtracked to ask, "If it's not your ex-wife or someone totally age inappropriate or an escort service, what's the big secret?"

"Jesus! Where do you come up with this stuff?"

I said, "I'm not asking out of nosiness. I might know her! She might be an alum —"

"And I might never see her again after one drink, so why discuss it at all?"

"I won't get invested. I won't even text you later to see how it went. That's how *un*interested I am."

When I returned with the trash bags, a broom, and a dustpan, Joel was wrestling with the large corrugated box that had housed the unassembled bed.

"Can't you put it on the truck without getting all neat about it?"

"That would be too easy," he said.

I was dabbing the floor with the broom as Joel watched.

"Who taught you how to sweep?" he asked, and when I didn't answer, he said, "If you must know, her name is Leslie."

"Thank you. Does she have a last name?"

"Probably. Okay, listen . . . I didn't think you'd love this part. Leslie has a sister who used to be married to Stuart."

I couldn't make immediate sense of that confession. "Stuart? *My* Stuart? Stuart Levine? You're in touch with him?"

"No, I am not."

"So you just ran into her somewhere, and she mentioned she had an ex-brother-in-law named Stuart, and you put two and two together?"

"Calm down. No. One of his mothers gave her my number."

"Stuart's mothers? When did you meet Stuart's mothers?"

"I didn't. Mom did."

"They met *here!* There wasn't any matchmaking going on."

"All I know is that at some point Mom mentioned what I do, since all it takes is a weather forecast, and they came away with a business card, and who knows how one thing leads to another?"

"What if you like her? What if you *marry* her?"

"Let that be your biggest worry," he said. "Now give me the broom. End of discussion."

Clearly I'd annoyed him. He was collecting not just the newly filled trash bags but also emptying every second-floor wastebasket. With arms full, he said, "I hope your guest will find his very heavy, solid ash, hard-to-assemble bed very comfortable. Would you prefer I leave by the servants' entrance?"

I said, "I'm sorry! You were a huge help with all of this." I propped the broom in the nearest corner. "Put that stuff down so I can give you a thank-you hug."

Post hug, post apology, over glasses of water in the kitchen, I asked, "Have you spoken to Mom today?"

"Why?"

"She told me she had to rush off the phone because it was now a business line."

"Oh, that," he said.

"What business?"

"It's bogus, a make-work project. She volunteered to be Dad's booker because he doesn't answer his phone."

I put an imaginary receiver to my ear. "Hello. Frankel Forgeries, Incorporated. And for your towing and plowing needs, you can also leave a message here for my only son."

"You think that's a joke? Tommy McKeon — you remember him? We used to caddy together? He told me that Mom was getting gas at the Pride station, and his dad was at the next pump. She called over to him, 'Snow predicted for tomorrow! How are you set for plowing?' He said, 'I do my own shoveling.' You know what Ma said? 'Does your wife know CPR?'"

I said, "I kinda admire that."

He helped himself to one of the apples I'd arranged in an artistic, nutritional fashion. "This new housemate," he asked. "He's a good guy?"

I said, "He was the only one who stuck up for me at work, at the inquisition. And this arrangement is very temporary, only until he finds what he's looking for."

"Maybe *this* is what he's looking for," Joel said.

Besides his duffel, Nick arrived with a suitcase, a knapsack, two boxes of books, an electric frying pan, and the contents of his wine rack. After another trip to his car, he returned with a bulging brown grocery bag.

I hadn't thought this far ahead as to whether we'd be dining family-style, sharing the cooking, or labeling yogurt and condiments in the unfriendly, proprietary manner of my Brooklyn roommates.

He said, "I didn't want to take anything for granted. Such as breakfast. I wasn't sure what you had for a coffeemaker. I guessed and bought ground. And half-and-half."

I'd been standing in the front hall, not meaning to block his entrance but frozen to the spot due to the sudden reality of Nick extracurricularly.

"How about a tour?" he asked.

I wasn't expecting to feel this self-conscious about everything, about my humble five rooms, about me in jeans, my hair in a ponytail. Had I thought this through? Would we be breakfasting in bathrobes? Commuting in one car or two? Using the same bar of soap? All of this seemed to be manifesting itself as social paralysis.

"Faith?" he prompted. "You okay with all of this?"

I said, "Yes, of course. And now the tour . . . this is what I call the parlor. This will be the dining room as soon as I get a dining-room table. This is my china closet. There's plenty of room if you have dishes. Or stemware."

"Hmm . . . stemware," he said. "I don't believe I do. But thank you."

Next was the kitchen. "It's probably self-explanatory," I said, but narrated anyway: stove, breadbox, sink. "It's soapstone," I said. "The original sink. I keep my cleaning products under it . . . Here. Whatever you need."

"And would this by any chance be the refrigerator and the toaster?" he asked.

I confessed that I was a little nervous. It wasn't his being here. It was seeing my very modest house through new eyes. Maybe he'd been expecting something bigger or grander or newer.

He said, "You're forgetting the large number of photos you showed me between your first visit and your moving in. So cut it out. It's great."

"Even if I don't have a microwave?"

"I'm antimicrowave. And I don't like big houses. They're so . . . big. So pretentious. So head of school."

"Whew," I said. "Thank you."

"Who's thanking who here? I could be at The Evermore. Or on Reggie's couch."

We ate turkey meatloaf he'd brought from his ex-refrigerator. I supplied macaroni salad and a corkscrew. Unsolicited, he confided that the meatloaf was from the deli counter at the Big Y. No one at his former address ever cooked anything. "Do I sound like a throwback? Like I expected my girlfriend to cook? I didn't. But she had so little interest in food that I think it was somewhat pathological."

As much as I would have enjoyed deconstructing that criticism, I thought it was best not to. I volunteered that Stuart had been a vegetarian, but called himself a vegan to win extra points. I helped myself to another piece of the meatloaf and pronounced it very satisfying, then ventured into the arena of meals in general. "I hope you know you can help yourself to anything in the refrigerator."

"Thank you. Of course, I want to contribute."

I said, "I think you're forgetting the service you're providing."

"Oh, right . . . as ghostbuster. When do I see the evidence?"

The dreaded album, he meant, which I'd buried out of sight in the china cupboard's creaky bottom drawer. "If you insist," I said. "But don't say I didn't warn you."

Had I expected that a man would be more stoic? He wasn't.

He closed the book after only a few seconds. "Are you fucking kidding me?" he said. "Pictures of babies' corpses? Who did this?"

"I don't know. Let's not say 'corpses.' It makes them sound so . . . I don't know . . . so *call 911*."

"You know for a fact that this album belonged to the previous owner?"

"Those infant seats were on my kitchen counter." I swept the room rather grandly. "These babies were photographed *here*."

It was at this point in the conversation that Nick put an imaginary phone to his ear, and said, "Ding-a-ling-a-ling."

"Huh?"

"You're calling the previous owner and getting to the bottom of this. We're practicing."

"She lives in Maui. It's the middle of the night there."

"Hawaii? Just the opposite. It would be . . . he checked his watch. "Five hours difference, or six? The middle of the afternoon." Then he repeated, "Ding-a-ling-a-ling."

"Are we role-playing?"

"Exactly."

"In that case . . . Hello."

"No, you're you, the caller. I'm the daughter. Pretend you're making conversation with a perfectly reasonable woman who sold you her childhood home. Think of fund-raising calls. Pleasantries first."

"That helps. Okay . . . 'Theresa? This is Faith Frankel, the woman who bought your house?'"

Nick said, his voice a cartoony half octave higher than real life, "Well, hello, Faith. It was a pleasure doing business with you."

I said, "No, it wasn't. She'd never say that because I paid way below her asking price."

"Okay, take two. Well, very nice to meet you, Faith — telephonically, that is. What is it that you're calling about?"

Already stumped, my first try was "Well, you know that the house went through an inspection, top to bottom —"

Baritone Nick stepped out of character to say, "No. Don't go there. Didn't she have to shell out a lot of dough for the repairs?"

"How about 'I found a photo album in the attic, in a cradle, and I thought maybe you'd want it.'"

"What would I want with a cradle?" he falsettoed.

"No, I meant the photo album. It was wrapped in a receiving blanket, and it had pictures of babies in it."

It was here that Nick's character snapped. He clutched a handful of his flannel shirt and whispered, "Dead? Are they dead babies? Have we been found out at long last? Is the jig up?"

Thus ended our wine-induced improv. "You get the idea. Just tell her what you found and could she explain it," he said.

We moved on to dessert, which was several flavors of ice cream I thought had male appeal, purchased on my way home. When I offered hot fudge, Nick said, "I may never leave."

20

I'm Not Blaming Anyone

I FELT OBLIGED TO LEAVE voice-mail messages on Theresa
Tindle's phone, hoping to sound upbeat, in the manner of
a satisfied owner suffering no buyer's regret. My first message said, more or less, "This is Faith Frankel, your buyer? All
is well. I found some mementos that I believe belonged to your
parents. I'll try you again." My second message, two days later,
changed "mementos" to "some photos found in an album, in the
attic."

Had I left my cell phone number? Apparently so. She reached
me at school, in my office, with Nick present. I expected she'd
be on guard, suspicious of the fussy buyer whose inspector had
found so much to flunk. But her first words were "Hi! It's Terry!
You called?"

"Terry?"

"Terry Tindle? Theresa? Mrs. Lavoie's daughter? The photo
album? Did you want to send it to me? Do you need my address?"

When waving my arm in in the air didn't get more than a puzzled look from Nick, I resorted to signage, scribbling, *Theresa, the daughter!* on a sheet of paper while saying, "Thank you for calling back. But could I ask you some questions about the pictures in the album?"

"Shoot!"

"First of all, if you're wondering which album, it's brown. The cover is tooled leather. Old. And empty except for . . . Polaroids. I don't know if you've ever seen them, but they reveal something you might find disconcerting —"

"Oh, shit," I heard.

I nodded victoriously for Nick's benefit. Surely Theresa was going to elaborate now that I'd reopened a hideous chapter of her sad early life.

"Who else saw them?" she asked.

"Just my parents. And my housemate."

"Are you trying to embarrass me?" Theresa asked. "Because, frankly, I'm surprised you had the nerve to call me."

How had this turned sour so fast? "I'm not blaming anyone!" I protested. "I'm not accusing anyone of anything. Maybe it's none of my business, but as the new owner, I really need to know what happened here."

"Is it really any of your business. And do you think this is funny?"

"Of course not. Quite the opposite."

"Throw them out! I don't want those Polaroids, which I can't believe anyone kept."

I said, "I really don't think I should throw them away."

"It's not your decision!"

"But what if they're some kind of evidence?"

"For what? Something they liked doing in the privacy of their own home?"

Was I horrified or just stumped, either of which must have

showed, because in a few seconds Nick was holding up a sign that said *WTF?*

I said, "Is it possible that we're talking about totally different photos?"

"I'm talking about pictures of my mother that no daughter would want to see!"

Was English suddenly a language I didn't speak? "Pictures of your mother?" I repeated.

"Naked! What else would I mean?"

Naked pictures of Mrs. Lavoie, who only existed in my mind's eye as a nonagenarian on her deathbed? What had I ever said other than "Polaroids" that invited such an unbosoming? "Why would you think that?" I asked.

"What else am I supposed to think? Disturbing photos? Or did you say disgusting? And I wouldn't be surprised if he used a Polaroid because Kodak certainly wasn't going to develop nude photos. Everybody knows that."

All I managed to say was "I'm a big believer in artistic freedom —"

"It was their own business. If it's your own husband, and he's not sending a roll of film to the local drug store, what's the harm? It doesn't make you an exhibitionist."

Now reduced to babbling, I said, "I know we tell the girls at school — never, never, never let anyone take naked pictures of you because it's going to end up on the Internet."

"That's now! This was between a married couple. Just like you said, it's art."

Thus I found myself discussing Polaroids I'd never seen, which might never have existed. "Do you know for a fact that your father or a stepfather photographed your mother naked?" — winning Nick's full eye-popping attention.

"Of course I didn't know. Okay, maybe I found one in a drawer after he died. Certainly not porn. I wasn't shocked! Looking back, I think they had fun together. It was a small house, and I slept directly across the hall from them. She was proud of her body — I'm sure you knew girls like that in college. You can just tell — the way they parade around. She was in great shape, even after having three kids."

Three. Babies. I'd done it. Unknowingly I'd forged a path that led us back to my starting point. I said, "Three babies?" And even more disingenuously, "So you weren't her only child?"

"Well, I kind of was. She was pregnant, but the babies didn't make it. I don't remember that much, and I didn't know anything about the birds and the bees. I was only six or seven. Later, much later, I asked what happened. Like, hadn't she gone to the hospital and had a baby?"

"Did she tell you?"

"She told me it was the Rh factor. A blood thing. She was Rh negative, and the babies triggered some fatal allergic reaction. They've figured it out since. *I* lived because I was the first baby. After that . . . well, look it up. It's about antibodies. Now it's fixable — they give the mother a shot or two, and it's all fine."

What does one say except "I'm so sorry. That must've been a terrible thing — to grow up under the shadow of that." And then, as if I weren't trading in make-believe: "If posing for photos gave your parents some solace or enjoyment . . . who is anyone to judge?"

"PTSD," she stated. "You know what that is?"

I said I did, yes.

"Plus my father's sudden death, and then the stepfathers. One day they're there, and the next day they're gone. Believe me, it's all taken its toll . . . Do you have a shredder? Because I don't want these photos. I don't even want them thrown out, lying around the dump."

I said, "I have a shredder at work. So sure . . ." But without conviction, as I considered telling the truth about the photos — that "disconcerting" did not apply to her mother posing naked. Would she want a photographic record of the true subjects, her departed siblings?

Then I heard "How's Mrs. Strenger? Still next door? She used to babysit me before she had her own kids."

I said, "Mrs. Strenger? Is she on my driveway side?"

"Yes, that's her. She had this amazing red-gold hair. They were newlyweds when they moved in and he worshipped her. Even as a kid, I could see that. She was a knockout, but he was nothing to look at. It's funny, isn't it — the way that can happen? They had two boys, who are probably in their fifties now. I babysat for *them*. I forget their names, but neither one got the mother's hair color. I wonder if they're on Facebook?"

What does one say besides "Thank you for calling back. I'll take care of everything."

Was there a name for this detached conversational hopscotching? Next time I saw Everton's school psychologist in the lunchroom, I'd ask.

21

Team Turpentine

R H FACTOR?" MY MOTHER REPEATED. "Why didn't *I* think of that?"

"Because you're not a doctor!"

"No, I meant I should've thought of that because *my* blood is Rh negative! They gave me a shot during the pregnancies and then another after I gave birth. It's no big deal now, but in the old days . . . well, never mind. You were never in danger. The good news, in its own horrible way, is that we know for sure that your house wasn't a crime scene."

Knocking against each other in my increasingly inefficient brain were these thoughts: A. *Why hadn't this occurred to her earlier?* And B. *If it weren't for medical science, I'd be dead, too.*

"Of course," she added. "It still doesn't answer the question why someone took pictures of those poor babies."

I said, "I'm at work, Ma. I can't really think straight now."

"Maybe the pictures were done professionally. By which I mean by the police. Because you call the police when some-one dies in your home and they send the medical examiner. Or maybe it was the undertaker, for cosmetic reasons, like how the babies looked closest to being alive."

"Still, who puts pictures like that in an album?"

"Oops. Your father's calling. Talk soon!"

I hung up and just sat there staring at the campus map with which I had replaced the map of the continental U.S.

"Not that I was eavesdropping," I heard Nick say, "but the photos? Maybe the parents were so crazed with grief that they couldn't let the babies go, and they happened to own a Polaroid camera. Must've been one of the first models. What year did you say this was?"

I said, "It was 1956. Thank you for that. Really. That's going to be my take-away. Please remind me never to mention those poor children again."

My mother texted me within minutes. **Dad's going to paint 2 cherubs floating in the sky.**

Why? I texted back.

To honor the babies! On spec.

I told Nick of this new artistic venture and, after a few swigs of now-cold coffee, that my mother had Rh-negative blood, the thing that killed the babies; well, the antibodies did, which meant I could have been a goner but for medical science, the cure, the medicine, the shots — good thing I wasn't born twenty-five years earlier . . . just like babies number one and two.

After a respectful pause, Nick asked, "And would this be the topic you're no longer dwelling on to the detriment of thank-you notes?"

I looked down at my morning's output. The one note I'd begun had gotten as far as *Dear Dr. Tseng, Everyone here at Everton Country Day* . . .

~ ❧ ~

Nick and I commuted in separate cars, rarely ate lunch together, discussed dinner off-handedly in the waning hour of the
workday. One of us would say, "I'm picking up a roast chicken"
or "I'm thinking of sushi," always prefaced by a variation of the
phrase "If you don't have other plans . . ."

So far, Nick's real estate search had yielded nothing. That
one on the dead-end street that sounded so good on paper had
no light or cell service. Another had wall-to-wall carpeting in
the kitchen. A so-called garden apartment overlooked an algae-
coated swimming pool. They were too small or too smelly or
had a dog barking in the next apartment for the entire visit. No
storage, no parking space, no counter space, no character. "I
swear I'm not fussy," he said, after each visit. "All I'm asking for
is half of a house, upstairs or down. I'm not looking for a palace,
just a few decent rooms. Who knew the inventory would be this
bad?"

I did. Mid-November was not when apartments became free.
One week at 10 Turpentine became two. He put apartment-
wanted signs up at school. Someone with an in-law apartment
called, offering a room over her garage, not technically a legal
apartment, plus there were parents arriving from Florida in
mid-May.

As a housemate, he was excellent. He took out the garbage before it overflowed or decomposed. He fixed things that I didn't
know needed fixing or desqueaking. He wasted no time buying various oils and ammoniated liquids, along with fine steel
wool, lightbulbs of various wattages, and a shiny black power
drill. So when he said, "All I'm looking for is half a house," I said,
"Sit down. Okay. This is a two-bedroom house and you've been
a model roommate" — an especially apt statement at this moment as he was collecting limp dish towels to be thrown into
the wash with his own load of whites.

He didn't answer immediately. After returning from the cellar and no doubt cleaning the lint filters, he announced, "I agree. This is definitely working. We're both easy to get along with. We've worked out the kinks. I just wonder if you think it would ever get awkward."

I said, "Such as?"

He poured a refill into the cup he'd already washed and sat down. "I'm not saying this is going to happen tomorrow, but we're two single people . . ."

What was I expecting? Something personal and declaratory? No. What he was working up to was this: "I mean, how awkward if one morning, at breakfast, there are three of us instead of two?"

A sleepover. With a woman. Or, in my case, a man. So I asked lightly, casually, like the neutered buddy and disinterested party I was pretending to be, "Do you have someone in mind?"

"No! The ink's not dry on the breakup. I'm just covering all contingencies."

Of course, bachelor Nick, handy, eligible, and good-natured Nick — handsome Nick, lest I'd failed to note that before — would undoubtedly meet someone, and in the natural progression of things, the new girlfriend would keep a toothbrush here. Because an answer was called for, I said, "I could deal with that."

Nick said, "I don't even know why I brought this up now."

"Covering all contingencies," I reminded him. "Who knows. You could start seeing Brooke again. Like a trial run."

"Did you forget that the only trial run Brooke wants is down the aisle?"

I could've added, *You're well rid of her*, but decided to take the high road. "Who knows what new girl or guy might be around the corner. We're both free now." Then, in case that sounded one iota flirtatious and inappropriate for a coworker, I lied, and said, "A few of my brother's friends are calling me, but I think it's too early."

"And Stuart?"

"Stuart what?"

"Any regrets?"

"His. I had to unfriend him. He kept sending me messages."

"Saying what?"

"Same old stuff. 'Heading south. It's cold up here. The credit card was rejected again.'" I stopped short of reporting the *love you*s expressed in emoji.

Nick said, "Never having met the douche, may I still say congratulations on the unfriending?"

With that, he rose from the table, walked his mug to the sink, rinsed it, then came back with a sponge.

I said, "You're an uncommonly good roommate."

"It's official then? I'll get the rest of my stuff?"

"Deal."

"No, not a deal until I know what half of your expenses are, by which I mean mortgage. *And* taxes. Plus utilities."

I couldn't think of a single reason why one-half of everything wouldn't be a fair share. I said, "Okay. I'll do the math. Nothing's due till the first of the month."

We shook on it, a kind of teenage-boy shake with thumbs and a fist bump. "Mind if I bring my vacuum cleaner, which actually picks up dirt?" he asked. "And can I now caulk around the tub?"

I nodded, but my face must have been registering *Did I just hear what I thought I heard?*

"What's that look for?" he asked.

"Cock around the tub? I'm not sure what that means."

"Caulk, you knucklehead! C-a-u-l-k. The stuff that comes in tubes. You haven't noticed there's hardly any seal left between the tile and the tub?"

"I'm not sure I was meant to be a homeowner."

"You're covered now. Team Turpentine."

I left the kitchen, heading for my coat, but returned to ask, "And speaking of teams, did I ever properly thank you for saving my job?"

"I'm pretty damn sure your job was never in danger."

"Then saving me from probation — during which they'd have hired somebody who played football with QB1."

When his pleasant expression clouded, I asked, "Did I hit the nail on the head? About firing and hiring?"

"Oh, sorry. No. Nothing like that."

"What then?"

"Nonsense. Reggie's."

"Such as?"

"He thinks he's so hilarious! When he saw that I was having my mail forwarded here, he started up with 'Didn't take either of you long to get over your exes.' That kind of crap."

I said, "Thankfully, he doesn't try that stuff with me."

"Because he's a twelve-year-old boy who can't talk to girls."

"And, don't forget — he's an idiot. We have to stage a coup."

Nick grinned. "No wonder he's scared of you."

"He should be. He knows the Frankels would come after him — mother, father, brother, plow. Not to mention the law firm of Franconi and Franconi."

"When do I get to meet the famous parents?" Nick asked.

"Any day now," I answered. *Maybe after I've told them you moved in.*

22

~∾⊱⊰∾~

Mind If I Look Around?

HOW HAD I NOT DEDUCED from Stuart's messages referencing sleet and low funds that he was aborting his mission? He'd only gotten as far as a gas station restroom in Missouri, right over the Illinois border, when he decided that he'd raised enough awareness and could fly home, thanks to his moms' air miles.

Nor had I realized that Nick was still following Stuart on Instagram until he announced at work, smartphone in hand, "What's this? Your ex-fiancé is giving a thumb's-up in line at a gate."

"What kind of gate?"

"Southwest Airlines. Getting on a plane."

"Hand it over," I said.

Sure enough. There was Stuart managing a selfie despite the camping equipment and carry-ons. The message said, "At Lambert-St. Louis airport. Need to get back to MA for personal reasons."

I read it aloud, and asked, "Do you think MA means Ma, like mother, or MA, like Massachusetts?"

"The latter."

Personal reasons. We hadn't talked in weeks, but those might involve me. I picked up my fountain pen and wrote two lackluster thank-yous for low-end donations. Nick was on the phone confirming an upcoming visit to an alum. Though typing as he talked, the conversation was animated, about some varsity hockey player's breakaway goal, followed by references to the alum's wife and daughters by name. He hung up and did a happy xylophoning with a pencil.

"What?"

"Ka-ching."

"How much?"

"Miss? Do I get in the car and drive to Connecticut for less than ten K?"

I went back to work, aiming for more oomph and personal engagement in the next few notes. Across the room, Nick continued his winning salesmanship, confirming more day trips, sending more regards to relatives, hinting at brass plaques on renamed buildings.

This time I checked Stuart's airport photo myself. "Posted fifteen hours ago," I told Nick. "One good thing: he didn't alert me to his homecoming."

Nick didn't ask for amplification, but I volunteered it anyway. "The fact that he didn't announce he was coming home or ask me to pick him up at the airport means he's accepted that we're done. Over. Finis."

Nick merely grunted, which was all I expected. We were co-workers, after all, not sorority sisters. I announced, after what I hoped would be perceived as a nonchalant interval and topic changer, "I'm thinking of making chili for dinner. You in?"

It was Saturday morning, not quite ten o'clock. His mothers must have told Stuart where to find me, which explained why, when I pulled aside the lace front-door curtain, a Lavoie leftover, there he was, bearded, grinning, and wearing a black watch cap. I could hardly pretend I wasn't home since only a windowpane separated us.

He pantomimed *Open the door,* so I did. Before I could say *Hello* or *Go away*, I was enveloped in a hug, definitely one-sided and reminiscently smelly. "Babe!" he was saying. "You look great!"

I wormed out of his embrace, and said, "You're back early." And even though I knew from Instagram hashtags, I asked, "How far did you get?"

"Pretty far. Hannibal, Missouri."

"Isn't Missouri next to Illinois?"

"Because I learned what I needed to learn! I met all kinds of people. And I mean all kinds."

"All kinds of people as long as they were old girlfriends? Did you bring home any sexually transmitted diseases?"

"That's such a ridiculous question that I refuse to dignify it. Are you going to invite me in?"

Without answering, I retreated to the parlor, perched on the upholstered arm of its only chair, and motioned toward the couch. Stuart followed, plopped down, looked around.

"Nice place! How many rooms?"

"Five and a half."

"Heating bills not too bad, I bet."

I didn't care to make small talk and told him so.

"You never liked small talk!" he answered. "Neither do I!"

I'd have offered any other guest a cup of something by now, but the only follow-up question I asked Stuart was "Exactly why are you here? I broke up with you. No matter how many times you e-mail me or text me or drop by that's not going to change." And before he could debate any of those points, I added, "You showed your true colors. And I didn't like them."

"Are we back to the women?"

"I never wanted to sound like a jealous fiancée, but now I can say that it was humiliating and highly annoying — posting pictures of yourself with your arms around busty women in every port."

"But I came back! Why would I come back if I didn't want to fix things?"

"Because you were cold. And broke! And probably bored."

"Babe . . ."

It was said softly, apologetically. What if the Instagram pictures and Facebook postings were nothing but bravado, putting the best face on a failed, forlorn hike? Maybe the real Stuart was the home game after all, not the away one.

"Why *did* you come back?" I asked, expecting his old self to say, *Isn't it obvious, Faith? You.*

But it was Stuart 2.0 who answered. With gusto, without a scintilla of Faith-based anything, he said, "I'd learned what I'd set out to learn — and one of those things was that you can't eat, sleep, travel, drink, socialize, fraternize, or publicize without money. In that sense, it was a confirmation. Mission accomplished."

Well, there it was, done and dusted. "You had to walk a thousand miles to discover that you can't get a tuna melt or whatever vegans put in a sandwich unless you have money in your wallet? You don't live in the real world. You're a case of arrested development."

"I'm starting a job on Monday. Doesn't that make me a resident of the real world?"

"An actual job?"

"I'll be working for my mother and Iona. They loved you, by the way."

I ignored that preposterous notion, having done nothing but insult their son during their unsuccessful visit. "Doing what?" I asked.

"I do intake for their clients, in their practice."

I wasn't interested enough to ask, *What do they practice?* but Stuart needed no encouragement. "They're psychiatric social workers. They met in graduate school, in fact. I never told you that? They specialize in adult eating disorders, mostly obesity. Their receptionist is on maternity leave and they were doing all the bookings and billing themselves."

"So you're the substitute receptionist?"

"I'm doing their social networking as well. Would you believe they don't have a web presence?"

"Yes, I would."

"Plus, I have a desk and a computer. I get to work on my memoir between clients. Believe me, it was no fun writing a book on an iPhone." He stood up, which I took to mean he'd noticed the cold shoulder and had had enough. "Mind if I look around?"

I said, "Yes, I do mind."

That led to his placing his hands on my shoulders and asking if we couldn't be friends. And don't friends give friends a tour of their house?

I said, "Let go of me." And after he stepped back: "Didn't your mother figures teach you to take your hat off when you're indoors?"

"Whoops," he said. "I've forgotten all my manners." He said again, "I'd love to look around. Any harm in that?"

Who could resist saying airily, after months of Facebook indignities, "I'd better ask Nick."

Wouldn't most recently dumped fiancés look perplexed at the mention of a strange man's name, let alone his domestic proximity? Not Stuart, who was probably assuming that a "Nick" under my roof would be short for Nicole.

"Nicholas!" I yelled in the direction of the stairs.

It didn't take long before he was descending the steps, looking like a relaxed full-time occupant — in jeans and a white T-shirt, his feet bare and his hair wet.

I said, "Nick, this is Stuart. Stuart, Nick. My housemate."

"Hey, man," said Stuart. "Housemate, huh?" And to me, "How many bedrooms?"

Before I could tell the truth, Nick said, "One. Why?"

"One," Stuart repeated. "What kind of house has only one bedroom?"

I shrugged. Nick shrugged. I said, "It must be why it was such a bargain."

Wagging his finger between Nick and me, Stuart asked, "Did Rebecca and Iona know about this?"

"He means his mother and her wife," I explained. And to Stuart, "It didn't come up. He hadn't moved in yet."

Nick said, "I've only been here . . . let me think . . . since Faith broke off the alleged engagement. Which coincided with my own breakup. Isn't that about right?"

"Since about Indiana," I said. "Or maybe it was Illinois."

"We share an office, too," said Nick, "so it was a logical next step."

I said to Stuart, "You couldn't possibly have expected that I'd want you for a housemate-slash-companion the way your mothers suggested."

"I kinda did," he said, "because another thing I learned on my journey was that where you sleep is not equal to where you are in your life."

"Whatever that means," I said.

He stared at me as if sorely disappointed that I couldn't grasp such a rudimentary doctrine.

"It's not even psychobabble," I said. "It's just Stuartspeak."

"What I meant, clearly, was people can coexist under one roof without having to be lovers or friends. You respect each other. You help out. *I'd* help out. I'm getting an advance on my first pay period."

"Of course you would, seeing who your bosses are. Are you staying with them, too?"

"For the time being, but it's only till I find my own place."

"Sorry, man," said Nick. "No room to coexist here."

"And frankly," I added, "even if there *was* room, I wouldn't have any respect for myself if I took you in."

How would he answer such a forthright confession? What was he taking away from our exchange? "You broke something off, too?" he asked Nick. "With a woman, I take it? Does she have a place?"

Wouldn't Nick take offense? Wouldn't his hackles rise?

No. What I saw instead was the half smile Nick reserved for a prize exchange with Reggie. This time, too, he was telegraphing *Pay attention; I'm going to have a little fun with this guy.*

23

Let Them Live Happily Ever After

TELL HER YOU JUST got back from a business trip, or whatever kind of trip makes you sound the least like a flower child," Nick advised Stuart.

"How many bedrooms?" Stuart asked.

"Two. The second one is her office, but it has a foldout couch."

"What does she do?" Stuart asked.

"She sells stuff on eBay. Designer stuff."

"Like clothes?"

"Like pocketbooks."

"Leather?" asked Stuart.

"I'm afraid so," said Nick. "Is that a deal breaker?"

I'd started out as a reluctant, mildly horrified party to the potential roommating of our exes but was now fully signed on as spectator. Wasn't I already a fan of Nick's nerve? Hadn't he called Mrs. Hepworth, then used the word *hellhole* about the very lockers her husband considered sacred, and made her laugh? I overheard and applauded such liberties every day.

"Are you allergic to leather?" Nick asked Stuart, so theatrically wide-eyed that I knew he'd never heard of a leather allergy.

"It's not an allergy," Stuart said. "It's a belief system."

I said, "I don't think you're in any position to be fussy."

Nick said, all innocence again, "I think it'll work. Stuart could impart some of his core values to Brooke."

"Brooke's been known to put too much value on *things*," I explained.

"Do you know for a fact that she's looking for a roommate?" Stuart asked.

Nick said, "She can't swing it herself; I know that much."

"Do I tell her that you gave me her contact info?"

I asked Stuart if he'd excuse us for a minute while I spoke privately to Nick about this matter.

"Good time for me to look around?" Stuart asked.

I said, "No. Wait here," and motioned to Nick that we conference halfway up the stairs, far enough for privacy while insuring that Stuart couldn't gallop to the second floor for a bedroom count.

I whispered, "Is this a good idea? Or are you just getting even?"

"The lease is in both our names and I'm still paying my share, so my motive isn't exactly altruistic."

"So she's actually in the market for a roommate?"

"We'll find out," he said.

Back in the living room, Stuart — in the approximate ninety seconds we'd been gone — had dozed off, his bulging backpack under his oily head.

"Hey!" I said. He snapped awake and sat up.

Nick said, "How's this? You tell Brooke that you have a friend at Everton Country Day and that friend knew I'd advertised for a new place and thus deduced that there was an opening at my former residence."

Stuart had begun shaking his head unhappily as soon as Nick said, "Tell Brooke that . . ."

I asked what the problem was.

"It's a lie. I'm sorry, but I don't lie."

"What's the lie?" asked Nick. He pointed. "Friend, check. Friend of friend, check. Both — Faith, me — Everton Country Day. Show me the lie."

"I don't know, man. I mean, down the line, I'd have a little too much to drink or smoke, and I tell her that it started here, face-to-face, with her ex-boyfriend. Because something tells me that this is nothing but a con. Here I am, just back, pretty grungy, and isn't that what you were discussing in private? Wouldn't it be hilarious to sic him on Brooke?"

His theory was so true that I didn't even attempt an answer. Nick said, "Is that what you think? Because I can disabuse you of that notion right away." He patted his jean pockets, then said, "I'll be right back." Taking the stairs two at a time, he was up and down in what seemed like seconds, his phone already to his ear. *Not answering*, he mouthed, then: "Brooke? Nick. I gave your e-mail address to a guy I know, well, a guy I met, just back from a cross-country trip, looking for a place to live. A safe guy, believe me — Buddhist, pacifist, you name it. Harmless. And employed. He's living at home with his mom. His name is Stuart." And just before hanging up, he said, "May I remind you that you promised to find someone to take over my portion of the rent ASAP."

Stuart seemed to be enjoying that voice-mail introduction and profile. He asked if he could give Brooke my name, too, as a personal reference. I said, "I'd rather you didn't."

"Is Brooke someone who holds grudges?" Stuart asked. "Like, is she judgmental?"

"Not at all," Nick said. "She's a peach."

Stuart said, "If it's meant to be, it'll happen. If it doesn't, no sweat. I'll explore other options."

"Such as?" — I couldn't help asking.

"My father and Linda have an extra bedroom. And I've been in touch with my ex since I've been back."

"I thought Faith was your ex," said Nick.

"I meant my ex-wife."

"In fact, she's a double ex. They were married and divorced twice," I told Nick.

"Quite the good no-grudge holder," Nick said.

Happily complimented, Stuart headed toward the front door, but not before bestowing hugs on both of us.

As soon as I heard his surely borrowed, rainbow-bumper-stickered Volvo leaving the driveway, I said, "You know he's going to go all feng shui on the place, and then there's the meat in the refrigerator and the leather in the closets. He's not mister live-and-let-live."

"Is that so? Poor Brooke. I'll be sure to cry me a river over that."

We'd moved to the kitchen table, coffee poured, toast in the toaster, newspaper divided. I started a few articles, not sticking with any, before I said, "You never told me you were still sharing Brooke's rent."

"Two months is all I promised. Three max. I figured she'd get a real job, or move, or ask her parents to pitch in."

I walked to the refrigerator for a milk-and-juice survey, this being Saturday and shopping day. "Should we stick with two percent?" I asked.

"Fine."

Still staring into the refrigerator, I confessed, "Stuart's something of a nudist."

"He would be."

"When she meets him, won't it be clear that you were playing a joke on her?"

Nick didn't answer. Instead, he grumbled about the dearth of the *Echo*'s reporting on Everton Country Day's football team's six-and-two season. Finally, he looked up and asked, "You never met Brooke, did you?"

"True."

"Here's what'll happen, vengeful joke or not. She'll answer Stuart's charming bullshit introductory e-mail. They'll write back and forth, and before finding out he doesn't have a pot to piss in and doesn't bathe, she'll decide to give it a shot."

I said, "Okay, fine. Let them live happily ever after for all I care." I sat down again, looked up from my shopping list to ask, "Any requests outside the usual?"

We didn't grocery shop together, since two people pushing a cart on a Saturday morning looked like a couple. He put out his hand, palm up. For a bold half second I thought of squeezing it, but instead I just passed him paper and pen.

24

Oh No, Oh No, Oh No

MUST THERE be a time in a modern parent's life when he decides that his adult children are mature enough to help unburden his tortured soul over lunch?

This is what Henry Frankel told Joel and me as the three of us tried to eat stylish luncheon fare at the café in the Boston Museum of Fine Arts: that he couldn't go on living a lie. Against all odds and defying logic, he'd met someone and they were — so sorry! — deeply in love.

Nearly in one voice, my brother and I demanded who, when, and why *now*.

"Her name is Tracy," he pronounced most reverently.

"Tracy! How old can someone named Tracy be?" I asked.

"Is that really important? And is that really what needs to be discussed?"

"How old?" I repeated.

"Almost forty," he said.

"Wait," said Joel. "You're telling us you're having an affair with a woman who's Faith's age?"

"Not Faith's age." He turned, and asked, "You can't be close to forty, can you?"

"No. But for purposes of this conversation, yes!"

"What about Mom?" Joel asked.

"Your mother's figured it out," he said quietly.

"When?"

"Over the course of the last few weeks. In terms of telling you two, our timing was deliberate. We didn't want to add to any of Faith's woes, but now all seems relatively peaceful."

"Until, like, sixty seconds ago!" said Joel. He gave his plate a shove, the plate holding the triple-decker sandwich with the bacon smoked over alder wood that he'd been so delighted to find on the menu.

"I didn't want to tell you over the phone." Dad sighed heavily. "And now I'm thinking this" — public space, eager ears — "wasn't such a good idea, either."

"Who is she?" I asked.

He started with "She's a housewife," followed by a correction that technically she was not a house*wife* because she was divorced, but that would have applied when she was married, with two daughters and a big house to care for. However, she was a law school graduate and member of the Massachusetts bar.

"So she's a divorcée?" I asked, putting as much old-school disdain into that word as I could summon.

"It was a very unhappy marriage," he said.

"Like we give a shit!" said Joel.

"And you met how?" I asked.

"And when?" asked Joel.

"We met in August when she commissioned me to personalize *Blue Angel* for her daughter's bat mitzvah —"

"Wait!" I said. "Is she the one who started this whole thing?"

"What whole thing?"

"Painting Chagalls, personalizing them, whatever you call it. Just when we thought you were all starry-eyed and professionally fulfilled. Turns out it wasn't art at all! It's infatuation."

"He's fulfilled all right," Joel said. "That's coming across loud and clear."

"This isn't infatuation," our dad said. "Infatuation burns itself out."

"The new Chagall," I ranted. "Getting Mom all invested so she sits home in case it's a future patron calling, as if she's your secretary. How'd you let that happen? How'd you let *any* of it happen?"

Dad assumed a look of misunderstood, lovesick confusion. Were his two adult children incapable of relating to love overwhelming, which in its own sweet, storybook way was guilt free due to its near-biblical inevitability — at least that's how I was translating his expression.

After a prolonged period of sitting without any of us touching our food, he tried again. "I couldn't keep it to myself anymore. Your mother wanted to run to the phone, but I said, 'No, let me tell them face-to-face.' I didn't want you to be shocked when I moved in with Tracy."

"Did you say 'move in with Tracy'?" I managed to repeat.

"With her barely teenaged daughters? Because good luck with that," said Joel.

"Where?" I asked. "Florida? Isn't that where this whole subspecialty got started?"

"Not Florida. No, that was different; that was a de Kooning I did in Aventura. Tracy lives in Newton. And, yes, with her daughters, two of them, fourteen and almost twelve."

"Won't that be handy," I said. "Live-in models for all the princesses and angels and that other moony crap you're peddling!"

Uh-oh. That was not exactly on topic. Within seconds, it was clear that the hush that followed was an unsteady one, that he was verging on tears, no doubt distressed first by our hostility and prudishness, and now by my artistic effrontery.

"Look," said Joel. "We're not babies. We know people have affairs and get divorced even after decades. But I don't want to see Mom curled up in a ball, crying her eyes out."

"She could be suicidal," I hissed, drawing glances from our fellow café patrons.

"I assure you, she is not curled up in a ball," Dad said.

"You know because you're talking to her?" I asked.

"Daily," he said. "More than that. And by the way, no one is talking about a divorce."

More shocked noneating followed. Joel said, "Do they serve liquor here? Anyone else want a drink?"

"What do you mean, no one's talking about divorce?" I asked.

"Exactly that. Your mother and I are not dissolving our marriage. I'll be living with Tracy, but —"

"Oh, like Tracy is going to love that you're not getting divorced. That's fine with her? She doesn't want to marry you?" I demanded.

"As a matter of fact, she doesn't. At least not yet. It would be complicated, financially. We're taking it one step at a time."

"Why can't you just seduce models in your studio like other artists do?" Joel asked.

Our dad's phone was ringing, or more accurately, wind-chiming. My father answered, then whispered, "Still. Can I call you back?"

"She has her own ringtone?" Joel asked. "Who showed you how to do that?"

Our besotted father then offered his caller a good-bye so tender that something shifted in my anger equation.

"What are you going to tell your girlfriend when she asks, 'How'd it go with the kids today?'" Joel asked.

"I'll have to be honest. I'll say, 'It didn't go well. To my great disappointment, Joel and Faith would rather I keep my new-found happiness to myself, preferring I just sneak around behind their backs.'"

"At this stage? Would that be so terrible? You were already living in separate cities, and Mom was okay with that, believing that you only flew the coop because you were painting 24/7," Joel said.

"If this makes it any better, that *was* the reason for my renting the studio. Meeting Tracy came months after I left Everton."

"Just like that? You weren't looking —"

"I promise you, I was *not* looking to have an affair. Your mother adjusted once she understood that I had this need, this itch to paint, and I wasn't moving out for personal reasons."

"Yeah, well, that itch didn't take long to shift south," Joel muttered.

"She told us you came for supper every few weeks and you stayed over, implying *conjugal visits*," I said.

"You asked me why I had to tell your mother about Tracy. That was precisely why. How could I sleep with two women, effectively cheating on both of them! Can you imagine what I was going through? After a marriage of almost thirty-six years, and then the fates or the stars or God sends me this overwhelming passionate new life!"

I said, "Um, Dad. I'd rather not go there."

Joel said, "Ya, right. God's big on people fooling around."

There was no letup. You'd think another male, in this case my thirty-four-year-old divorced brother, might be the more likely ally, but he demanded, "Did you screw around on Mom before this? Because I remember wondering about what's-her-name, the woman with the crazy eyes who worked for you and drove a Mustang?"

"I don't know who 'crazy eyes' refers to, but it doesn't matter, because I never had an affair with anyone in my office."

More to ponder, more to rewrite about my parents' allegedly happy marriage. "No affair with anyone *in* the office" sounded like words chosen carefully in grand-jury-testimony fashion, suggesting adulteries elsewhere. I closed my eyes.

My father continued, "Your mother had a sense. I don't mean back when I first moved. I mean lately. She'd picked something up."

"Such as?" Joel asked.

"Something indiscreet that was left on voice mail."

"By Tracy, I take it," I said.

He nodded. "Nothing big. Just an endearment and a reference to an upcoming date."

"Oh, really? That's all? A *date?* Why would that make any wife suspicious?" Joel sputtered.

"You don't think Tracy left that message on purpose?" I asked.

"It's done," he said. "There's no point in second-guessing —"

"It sure did the job, though, didn't it?" Joel said.

A waitress was at our table, her apologetic body language conveying that so far she'd sensed no good moment to be asking any of the usual questions, but duty obliged her . . .

"Just the check," said our father.

I said, "I'm going outside to call Mom."

"Can you wait until you've heard me out?" Dad asked.

"There's more?" Joel asked.

"Just what I came here to assure you of. Nothing changes. Your mother and I both love you, and just because —"

"Jesus!" Joel yelled. "That's what you say to your eight-year-old when you're moving out — 'Mommy and I aren't happy together, but we both love you very much, blah blah blah.'"

My father was looking at me, pleading for something . . . anything that was less than antipathy. *Don't go all soft,* I scolded myself. *Don't jump ship.* But seeing his watery eyes, I shushed Joel, then heard myself say, "I guess I sort of get it."

"Just like that?" Joel asked.

"What's our getting so pissed off going to accomplish? If we stop talking to him, do you think he and Mom will renew their vows and that'll be the end of Tracy?"

Joel's one-shoulder shrug was unhappy but faintly obliging. I reached over and patted my father's dejected hand.

"Please don't forget I was in insurance," he pleaded, "always factoring in life expectancies."

Joel and I exchanged newly worried glances.

"I don't want to hang my hat — or more precisely my heart — on actuarial tables. We never know how much time we have left, do we?"

"Are you ill?" I asked. "Is that what you're trying to tell us?"

"No! I'm fine. I'm great. Ironically, I've never felt younger . . . 'in this short Life that only lasts an hour.'"

"Huh?" Joel said.

"Emily Dickinson, of course," Dad supplied.

We didn't give him our blessing exactly. But *this?* We'd never before heard Henry Frankel quoting poetry.

25

A Lot for a Daughter
in One Day

I DROVE STRAIGHT FROM BOSTON to what I'd previously considered my parents' home, dropping Joel off before-hand as he was insisting this condolence call needed to be woman-to-woman.

Finding the back door unlocked, I let myself in, calling, "Mom!" then "Nancy!" from room to room before heading partway up the stairs, tiptoeing like a daughter who hoped her mother was merely napping and not dead by her own hand.

"Faith?" I heard, and though far away, it sounded normal, even pleasantly surprised that her overly busy daughter had dropped by unannounced. "I'm down cellar. Be right up."

"You okay?" I called.

"Laundry," she answered.

I didn't wait, but hustled downstairs. First impression: not a good sign that in late afternoon she was dressed in a flan-nel housecoat and slippers. "You okay?" I asked, watching her rather nonchalantly pretreat stains before I blurted out, "I

know everything! I'm still in shock!" Within seconds, uninvited, my arms were around her neck and I was blubbering condolences and apologizing for being the daughter of a man who
would do such a thing.

She didn't melt into my embrace or even pat my back. Instead, she untangled soggy me from around her neck. "Buck
up," she said.

Did my betrayed and forsaken mother just tell me to buck up?

"I don't need you falling apart," she continued. "Now let me
add the fabric softener and we can talk upstairs."

Having presumed too much, having miscalculated the toll
my father's sins were taking on my mother, I obeyed. I went
straight to the living-room couch, flopped down, then sat back
up so I would appear less annoyingly wounded.

I could tell from her opening line that she'd prepared for this
moment. "This can't be easy for you and your brother," she began, "but, you know, just because your father and I will no longer be together, it doesn't mean —"

I said, "You, too? Divorce 101? Dad said practically the same
thing! It's not about how *we* feel. It's about how you're taking all
of this! I think you're trying to be strong. You don't have to be!"

She sat down next to me, hip to hip. "I've known for a long
time," she said. "Longer than you think . . . now let me get
dressed. I'll be right back and we'll go for a walk."

"In the dark?"

"We can just go around the block a few times. I haven't been
out of the house for two days."

Just when I started worrying about pills she might have
stockpiled, about life ebbing out of her upstairs, she reappeared,
wearing a long black sweater over houndstooth leggings, hair
combed and lipstick tomato red.

"Is that coat warm enough?" she asked me. "And no hat?" She produced one that had wool braids hanging from earflaps that I'd never have agreed to wear on any other day.

"Toasty," she said. "It's alpaca."

I said sure, of course. Thank you.

Before we got from the brick path to the sidewalk, she said, "I hate him, okay? Is that good enough?"

Well, yes, certainly good enough in terms of a breakout from her otherworldly calm, but with more propulsion than I expected. "Because of the affair or for longer than that?" I asked.

"Don't ask how long I've suspected he had women on the side. Of course, he denied that every time."

I said, "This is a lot for a daughter in one day . . ."

"I'm not supposed to talk to you like you're a child, remember? I'm sure your father let you in on the gory details."

I said weakly, "He told us that he'd met someone, that he hadn't been looking to fool around when he moved to Boston. Then it happened. Her kid was having a bat mitzvah and the home wrecker needed a fake Chagall."

"Well, that's interesting, because you know how he broke the news to me? With a lie. He sat me down on the porch glider and told me he wanted an open marriage! Your father! I knew that was an excuse, so I said, 'Who is she?' Just like that. *Who is she, Henry?*"

Open marriage? Even as a fictional bargaining chip, those were not the words a daughter wants to hear. "But it was just his way of leading up to the Tracy news, right?" I asked. "He didn't mean literally an open marriage?"

"He said it! And you know what *I* said?"

I didn't. I couldn't even guess. A neighbor was approaching, her big white dog crowding us into single file. "Marion," my mother said, "you remember Faith. She bought a house on Turpentine. Faith, this is Marion and Koochie."

There I was in an embarrassing hat, never less interested in chatting with a near stranger than at that moment. "Don't let us keep you from your appointed rounds," I said. And for added incentive, "*Brrrr.*"

Marion and Koochie moved on. I put a finger to my lips, signaling *Wait; don't blurt out anything until she's out of range.*

"Why should I care if the neighbors hear! They had their suspicions about our marriage when your father went off to find himself. I might as well send a group e-mail telling them they were right!"

A huffy block-long silence followed until I prompted, "You were going to tell me what you said after you heard 'open marriage.'"

"I didn't know I had it in me. Without missing a beat, I said, 'If you must know, I've been conducting an open marriage myself ever since you moved to Boston.'"

"No, you were not!"

"Of course I wasn't. But I couldn't resist." The near triumph in her voice quickly dissipated to a mutter. *Son of a bitch,* I heard. *Son. Of. A. Bitch.*

Was I supposed to agree, disagree, or mount a daughterly defense on behalf of my deliriously fulfilled father? I did neither. Because it had started to snow, I noted, "Joel must be happy to see this."

"Happy," she snapped. "To see his father make a fool of himself?"

"No! Not that. God, no. I meant the first snow of the season!"

"How come Joel didn't come with you to see me straight from the Boston confession?"

I said, "He must've wanted to get home to his plow. But trust me, he was furious, yelling at Dad — and this was in the café at the MFA where it's so beautiful and calm, all air and light. I had to shush him. There was no boys-will-be-boys thing going on."

"How did you leave it?" she asked.

I said, "Well . . . I'd have to say in fairly civilized fashion. By the time the check came, we realized — Joel and I — that Dad didn't need our approval, maybe just less hostility. Plus, we only have one father and . . . you know . . . life is short."

"Was *she* there?"

"No, of course not."

"That's next. Mark my word. Did you see the painting that was the catalyst? It had other symbols in there that only the artist and his patron-paramour could translate . . . hearts, arrows, and apparently a bed floating in the sky. The nerve!"

I'd looped my arm through hers, pretending it was weather related, the sidewalk slick. I said, "I can't tell — are you more sad than angry? Or vice versa?"

"I'm filing for divorce is how I am! I want the house and alimony and whatever else I can get."

"We have no-fault divorce here," I reminded her.

"I don't care! There must be a loophole! And don't worry — I'm not using Joel's spineless divorce lawyer. I'll drive to Boston if I have to. I want a shark."

"Is a divorce worth the trouble? At this stage of life?"

"What stage? The stage where your husband thinks he's forty years old and can't keep it in his pants? That one?"

I said, "I think I'm getting a clearer picture of angry versus sad."

"It's bubbling up. In a good way. Maybe I just needed some fresh air and a sounding board."

I asked if she'd told anyone else.

"Not yet. I considered confiding in Aunt Elaine, of course. And Marjorie and Naomi. But then I thought, *Everyone knows that my husband moved out.* They didn't like that one bit, but they got used to it. So I decided to let sleeping dogs lie. Do I really need to say, 'I have an update. Henry has a girlfriend, in fact, his soul mate, and he's moving into her swanky house with her and her two children.'"

I said, "I wish you'd come to me when you found out."

"But you were a mess — first that nonsense with the job, then your nerves about buying the house, then breaking up with Stuart."

"It would've taken my mind off all of that."

She patted my arm and said I seemed to be doing better, parents' divorce notwithstanding. And she wanted me to keep the hat, which made me look like a Lapland schoolgirl — in a good way.

By now we'd walked all the way to Turpentine. "Do you want to come in?" I asked. "Or do you want me to drive you home?"

"That's going to be hard since you left your car in my driveway. But whose car is this?"

"Nick's. My coworker's. He lives here now."

"Well, well," she said.

"Not like that. He needed a place, and there wasn't anything good on the market."

"Have I met him?"

Had I dragged her to a recent ECD fund-raiser/game/dance recital/theater production/reunion? *If you'd met Nick, you'd remember,* I thought. "Unlikely," I said.

She asked the time. I checked my phone. "Almost six."

"Let's have a drink," she said, on the porch now, hand on the doorknob. "A good stiff one."

"Is it all right to speak freely in front of Nick — about you and Dad?"

"I look forward to it," she said. "You know how long I've had to keep this quiet?"

"Weeks."

"At least."

"Nick?" I called, as soon as I closed the front door behind us. "My mother's here."

"Nancy," she corrected.

"Want me to come down?"

"Please do," my mother called back. "I'm dying to meet you. Do you have any vodka?"

Within seconds, Nick was descending the stairs in jaunty fashion, looking Country Day casual in corduroys and flannel. Halfway down, he asked, grinning, "On the rocks?"

"Way past that," my mother said. "Heading for divorce court."

I put my arm around her shoulders and gave her a squeeze. "My father is having an extramarital affair. She's doing amazingly well, though, aren't you?"

"She's half his age!" was her next outburst. "I'm usually a dignified person, but it's been bottled up for weeks."

"I know it's very hard," said Nick. "I haven't gone through a divorce, but I've recently broken up with someone. Maybe we should have that drink and toast . . . what shall we toast? Eyes forward? Happier days ahead?"

Was that a nudge from my mother's elbow? Probably.

Many hours later, after vodka martinis, a bottle of wine, all the cheese, salami, nuts, and crackers on hand, and back-to-back Spencer Tracy movies on Turner Classics, my mother was still there. The snow was coming down, wet and heavy. Nick's car didn't have snow tires, his blood-alcohol level was DUI-worthy, my mother hadn't worn boots, and multiple calls to Joel had gone straight to voice mail.

"Nights aren't great," I heard her confide to Nick.

He had toothbrushes at the ready for potential lady guests. I lent her a nightgown. She got my bed, and I slept on the couch.

26

·❧·

What's This About?

HUNGOVER AND ACHY from a lumpy night on my three-cushion couch, did I need the doorbell ringing at 8:35 on a Sunday morning? Barefoot and annoyed, I padded to the front door. Pulling aside an inch of its curtain, I recognized Brian Dolan, who, like everyone else, was an acquaintance if not a classmate of my brother's. Less pleasant update: he was now on the Everton police force, in full uniform and unsmiling on my front porch.

"What's wrong?" I asked, hoarse with sleep and alarm, having opened the door a half inch. "Is Joel okay?"

"Joel? Haven't seen him since the playoffs. I'm here on another matter. Mind if I look around your basement?"

"My basement? What for?"

"Just a look-see."

"Out of the blue you want to inspect my basement? And I *do* mind — I'm only in my nightgown."

"I can wait."

I told him that my mother was sleeping in my bedroom, and if I went upstairs for some clothes, I'd wake her. Could he come back in an hour?

"How about throwing on a coat? It won't take me long."

"Okay. Give me a minute." Upon returning, parka zipped, I said, "Should I be asking if you have a search warrant?"

"A search warrant is your right," he said. "Of course, being Sunday, I'd have to wait till tomorrow for a judge, so I couldn't come back for a few days. Aren't you at work weekdays?"

I said, "In that case, I'll let you in, but I need to know why you want to look in my basement" — my lack of hospitality due to nervous knowledge of Nick's Ziploc bag of pot, probably in plain sight upstairs.

His sigh suggested that this was harder work than anticipated. "I can tell you this much: we got a phone call . . ."

"From?"

He took out a small notepad, and without leafing very far back, announced, "It was anonymous."

"About me?"

"Not you. The house. The caller was very specific: 10 Turpentine Lane."

"And what was the tip?"

"It concerned things that might have transpired . . . in the past."

"In my cellar?"

"Possibly. Which is why I'd like to take a look."

"No clue as to what you'd be looking for down there?"

Brian said, "I think you can guess there might have been criminal activity."

I asked, "Are you a detective?"

He stood a little taller. "Since August."

I said, "Here's the deal, Detective Brian. I'll let you go downstairs without a search warrant, but first you tell me what the tipster said."

"Faith," he said. "You know me. You know my sisters. It's freakin' cold out here."

I opened the door immediately. "Sorry. I'm a little foggy — wasn't expecting the police at my door at eight o'clock on a Sunday morning. Come in." Then: "What did you say the tipster left on the tip line?"

"Good try. I haven't said."

"C'mon. I'm not asking for the who of it. Just the what of it. That must be for public consumption. Or at least owner-of-the property-in-question consumption."

"It might be nothing. Or it might be more than you want to know."

"'More than I want to know'? That's a little patronizing, don't you think?"

That proved to be an excellent gender-sensitivity strategy because he said, "Sorry. Okay . . . the caller said that some events that transpired in the '60s and '70s, deaths actually . . . might not have been from natural causes. That was basically it, plus this address."

"Nothing to do with babies?"

"Babies? Nope. Men. Two of them. Husbands of a previous owner."

Of course, that was the moment my mother, fully dressed, a lip gloss of mine applied, sweater over leggings, was descending the stairs. Where another mother might ask, at the sight of a uniformed policeman in her daughter's foyer, "What's wrong?" mine was saying, "Hello, Brian. When did you come by?"

"Five minutes ago," I said.

"How are the roads?" she asked.

"Ma! He's following up on an anonymous tip."

Her initial perplexed expression turned into the hopeful question "About Faith?"

I was tempted to joke about my recently alleged embezzling at Everton but didn't in case Brian missed the irony. "He wants to check out the basement," I said.

"Is he telling us why?"

"Police business," he said.

"Should one of us accompany you?" she asked.

"It's your property," Brian said. "Your decision."

I said, "She doesn't live here. It was just a weather-related sleepover." I pointed toward the kitchen. "Cellar door's that way. Light switch is on the right. Use the railing. The stairs are ridiculously steep."

"Are you thinking there are bodies buried down there?" my mother asked.

Detective Dolan smiled. "Highly unlikely."

"So what are you looking for?"

I had started my ascent to the second floor, but stopped halfway, torn between waiting for his answer and hustling upstairs to warn Nick that we had a detective on the premises.

"I'm just going to take a few pictures," he said.

"Are you married?" she asked.

"Yes, ma'am."

"Let him get on with it," I scolded, and in case I looked like someone in a rush to hide evidence, added, "*Must* get dressed."

Upstairs, I knocked — three quick raps on Nick's door. "Can I come in? You decent?"

When I heard a groggy yes, I slipped into his room and closed the door behind me. "A cop is here. He's in the cellar, but just in case . . . you know . . . your refreshments?"

"Why is a cop in the cellar?"

"An anonymous tip — something criminal that might've happened here."

"When?"

"Nick! If he finds your pot and arrests you, you'll lose your job! And maybe I would, too, as an accessory."

"Relax," he said. "It's in my sock drawer. You need a warrant to look in someone's sock drawer. Does he even have one?"

"No. Okay. Never mind. I'm getting dressed."

He sat up finally. No garment was in evidence. Had I ever seen Nick's chest unclothed? Of course, passing each other in the hallway. But in this particular setting, it seemed especially naked.

"What's with the parka?" he asked.

I flashed it open and closed quickly for a second's glimpse of the nightgown that needed concealing.

"Is the cop asking for all hands on deck?"

"No! He doesn't even know you live here. I was just being your lookout."

"Thanks. Stop worrying. Get dressed, go back down, find out what's what. And Faith? Be cool."

Water for my mother's tea hadn't even reached a boil when I heard Detective Dolan ascending the cellar stairs. "All set . . . thank you," he said, closing the door behind him with what looked like gumshoe meticulousness.

"Any luck?" my mother asked.

"She means did you see anything suspicious?" I asked.

"Clean as a whistle," said Detective Dolan.

Only weeks later would I realize that he wasn't answering my question as it related to the anonymous tip. He was cleverly complimenting and distracting me about the admirably neat state of my basement.

27

Too Much? Too Close?

BACK IN MY MOTHER'S DRIVEWAY I found a note under my wiper. *Could only plow ptway. Where are you & where's Ma? J.*

"Obviously he was worried about you," I told my mother, who was energetically scraping ice off my back windshield despite my protests.

"Not *that* worried," she said.

"It was a big night for him," I said. "Land-office business, I bet."

"Wouldn't you think he'd have come straight here after getting the news that his father had taken up with a teenager?"

"Ma, we covered that. He's a guy. They're not good at that stuff. Then it snowed — all night, all for the good."

"Call him," she said. "Tell him I'm back at home, having spent the night with you due to inclement weather."

I said, "You call. I've already left too many messages."

Scraping and sighing, she said, "In the old days, everybody picked up. Your phone rang and you answered it, period."

I slipped her big purse off her arm, fished inside, and came up with her cell. "Except in the good old days you didn't get to make phone calls from your driveway. Here, call him. I'm going home." I opened the car door, and just before climbing in, I pointed toward the house. "Notice that your terrible son shoveled your walks, front and back."

"What if I *do* reach him?"

"Isn't that the point?"

"What if he says something like 'Dad wasn't living at home anyway. It's not that big a deal.'"

"He won't say that. I told you how upset he was, which is probably why he's not picking up. Now go inside. Take a nice soak in the tub, read the Sunday paper. I'm around if you need me." *With my phone turned off,* I thought.

"I might call him," she said. "So just warning you."

"Isn't that what we're talking about?"

"I meant your father. I'd enjoy giving him a piece of my mind. Do you know the saying 'You can't dance at two weddings with one *tuchus*'?"

"Now I do." I turned the key in the ignition and was relieved to hear the engine turn over. I waved good-bye and tried not to think about the forlorn return wave in my rearview mirror. Five minutes later, as soon as I'd pulled into my driveway, my next-door neighbor, Mrs. Strenger, was hurrying down her back porch steps in a puffy down coat and unbuckled overshoes, calling, "Is everything all right?"

I said, "Yes — at least since I left twenty minutes ago."

"I saw the cruiser in your driveway . . ."

"Oh, that — it was just Brian Dolan, a friend of my brother's."

"Off duty?"

"Well, no . . . on. But it was nothing. Well, nothing about me

. . . some ancient history he was looking into." Then, casually, as if an unrelated topic, I asked, "How long have you lived here?"

"Fifty-three years this month."

"Wow. Very precise."

"I know exactly because we moved in the week of the president's assassination. Not a good way to start a new life together." She must have sensed I was about to express my sorrow for such unfortunate timing because she said, "I don't want to give you the wrong impression. It's been a lucky house for us: a marriage that lasted through thick and thin. Two handsome sons, five grandsons — would you believe that? All boys! — and if we were to sell it tomorrow, it would bring many times what we paid for it."

Could she know what a pittance I'd paid for my little shitbox next door? I wondered.

"You said Donna Dolan's boy was here about ancient history. Do you know which ancient history he meant?" she asked.

"*Ancient history* was my term. It seems . . . I don't really know. Maybe" — and now this was Amateur Detective Frankel leading the witness — "it referred to deaths in the Lavoie family?"

"I wouldn't be surprised! She lost all three of her husbands."

"Lost?"

"Passed away. Who can live through something like that? And I'd heard — it was before I lived here — that she lost twin babies. No wonder a person can't go on living."

Except that she went on living until she was at least ninety, I refrained from saying.

"I wasn't here yet when the first husband died," she continued. "But the other two were accidents." She lowered her voice to a whisper, unnecessary in the wide-open cold air. "I think they were drinkers. At least I heard awful rows. And the little girl — little then — used to come over to my house and just sit on my porch swing. Both of the stepfathers were falling-down drunk when they died."

"Is that what you heard?"

"You'd think being drunk would relax their muscles and they wouldn't get hurt, but they both died from the falls — three, four years apart. One I think went to the hospital but died there. Not a lucky house. Not for her, at least."

"Was it the cellar stairs?" I asked.

"I hope you've carpeted them," Mrs. Strenger said.

Nick was reading the Sunday paper at the kitchen table. I repeated as faithfully as I could, and rather breathlessly, the entire conversation I'd just had with our elderly next-door neighbor.

He listened, reflecting none of my astonishment at the house's continuing bad karma, then said, calmly, "The wife pushed them. Clearly."

I said, "I thought that, too! But wouldn't that be the first thing the medical examiner would conclude when someone's third husband died the same way as the second?"

"You should ask your friend the cop."

"What about autopsies? Couldn't they tell the difference between a push and a fall?"

Nick said, "I'd put Nancy Frankel on the case. It would take her mind off Tracygate."

I said, "Was it too much last night — the Frankel family soap opera?"

"I tuned a lot of it out."

"Good," I said, but at the same time I wondered how much of our conversations, at home and at work, did he tune out. When he appeared to finish the section he'd been reading, Technology, I asked, "What about *your* mother? I never hear about her."

"No longer with us," he said.

"Sorry..."

"Cancer. Almost ten years ago. My father remarried — a woman he'd dated in high school, the one that got away."

"Let me guess. They reconnected on Facebook?"

"Nope, at a class reunion — which *I* made him go to. He waited a very respectable amount of time before he even asked her out. They're in love. It's very cute, actually. She's no genius, but it works." He smiled. "Needless to say, I was his best man."

"And this is where?"

"Chicago."

"Where you grew up?"

"Correct."

I said, "Thank you — it's like a short story — it starts with a loss, with lemons, then life gives you lemonade and it ends with a wedding —"

"I knew you'd like that," he said from behind the paper.

Still in my coat, still standing by the table, I said, "I'll let you read. I'm going to do a little work."

"In other words, *I'm going to try my brother again?*"

"What? Too much? Too close?"

"The family dynamic... you're all so... hovering." He shook his shoulders as if releasing unwanted possessive hands.

I said, "We aren't usually on top of one another like this. It's been a very traumatic fall and winter."

"Believe me, your brother's fine. He's probably sound asleep."

I said, "Thank you. A male perspective is very helpful."

I could tell he was trying to sound offhanded when he said, "I might call my dad today. He doesn't even know I have a new address. Or that I broke up with Brooke."

"When was the last time you talked?"

"A month? He doesn't do e-mail. If his wife answers, I can't get her off the phone . . ."

"But you're not estranged or anything?"

"Nope."

"Did he know Brooke?"

"He'd met her. At his own wedding, in fact."

"Don't you think he should at least have your new address?"

"He should, especially here, the scene of many alleged crimes — he being my next of kin."

"Why did I buy this place?" I moaned.

28

Woe Is Us

LATE SUNDAY AFTERNOON Joel finally texted back, **will call Mom.** I refrained from word choices such as *For Chrissake, took you long enough.* Instead, I wrote back, **Come for dinner tonite? Frankels & beans?**

That worked. It was what as kids we'd called our Sunday night suppers with Heinz and Hebrew National, a family tradition . . . when the Frankels were still a family.

Nick had hockey every Sunday night. He led up to his departure with the weekly grousing about the bumpy Everton ice, the know-nothing refs, and why did he let Reggie talk him into signing up. "Have fun," I said. "Don't get any teeth knocked out." I added that his timing was good: Joel was coming for dinner and no doubt he'd had had quite enough of Frankels singing the blues.

"A pity to miss that," he agreed.

Only when pressed and after a beer, and with me avoiding parental topics, did Joel confide that he'd kept a third date with Leslie, Stuart's ex-sister-in-law.

"Did the subject of Stuart come up?"

"Nope."

"Never? Even though his mothers put you two in touch?"

"Maybe on the phone before we met. I can't remember."

"Did you get any impression about whether Leslie likes him?"

"Stuart?"

"Does she hate him?"

"Do *you?*" he asked.

"He deserves it."

Here was where a brother who didn't want to talk about his own personal life moves the conversation forward with "Who picked the fancy beer?"

I said I did; it was brewed in Brooklyn.

There was a pop from the saucepan, a knockwurst bursting its skin. "Dinner is served," I said.

We helped ourselves from the pots on the stove then took seats at the kitchen table.

"Where's the housemate?" he asked.

"On campus, playing hockey. The faculty-staff game is every Sunday night. He's the goalie so he has to show."

"Decent," he said.

"Speaking of not so decent, have you heard from Dad?"

"Nope. Only Mom."

"How'd that go?" I asked, knowing full well every sentence they'd exchanged.

"She called him, you know."

"She warned me she might . . ."

"She told him, 'Don't go around telling everyone we're *not* getting divorced. Because we are. I'm not the one who has anything to be ashamed of! This isn't the 1950s.'"

"Ironic," I said, and pointed to my 1950s Formica counter,

where my mother's Eisenhower-era lemon squares were defrosting.

Joel muttered a *hrrmmmph* that sounded like a rebuke.

"Can you translate that?" I asked.

"It meant you should move back to Brooklyn."

"Because Mom bakes me *cookies?*"

"No. What's here for you? Everton Country Day? Mom dropping by every two minutes?"

"And what would I be going back to?"

"New York! Stuff to do and see. First-run movies! Public transportation."

"Why don't *you* move to Brooklyn if it's too claustrophobic here? Or Boston? Or, I don't know, Honolulu, Hawaii? Aren't you in the same boat as I am?" Then, for good, illogical measure, I threw in "Plus dating a woman whose family I wouldn't want to sit with at your wedding!"

"Well, *that* makes total sense." He leaned over and gave me a friendly cuff on the shoulder. "What else ya got?"

"Not much."

"There's always the old favorite, *How about taking some courses and working toward a degree? Shouldn't you have a PhD by now? And a couple of kids?*"

I said, "You don't get that from me. And Everton makes perfect sense for me now. I have a house, a job I mostly like, a very good tenant —"

"That's how you think of him? A tenant?"

Ignoring that, I moved on to "I have a car; I have what New Yorkers would consider a yard. And even if Mom is underfoot, what's better: being a mile away or spending a fortune getting up here when she needs a little . . . boost?"

"You call this a boost? She told me she slept here."

"Only one night! And only because we'd had too much to drink so we couldn't drive her home, and we weren't going to let her walk in the dark, in a blizzard."

Thus, conversation was reset to the weather forecast and the batch of new plowing patrons, old faithfuls who were once on his paper route. I cleared the plates, and from the sink, I heard, "Mom likes your tenant."

I said, "She told you that?"

"Obviously." Then — as if it were the logical follow-up to a Nick compliment — "I told her he was gay."

I squeaked, "You did? Why?"

"You know," he said.

"No, I do *not*."

"I think it was after she said she hoped you weren't falling for him. Or maybe the other way around — Nick falling for you. I figured I'd throw her off the scent. It'll save us both her stewing over the Gentile factor."

Where to start refuting, correcting, scolding? I huffed first about my own various troubles, then the paternal trauma we'd all suffered the day before, plus his buddy Brian Dolan's showing up to investigate some murders that might have been committed in my cellar. "And after all that," I ranted, "that was her takeaway? That was her big overriding worry? Nick isn't Jewish?"

Joel shrugged — a yes if ever I'd seen one.

"Did she tell you he sat there and listened to her tales of woe? What guy does that? Nick, who saved my job —"

"She thinks *we* saved your job —"

"Who always pays his share of the mortgage on the first of the month and never leaves a dirty dish in the sink? Not that anyone's falling for anyone. It's just the principle of it. The prejudice. After Stuart? Jewish! What kind of selfish hippie husband would he have been?"

"I said all that, believe me. I also said, 'Good luck with the Jewish husband campaign, Ma. Good luck in this century, in Everton, Massachusetts. And, let's face it, ticktock."

I didn't love any of that, but what was there to contradict? "Did she believe you when you said he was gay?"

"She'll forget about it. And when the time comes, you can tell her I made it up to throw her off course."

"When what time comes?"

"Gee. Let me think on that. Oh, I've got it: when you two are sleeping in the same bed."

"Not gonna happen. We work together. It's against the rules."

"I'm sure. And there's a nanny cam recording your home life for the board of trustees?"

I abandoned the table to plate the lemon squares, which were still a little glacial. "These need more time," and then, glancing at the clock, I asked, barely audibly, "Think we should call Dad?"

"No! Why would we?"

"Because we were a little brutal yesterday?"

"Aren't you the enabler! He's got *Tracy*" — pronounced as scornfully and dismissively as two syllables could be spoken — "for all his needs. She's probably saying right now, 'What horrible, selfish children you have. Don't they want their father to be happy?'"

"Okay. We won't call him. I don't want to be an enabler."

He asked if he could take dessert to go — needed to hit the hay . . . late night, then early plowing, not to mention the sanding and the shoveling. At the door, he said, "About Brooklyn? Maybe I was thinking *happier times*. You got back here and, *whammo*, the job, then the Stuart thing imploded, then Mom and Dad split. Plus your haunted house . . . speaking of which, I don't see why you have to give a crap about who died here fifty, sixty years ago. Now get a good night's sleep. You look like hell."

I said, "Gee, thanks," then threw out, "*You're* gay. I'm telling Leslie before she gets in too deep."

"Ha! This is Massachusetts. You gotta do better than that."

Against Joel's advice and my own better judgment, I texted my dad. I typed, erased, typed, revised, and finally came up with only **Dad — not the easiest lunch I ever had but better to know.**

Uncharacteristically, he answered quickly. Why did I get the sense that it had been dictated by Tracy? Maybe it was the use of full sentences and its pedantic tone. **You're right, Faith. It wasn't the easiest lunch for me, either. I need some time to settle in at Tracy's & to let our conversation at lunch metabolize. I'll be in touch.**

Let our conversation *metabolize?* What did that mean? I'm the one who will be in touch when I feel like it. I, the professional scribe rarely at a loss for words on paper or screen be they personal or professionally shopworn, did not write back.

29

How to Avoid Thanksgiving

NICK DIDN'T SEEM to be noticing the unavoidable holiday hurdle ahead despite the turkey-themed decorations in the school cafeteria. Finally, I asked at breakfast, ten days before he'd need to get on a plane, "I don't suppose you're thinking of spending Thanksgiving with your own family?"

"Thanksgiving," he repeated. "When is that again?"

Doesn't everyone know it's the fourth Thursday in November, and didn't every family start chafing for RSVPs the first week of that month? I said, "It falls on the twenty-eighth this year."

"And we get Friday off, right?"

"Of course! And a half day on Wednesday."

"Love that," he said.

I asked, not my trademark diplomatic self, why he sounded as if he'd just stepped on American soil for the first time.

"The usual reasons: marshmallows on the sweet potatoes, a big-mouth homophobic uncle, cranberry sauce in the shape of its can . . . my widowed dad roasting the turkey for twenty-four hours."

"I thought he remarried."

"True. So now it's a huge thing with all of her relatives. At this point, I couldn't book a flight even if I wanted to. And I don't want to."

I said, "My mother's probably counting on Joel and me — this being the first holiday since my father dropped the bombshell."

When Nick didn't respond, I said, "Would you like to join us for Thanksgiving? My mother makes three pies, and her own cranberry sauce, in which you can see actual cranberries."

He asked, "Do you need an answer now?" then returned to the sports pages.

I said no, of course not. No pressure. None.

Later, at my desk, while I was trying to find the euphemisms to inform a scholarship donor that his recipient was on social probation for peeing off the roof of the science building, Nick said, "Okay! Here we go. Thanksgiving solved."

I looked up.

"Check your e-mail. The Smilowitzes had to back out of the New York field trip. It's an appeal from the Student Activity Office — chaperones needed or the trip is off."

Well, there went the possible even number at my mother's table. "You'd want to drive a busload of kids to New York and make sure they don't wander off and buy drugs and stay up all night so that the hotel security knocks on your door at two a.m.?"

"Very bad attitude. It could be fun." He read aloud as he typed his reply, "Alison — can I have the names of the kids who are going? Thank you, Nick Franconi, responsible adult, Office of Development."

I said, "If you're serious . . . good luck."

"I don't think you heard me. The Smilowitzes had to back out. Smilowitzes, plural. They need two subs, male and female, due to the genders of the students who have signed up: girls and boys."

I said, "Ask her for the itinerary. If it includes my tenth trip to the Museum of Natural History, I'm not interested."

"It's right here in the first SOS. Tickets already in hand for the Matisse cutouts. Orchestra seats for *The Curious Incident of the Dog in the Night-Time.* A tour of the Tenement Museum. Wait. There's more. Thanksgiving dinner in Harlem at a famous restaurant whose specialty is chicken and waffles and sweet-potato pie."

I asked where these substitute chaperones would be staying.

"Not the five-star accommodations on Turpentine Lane in the style to which you've become accustomed, but perfectly adequate."

"Such as?"

"A Holiday Inn."

"But I can't just run off. I have a heartbroken mother to think about."

"I've spent a drunken evening with that mother of yours. I'd say she's doing remarkably well with her heartbreak."

I looked down at the note I was trying to write. "Miss?" I heard. "Focus, please. Can I tell Alison you're in?"

"I suppose my mother could go to Aunt Elaine's. And Joel wouldn't care."

"You could just announce it — off to New York over Thanksgiving, Ma, done deal — without asking her permission. Some adult daughters might consider that."

"Message received."

"Here it is: the list of kids."

"Read me the names," I said. He did. All seniors. No troublemakers, at least not notorious ones, including a boy whose debate prowess and straight A's were topics of my semiannual notes to his scholarship benefactor.

"You're going," Nick said. "Watch me call Alison right now and tell her she has snagged two chaperones."

"Are we paying for these tickets and meals and everything else?"

"Read the e-mail. It comes out of the student activities budget. Apparently it has to be used before the end of the year or it disappears."

"It's a huge responsibility."

"Eight honor-roll kids, one van, two chaperones? It's like an away game with the chess team."

"You'd drive? Because I've never driven a van."

"Is that a yes?" Nick asked.

"What if we have to share a room with a kid?"

"We won't. And when was the last time you got out of Everton?"

"Feels like never," I said.

Our three and a half days didn't exactly fly by. We dealt with two roommate reassignments, one inhaler overnighted from Everton, one pink eye, and two days of rain. We imposed a midnight lights-out rule, at which time Nick and I repaired to the hotel's drab bar for wine disguised as coffee in Styrofoam cups. We adopted the motto "Divide and conquer," which meant occupying two tables, one adult per four kids at every meal, except for Thanksgiving dinner at a teeming Harlem restaurant, where all ten of us ate family-style. Noticing that neighboring tables were saying grace, one of our girls asked, "Shouldn't we do that?"

"Sure," said Nick. "Anyone?"

I closed my eyes, waiting for secular inspiration, since I only knew one blessing and it was in Hebrew.

The drama club president and frequent leading lady, Carlee, obliged. "Let us give thanks for the plants and animals who sacrificed themselves so that we can enjoy Thanksgiving dinner," to which suspected admirer Rafe added, "In New! York! City! People!"

One by one, they spoke — some sounding prayerful, but the majority expressing gratitude for not having to set the table, clear the dishes, load the dishwasher, peel potatoes; for not having to starve all afternoon while the turkey was roasting; for getting to see the Macy's parade in real life, even though it would've been awesome if one of the floats had, like, broken free and got caught on the Empire State Building!

"Inside voices, children!" one of them called out, earning laughter from the moms at the next table.

Nick said, "So far, so good, you guys. I think I can speak for Ms. Frankel, who had to be convinced that this wasn't the worst idea I ever had, that we are not sorry we signed on for this. So thanks, and keep up the good work."

"A-men," I said. "And let's not forget to thank the generous alumni who funded our trip."

"Thank you, rich people, wherever you are! Keep it comin'!" said our heretofore quietest boy.

"Planting the seeds of stewardship," said Nick, with a wink.

One wink across the table in my direction? Who would even notice that?

The girls started it as we left New York on the ride home. "You two married?" one of them called out from the giggling back row.

"No. That would be Mr. and Mrs. Smilowitz, the chaperones who had to drop out," said Nick.

"You know we're not married," I said.

"You share an office, right?" Carlee asked.

Then the debater I knew via my thoughtful stewardship updates offered, "Yah. And it's, like, microscopic."

Nick said, "Not true. Nor am I appreciating the subtext of that inaccurate description."

I said, "People! Let's talk about the play. How many of you read the novel ahead of time?"

Silence. "Nada!" someone finally yelled.

I told them that I owned a copy and would be happy to loan it. Which is when I heard a whispered "They live together."

"And you know that how?" I asked.

"Her grandmother lives on your street," Hayley answered.

I couldn't deny our housemate status. I told them yes, we shared a house. I knew what they were giggling about, but they were crossing boundaries.

Someone asked if we could give out demerits like teachers could. Nick said, "No, but we can get you all expelled," which only added to the merriment.

We asked for a change of topic, or silence and mercy. Why weren't they texting or plugged into their music like every other kid on campus?

"We're team building," said Amanda. "It's the whole reason for field trips."

"Bonding," said her Holiday Inn roommate.

"For the last time," I said, "Mr. Franconi and I are coworkers and teammates. And don't you think it's retro and unhip to tease two people because they work together and happen to be of the opposite sex? Wasn't the Tenement Museum about many unrelated people who lived under one roof?"

"They had no money. They were immigrants. They worked in sweatshops."

"They had to share beds!" someone said, to more hilarity.

I said, "Okay. Enough. These jokes are getting very tiresome."

Was "tiresome" funny? Apparently so.

We didn't get silence or mercy. We got whispers, guffaws, and, finally, "We saw you slipping out of Miss Frankel's room last night," another wisenheimer tried.

Before I could protest, Nick said, "Or maybe you saw me slipping out of the police station where I'd just reported you delinquents to the authorities."

Jeers and laughter. What fun these two nonfaculty chaperones were!

I whispered to Nick, "That wasn't exactly a denial. Maybe you should have been more direct." He took one of his hands off the wheel and snapped his fingers. "Delinquents? Listen up. Ms. Frankel wants you to understand . . . wants *me* to make it very clear that I was not slipping out of her room. That is uncalled for and — don't quote me — bullshit. In fact, I don't even know what room she was assigned to. Ms. Frankel? Would you like to add anything to that?"

I swiveled around in my seat. "Yes, I would. I know you're all having fun. I know you think you're hilarious. Mr. Franconi and I happen to live in the same house, but that is a financial arrangement. And I think there's a teaching moment here (boos) . . . no, wait, it's challenging the antiquated notion that two people of the opposite sex sharing an activity or an office or a van have to be a couple. It never occurred to us that if we agreed to chaperone this trip, we'd be . . . what? Accused of hooking up?"

That phrase appeared to be highly amusing, too.

"Settle down," Nick said to them. And to me, quietly, "They're having fun. They're harmless. And I don't mind."

Truthfully? I didn't mind, either.

Parents were waiting when we returned. Each one said, "Was Amanda/Pilar/Kayla/Carlee/Hayley/Jordan/Rafe/Khaled good? Well behaved? No trouble?"

Nick winked at whichever son or daughter was fending off a parental embrace. "Couldn't be more delightful," he said every time.

Heading home I asked, "Do you think we'll never hear the end of this?"

"So what? They're all seniors. They'll be gone in six months. Until then, we'll just keep being the consummate professionals that we pretend to be."

Pretend to be? Which part were we faking? I said, "It doesn't make sense, does it — how all eight of them were singing the same tune?"

We turned onto Turpentine and then into our driveway. There were a few moments of silence before he unclicked his seat belt. "Not so hard to grasp," Nick finally said.

Did he mean something other than blatant senior silliness? Us, for instance? I chose not to ask.

30

·❧·

Bratty Brooke

UPON RECEIPT OF E-MAIL invitations to Stuart and Brooke's Christmas-Hanukkah-Winter-Solstice open house, I asked Nick if he'd known that our exes' housing arrangement had worked out.

"Only because she had the decency to tell me that my half of the rent was now covered."

After the RSVP deadline had passed, Stuart sent a reminder, asking whether I was attending and was I bringing a guest. **No and no**, I e-mailed. Only then did he plead his case: that he and Brooke didn't know many people in Everton, and could I please put our differences aside and come? Nick hadn't RSVP'd, either. Could I tell him the same thing: guests needed.

When I relayed Stuart's message across the office, Nick said, "I have zero interest in doing Brooke the favor of making her party *not* a bust."

I asked, "Do those double negatives add up to a yes or a no?"

"A no. N-O."

"Me, too," I said, returning to the list of names need-ing to be thanked for end-of-year donations. "What do I say to someone I happen to know has a summer home on Mar-tha's Vineyard and a ski lodge in Stowe, and donates twenty-five dollars?" I asked. Without waiting for an answer, I nar-rated, pretending to write, "Dear Cheapskate, Are you *kidding?* Twenty-five dollars? Why even bother? Homeless alums give more than you do. Sincerely yours, Faith Frankel, Director of Stewardship."

And suddenly there was Reggie at our open door. His eaves-dropping had become chronic since Nick moved to 10 Turpen-tine, when, conscious of appearances and without consulting each other, we'd been keeping our office door conspicuously open.

"Whoa," Reggie said. "You can't write that!"

"I can't? Oh, dear. I always say that if the donation is two fig-ures."

"They deserve it," Nick said. "Twenty-five lousy bucks? Who needs 'em?"

"But, but — we never call our donors cheapskates! We don't question the amount of their contribution. No matter the size of the check, it's good for our yield."

I fluttered the blank notecard in the air. "Reggie? Seriously? Do you really think I'd write that? Or — just maybe — could I have been kidding?"

He walked over to my desk and pawed through a few blank notecards. I gave his hand a light slap. "Do you mind? I was joking!"

Of course, he had to say that he knew it was a joke, knew I had to be kidding. Ha, good one!

"In that case, you'll excuse me while I get back to thanking"

— glancing at the top name on my to-do list — "Tanner Rowland for his generous gift to his beloved alma mater."

Reggie still didn't move. "Now that there's nothing to worry about," I said, "you can amscray."

He glanced Nick's way then back to me. "You two have some kind of holiday party you're going to? Not our department party. I mean, a private one?"

"Very private," I said.

"Which I'm skipping," said Nick.

"Did I hear 'open house'? Like you can bring a guest?"

"*I'm* not going," I said. "*He's* not going," pointing at Nick. "So you can hardly be a plus-one."

"Who's throwing it? Anyone I know? Alums?"

"No," said Nick.

"Is it the kind of party where an invitation is transferable?"

"Doubt it," I said.

"Whose party again?"

"You don't know them," said Nick.

Case closed, topic moot, I granted, "Stuart Levine and Brooke somebody."

"Stuart and Brooke?" Reggie repeated. "I know those names."

I pointed to the wall where the map of the continental United States once hung. "He's the friend whose walk across the country I was tracking."

"Friend? Aren't you going to marry the guy?"

"Not anymore."

Nick said, "She realized around Illinois that it wasn't meant to be."

"And why does the name Brooke ring a bell?" Reggie asked.

Nick shrugged. I shrugged. At this social dead end, Reggie returned to his default jock goofiness. "Your good friend here,

Elinor Lipman

Mr. Can't Make a Save to Save His Life, allowed four goals last night."

"Do I care?" said Nick. "I shouldn't be in the net anyway."

"C'mon. Two more games. You're no quitter. You just need to focus." Then, fond as he always was of his coach mode, Reggie turned back to me. "None of my business, Frankel, but here's what I'm thinkin': you should go to that party."

"Really? Why is that?"

"Don't make me say it," said Reggie.

"Not 'do it for the school' so I can network there?"

He lowered his voice. "Seriously. Do you get out? Do you go to parties? Lots of people call off weddings and they move on. Would a little social life kill you? I mean, if you went to a party, you might — you know — meet someone."

"Is that how you met the nonexistent Mrs. O'Sullivan?"

"I'm a guy. We do just fine."

I looked over to see if Nick had heard. His face and posture registered nothing but full attention to fund-raising.

I said to Reggie, "Surely you know you're not supposed to ask me about my personal life. And, just for the record, I go to plenty of parties. Have I missed one single reunion gala or trustees' cocktail party?"

Reggie said, "That's not partying. That's work. We don't even drink at those things."

I said, "I have a ton of work, so if you'll excuse me . . ."

"Okay, sure. Just sayin'."

"Just sayin' what?"

He smiled. "You could do okay out there."

"Bye," I said. "And close the door behind you for once." I waited for the sound of Reggie's footsteps to fade. "From now on, we work with the door closed. No more eavesdropping for that yenta," I said to Nick.

"It's reportable," he said. "You don't ask employees about their personal lives. Ever."

Of course, he'd heard every word.

Brooke's apartment was crimson walled, with odd objects hung in the living room: a toy ukulele, a mangy fur-trimmed cardigan on a hanger, and a framed *Boston Globe* front page featuring Jackie Kennedy's marriage to Aristotle Onassis. Brooke *may* have realized that the woman in the black-velvet tunic over lacy tights from a Soho boutique, with freshly cut and blown-dry hair, was me, but she clearly wasn't in the business of greeting or welcoming her guests.

"Mulled cider on the stove," Stuart told me. "Cups somewhere close by. We figured it would be do-it-yourself. So great you came!"

The kitchen was merely one end of the living room, with a counter dividing the space, and a mess of epic proportions. It was as if every pot, pan, and utensil used in the preparation of the buffet offerings was on display, unwashed, on every surface and piled high in the sink. A few onion skins and potato peels decorated the floor.

This was when Brooke found me, staring — perhaps a little smugly — at the inexplicable mess. "Disgusting, right?" I heard.

I said, "No. No. Perfectly understandable. This is what a kitchen looks like when you're getting ready for a party."

"I should've started earlier. Did you ever make lotkeys?"

"Um, excuse me? Did I ever make what?"

"For Hanukkah? Potato lotkeys. It didn't sound like such a big deal until I did it. What a mess. I was still in the shower when the first guests showed up."

I said, "It was nice of you to acknowledge Hanukkah."

"It was Stuart's idea. He's Jewish."

I said I knew.

"How do you know him?" she asked.

Really? I took the opportunity to downplay my embarrassing and unaccountable romantic alliance with him by saying only "I supported his walk across . . . the early states."

"I'm Brooke," she said. "You probably figured that out already."

"I'm Faith Frankel."

A curtain of ice dropped between us. "You work with Nick," she said. "Side by side, I understand."

Maybe if there had been congeniality rather than accusation in her tone, I wouldn't have answered as I did. "That's right. I work *and* live with him."

"Thanks a lot. Thanks for everything," she sputtered.

I'd like to report that I'd answered cleverly, but I was too stunned to speak. And I may also have failed to report that Brooke, by any standard, with the blond streaks in her abundantly perfect hair and dewy everything else, was exceedingly, scarily attractive.

"Saint Faith," she spat. "The perfect coworker and . . . and" — with a sweeping gesture that took in the mess — "so organized! Okay, and smart. Well, thank you, because I left a really good job and moved here because of him and that stupid school!" And with that, she strode to the refrigerator, where I watched her root around for something that turned out to be a carton of sour cream.

I finally said, "I'm not Saint Faith, not by a long shot."

"Oh, believe me, I know that! I'm not stupid. Do you know what he likes? Need any tips?"

Of course, I could have protested the sexual innuendo, but the inner actress I didn't often summon said, "No, thanks. I'm doing just fine."

Before a frosty good-bye, I added, "FYI? Applesauce should be served as well as sour cream."

Did I even need to find Stuart for a good-bye? No. Let bratty Brooke tell him that I'd been the target of her tantrum.

I went straight to the smaller bedroom where I found my jacket and scarf buried under someone's big raccoon coat. I was still buttoning up and arranging my outerwear in a mottled mirror when I heard "Faith?"

Reflected in the mirror was the round, hopeful, unadorned face of Rebecca, Stuart's mother. She launched her coat across the bed, revealing a blue and white sweatshirt, decorated with a puffy dreidel, then enfolded me in a hug.

I extricated myself at the shortest possible polite interval, and said, "Happy Hanukkah."

"Iona will be so delighted to see you. Shall we mingle?"

I said, "No, sorry, I'm leaving."

"You can't!"

"I have to." And not because I was looking for sympathy but only to squeal on Brooke, I announced, "Your son's cohostess was unaccountably rude to me after I told her who I was."

"What did she say?"

"She called me Saint Faith —"

"Which could be taken as a compliment!"

"Believe me, it wasn't. She was extremely sarcastic and she called Everton Country Day 'that stupid school.'"

"Are you quite sure she wasn't saying it in a joking, affectionate way? Like I might say" — she pointed to the dreidel — "my wife bought me this stupid sweatshirt.'"

"Believe me, it's not about the school. It's because Nick, my office- and housemate, used to be her live-in boyfriend. And it ended badly."

"Maybe it's just her manner," said Rebecca. "Some people

come off as cold. It's cultural." She whispered, "Her last name is Winthrop. And why would she invite you to her party if she disliked you?"

"She didn't invite me. Stuart did."

That answer seemed to make her happy. "Are you keeping in touch with him?"

"*He* is. I don't answer."

"He's buckling down," said Rebecca. "You know he runs our practice?"

"He told me he was your substitute receptionist."

"Exactly. Receptionists run the world!"

I said, "I can't stay. Say hello to Iona . . ."

"I'm sure there's an explanation," said Rebecca.

"For what?"

"Brooke's lashing out." She paused. "It could be the green-eyed monster. Stuart might have confided in her. About you, about his feelings —"

It was then that Stuart appeared in the doorway, clueless and grinning, holding two plastic glasses of eggnog. "Two of my favorite women!" he boomed. "I wondered what was taking so long in here! C'mon in. Brooke just brought out the potato latkes."

Rebecca said, "I've been having a heart-to-heart with Faith." Then, turning to me: "Do you want to tell Stuart what you felt transpired earlier?"

I said, "No, I don't," and to Stuart: "Gotta run. I have another party to go to."

"C'mon," he said. "Five more minutes. I was hoping everyone would be here for the announcement."

"Announcement?" I repeated.

"We're excited," said Rebecca, beaming.

I didn't quite leave, but stood by the front door, a mittened hand on the doorknob, listening to the breaking news. Stuart, tall and messily handsome, his walkathon tan not entirely faded, his hairline unreceded, announced in a wobbly voice, hand on heart that he, Stuart Ira Levine, had the honor of being chosen to father a child by two friends of his moms! Granted, he wouldn't have any legal standing, but what a thrill to help two wonderful women become a family. How could he not share such happy news, which he'd just found out himself yesterday, that his enzymes had worked their magic. The baby was due in August, the very month of his own birthday! Another Leo! He raised his glass. "To the future! To a little Levine — not that he or she will have my name, but still mind-blowing. And so flattering, to be chosen over an entire sperm bank catalogue! And what better present this holiday season: to be a biological dad, even the silent kind, at forty! *L'chaim!*"

Except for his two moms, the most common expression on the faces of this small crowd was perplexed. Who gets excited about being a sperm donor? Surely everyone else was entertaining the same thoughts that were running through my mind. *How much money changed hands for this donation, how did the job get done, and who in all of Everton, Massachusetts, was a bigger jackass than Stuart Ira Levine?*

31

Table for Two

I F I WAS RACING OFF to anything, it was back home to regale Nick with tales of Brooke's breathtaking rudeness. But somewhere between the party and my driveway, I thought better of that inclination. Gossip is never becoming, I reminded myself. I knew how to be diplomatic. Didn't I engage in it daily, testifying to alums that Everton Country Day was ever so grateful for their paltry contribution or their donation of a bat, ball, and glove?

Home by eight o'clock, I found Nick in front of the TV, watching the original *Miracle on 34th Street*. "How was it?" he asked.

"Not great."

His next question, eyes never leaving a colorized Kris Kringle, was "How did you find Brooke?"

I said she'd been busy with her cohost duties, that we'd only talked briefly while she was putting out the latkes. "First time she made them," I continued. "They weren't bad ... under-salted and a little undercooked. But nice of her to make the effort, don't you think? That's all I've eaten since breakfast: one latke."

When he didn't take the hint, I asked if he'd had dinner, and if not, did he want to go out?

"Where?"

"The Terrace? Or La Grotta?" I patted my velvet tunic and said it was a shame to waste the outfit.

Nick said rather formally, "You look very nice." And then, "Was Stuart being Stuart?"

"Oh, boy. Do I have a story for you."

He waited. I said, "Not now. I'll describe the grand finale over dinner. Can I talk you into it?"

His answer was un-Nick-like and off topic. "Maybe I should've gone with you. I just hung around. I read the paper. I did some Christmas shopping online. I called my dad, who was heading for mass in a rush. I forgot he's a lector. He wished me a merry Christmas and a happy new year — like that was it, as if we wouldn't talk for another month."

His pronunciation of "a merry Christmas" had a particularly ironic spin. Looking around, I noted the complete absence of anything that acknowledged a holiday. Any holiday. I did have a menorah in the china closet, but Hanukkah had come and gone in early December without one candle lit. Here I had a roommate who was a legitimate observer of Christmas, whose father went to mass on a Saturday night, and I'd done nothing.

He asked what I was appraising so studiously.

I said, "I just decided. We're getting a tree." I told him that when I was in high school, I'd go to Marisol Pérez's house where I got to put the tinsel on the branches because they knew I loved that and had no tree of my own.

He said, "Here's the part I don't like. We'd be that family in a G-rated movie who gets all cemented by a last-minute Christmas tree acquisition."

"I love those movies."

"Of course you would. No Christmas baggage weighing you down."

By now, he'd picked up the remote and snapped off the TV, but still hadn't said yes or no to my invitation. "Dinner?" I tried again.

"I could do that."

"Then we get the tree and ornaments? Or before?"

"No, too much work for tonight."

"Bringing home a tree is too much work?"

"Only in the movies is it no sweat. The perfect family buys a perfect tree, then magically it's all set up and looks like it could be on the White House lawn. Their singing — I'm guessing "Silent Night" — swells and the camera pulls back. It's snowing. Roll credits. In real life, it's a job. We'll need the stand, the lights, the ornaments —"

"The tinsel."

"The tinsel. Too much work on a Saturday night. Especially for a girl in fancy clothes. Let's do it tomorrow."

"Go change," I said, "just in case we can get a table at La Grotta. I'll call right now."

"Use my name," he said.

I was in my coat, reservation secured, waiting at the front door as he made his way downstairs. My first glimpse of his lower half showed him still in jeans, then, as he descended farther, I saw he'd put on his tuxedo jacket. "Very smart," I said, at the same time wondering, *What's this about?*

I told him they had a table in fifteen minutes and how perfect was that . . . as long as La Grotta wasn't going to make him uncomfortable.

"You mean was La Grotta our place?" — air quotes around the last two words.

"Just sayin'. Whoever answered there sounded very happy to hear the name Franconi."

"They're good at that," he said.

When we two were led to a good-size table for four, Nick asked, "Anything smaller?"

"Of course, of course," said the maître d'. He led us to a small round table and lit its votive candle with a pocket lighter. Minutes later, before we'd even opened the menus, two small glasses of a pale raspberry-colored liquid were put before us. "*Aperitivo!* Compliments of Claudio," the waiter proclaimed.

Nick raised his glass in the direction of the maître d' and nodded, smiling, at the same time he was murmuring to me, "His kids go to ECD. He doesn't quite get that I'm not someone he needs to kowtow to instead of the other way around."

I raised my glass in the same direction. "He's getting a thank-you note on Monday."

"Monday's Christmas," Nick reminded me.

Of course, that launched me back into my Christmas MO. The tree, the ornaments, all that other stuff we'd have to buy.

"Look . . . I'm not a kid. I don't need to get all decked out," Nick said.

"C'mon. We'll get a scrawny tree and a few ornaments from the closest purveyor of ornaments."

"Even that — the scrawny tree. Charlie Brown's? What else — you'll be stringing popcorn?"

"Yes, and cranberries. Plus those chili pepper lights the Pérezes had."

The waiter was approaching. I said, "We need another minute or two."

"No, we don't," said Nick. "May I?"

May he what? I said, "I guess so."

"*Hmmm.* Okay. The veal with artichokes. And the eggplant parm. You like eggplant, right? We'll share a pasta to start. Bolognese okay with you?"

"Very okay."

We ordered wine, a red from Sicily, the name of which Nick pronounced beautifully. And then, over our first pour, he said, "Now, the high point of Stuart's party, the grand finale, which you were saving for dinner. Will I want to hear it?"

I said, "It had nothing to do with Brooke. It was pure Stuart."

"About brotherhood and sisterhood and planets aligning?"

"Just the opposite. It was all about him."

"Let me guess. He found a publisher for his book."

I'd forgotten about Stuart's alleged book, which was undoubtedly in the first person, undoubtedly horrible, in text-message English, doodled between scheduling appointments and collecting copays. I said no, not that.

"Good news? Bad news?"

"Brace yourself," I said.

"Quite the buildup. You'd better deliver."

"How's this: Stuart announced, on the verge of tears and with his hand over his heart, that he . . . how should I put this? . . . successfully fertilized the egg of a lesbian."

"Whaat?"

"You heard me. He artificially inseminated — well, I assume it happened artificially — an ovulating friend of his mothers'."

"Wait . . . please tell me he confided this to you in private?"

"No! He gathered everyone around, got up on an ottoman, and clinked a glass to get our attention."

"And his guests said what?"

"Except for his proud mothers, everyone looked bewildered, as in *why is he telling us this?* Especially because the recipient is something like one day pregnant."

"And that's standard — the sperm donator finds out whether he hit a home run?"

"Probably not."

"Is he going to be the kid's father? I mean obviously biological, but involved with him? Throwing the ball around? Christmas and Thanksgiving and alternate weekends?"

"From what I could tell, no, no rights. Although, who knows what he's dreaming of."

Nick then asked — rather delicately, I thought — what Brooke's reaction had been.

"I wasn't watching Brooke." Made brave or just undiplomatic by *aperitivo* and wine, I then presented that which I had resolved to keep to myself: a faithful reconstruction of Brooke's sudden misplaced rage.

"Believe me, I know," he said.

"Know what?"

"Her opinion."

"Of what?"

"This. Us. The fact that we share an office *and* a house."

We were at the restaurant's smallest table, against a back wall, clearly earmarked for two people on a date, concerted effort needed for knees not to intermingle. I had no right to ask how often he and Brooke spoke, and about what, so I just dipped morsel after morsel of bread in the saucer of olive oil, commenting on nothing.

Nick, facing the entrance, said, "Oh, shit." I turned to see Claudio greeting a man with a guitar and two female companions, all dressed like carolers on an antique Christmas card.

"Oh, crap," Nick murmured. He shook his head strenuously in Claudio's direction, but it was too late. I heard a note from the guitarist's pitch pipe, leading to nods and then, "Come, they told me . . . pa-rum pum pum pum pa . . ."

"Not your doing, I trust," said Nick. "As in your holiday guilt?"

"Carolers? Wouldn't know where to start," I said.

"They're not bad," Nick said. "But where's our Bolognese?"

Weren't we on the topic of Brooke's bad behavior? When the singers stopped for a guitar tune-up and sips of water, I told Nick, "Now I'm going to say something that takes chutzpah. Ready?"

He leaned back in his chair. "I'm all ears."

I said, "Maybe I'm way off base, but Brooke seemed . . . jealous."

Did Nick answer on point? Did he confirm that Brooke's possible jealousy was either a figment of my imagination or had a basis in fact? Neither. "Oh, she can be irrational all right" was his inadequate answer.

"Something's wrong with her," I persisted.

"And you don't think I know that?"

"Yet . . . ?"

"Yet nothing."

"Because you seem . . ." I wanted to say "vulnerable," but downgraded that to "not quite detached."

"I am not the slightest bit interested in getting back with Brooke —"

"Even if she said, 'I don't need a proposal. I don't need a ring. I'd be happy just . . . living with you'?" I must've pronounced the last sentence in a voice that sounded scratchy, because Nick did something that he'd never done before. He came forward from his near recline, touched my wrist with his index finger, then ran it lightly down to my knuckles.

I looked up. Nick wasn't smiling, but was staring most intently.

Was this a friendly gesture or something else? I must've looked confused, because he added, "That wasn't the alcohol talking."

I knew it was my move. I let one of my heretofore restrained knees rest against one of his outstretched legs. We didn't speak, but just sat there like that.

The carolers, mistaking our silence for musical appreciation, moved closer. If they weren't singing "O Holy Night," they should've been.

32

⚬~⚬

December 23–24

SOMETIMES, BY MUTUAL AGREEMENT, two people have to table a consummation. Very much in the don't-do-anything-rash column was our success as house- and officemates. It wasn't merely inadvisable to take up with a co-worker, but at Everton Country Day, sexual congress with almost anyone has been actionable since the 1990s when Anita Hill was our commencement speaker.

We proceeded thoughtfully, which is to say nothing happened on Christmas Eve eve. After sharing Bolognese, scaloppini, eggplant parmigiana, and tiramisu on the house, back on Turpentine Lane, at the top of the stairs, we kissed good night, almost chastely, before backing into our respective rooms, smiling. The next morning, I came to breakfast in a diaphanous nightgown I'd once purchased optimistically. It was lacy in the bosom and pale pink, a color they call blush. For modesty's sake, I added a cardigan. Nick was at the stove, frying eggs over easy. Odd to see him clean shaven this early. And in nothing but

Christmas-themed boxers, as if there had been an emergency call to the stove.

I said, "Hope I didn't keep you waiting. I was taking a bubble bath . . . peach and passion fruit."

Once he was seated, I slipped off the sweater, and asked, "Is it warm in here, or is it just me?"

He was buttering a half piece of toast but also whistling in what seemed both a jaunty and suggestive manner.

I said, "I noticed you're wearing nothing but underwear to breakfast. That's a first."

He looked down, then up at me. It was an expression I'd seen the night before at La Grotta — solemn, as if to ask, *Would this be the kind of first you'd welcome?*

The next thing I said was "I'd really like to kiss you."

"We can do better than that," said Nick.

I closed my eyes — not a hesitation, but a time-out, the kind you need upon grasping, *My fondest wish has come true*.

Then one or both of us whispered, "Upstairs?"

Eggs and cereal abandoned. "Yes," we both said. *Yes*.

33

I Wasn't Even Born Then

PPARENTLY DETECTIVE BRIAN DOLAN never meant to imply at his first visit to my house that it was off the hook. His parting "clean as a whistle!" led me to believe that Mrs. Lavoie wasn't being posthumously investigated for manslaughter in my stairwell, and thus my cellar was no longer of interest to the Town of Everton.

But in mid-January, my first day back after a long weekend, I returned home to find state and local police cars parked in front of the house, and my mother greeting me like a surrogate hostess.

Still in coat, hat, and scarf, I charged to the back of the house and yelled my displeasure downstairs to what I assumed was the occupying Detective Dolan. He trudged upstairs and rather patiently let me rant. "This is what you do?" I yelled. "You just break into someone's home while she's at work and — what? — start tearing her house apart like she's a common criminal?"

Brian said, "First, no one's tearing your house apart. And second, a search warrant *does* allow us to enter the premises. But when no one answered here, I thought the neighborly thing to do was call your mom or brother, figuring one of them would have a key."

My mother was still looking hospitable and pleased to be of service while my own thoughts traveled upstairs to Nick's stash of pot. I asked, in what I hoped was entirely innocent fashion, "Um, what are you looking for?"

"Blood," he said. "Actually, bloodstains. I have it here," and with that, he produced a piece of paper that was indeed a search warrant.

"Blood? Whose blood?"

"We don't know yet."

My mother chimed in, informing her buddy Brian that he wouldn't find any such evidence because Faith was down there several times a week doing laundry, as was her housemate, and surely one of them would've noticed blood. And there had been a thorough inspection — hadn't he gone to Everton High with Wally Roche of Tri-County Inspection? How does an inspector miss bloodstains?

"We think they were covered up," Brian said.

I managed to ask if any other kind of human remains were also in my basement.

"We'll see."

It was then that a woman looking very forensic in white protective gear, helmet, and goggles came up from the cellar.

"Sir?" was all she said, but it sounded to me like *Found what we came for.*

"Hold on to the railing, for God's sake," I called after them. "I don't want to be charged with anyone's murder."

"Aren't you funny," I heard back.

I texted Nick, now at an Everton swim meet in his school-spirited, parent-cultivating way, **Not to worry, but cops here,**

had search warrant. In cellar (remember the husbands Mrs. L might've killed?) XOXO.

In the exact number of minutes it would take a person to climb down from the bleachers and drive back to 10 Turpentine Lane, Nick was bounding up the front steps. My mother, the self-appointed doorman, chirped, "Nick! How was your day?"

"Good. Thanks. Where's Faith?" I waved from the kitchen then hurried toward him. He motioned with his chin, *Do we worry about what's upstairs?* I said, "They're not interested in anything else on the premises."

"Anything else but what?"

"Blood. It says so on the warrant."

My mother, now at our elbows, asked, "What are you two whispering about?"

I wouldn't have told her the truth, but Nick said, "I have a little pot upstairs. Can we put it in your purse? I mean, just while they're here?"

My mother looked positively delighted to be colluding with us. "Where is it now?" she whispered.

"In my room. Bureau. Top drawer."

She winked. Then, in an unnecessarily loud voice, said, "May I use your bathroom? I'll be back down soon. Now where did I put my purse? Have to freshen up!" Smiling proudly, she headed for the stairs.

Back in the kitchen, Nick and I heard the murmur of many voices from downstairs, but nothing discernible.

"Think it's okay if we have a glass of wine?" I asked him.

Nick said, "Let's wait for our mule to join us."

We did wait, a longer time than locating pot and slipping it into one's purse should have taken. "I'll go up and see if she found it," I said.

Which is when spokesman Dolan returned to announce that

the racket we were about to hear would be his partners excavating. With crowbars and a concrete cutter.

"What's there to excavate?" I asked.

"I'll go down," Nick said.

"Please."

He then bestowed a comically dramatic, backward-tilted good-bye kiss as if going off to war. "Bye, baby. We'll always have Paris" — at the precise moment my mother appeared.

"Nick's checking on what they're doing," I explained.

Was she looking less happily conspiratorial than before her assignment? I said, "That was him being funny, the kiss. That was a line from *Casablanca*."

"Who doesn't know that?" she asked.

Purse strap over one wrist, she repaired to the sink, where she found breakfast mugs and glasses to wash.

"Sit," I said. "Leave those."

"I don't like leaving dishes in the sink."

"Are you angry? You sound angry." I lowered my voice. "Are you upset that he smokes pot?"

She shook her head.

"But it's something."

"I wasn't snooping . . ."

"But?"

"Upstairs? Nick's room? It struck me as very . . . unlived in."

Should I say yes, he's neat as a pin, never a thing out of place? Instead, an involuntary smile escaped.

"On the other hand," she continued, "*your* room looks very lived in. Your bedclothes . . . tousled. Water glasses and books on each night table."

"And that's bad?"

"I'm confused, to say the least."

"Ma? What do you think two water glasses mean?"

She said flatly, "Two people sleeping together."

"And that's so confusing?"

She finally turned off the faucets and dried her hands. "Either your brother got it very wrong, or he was teasing me. Or you're being played."

"What are we talking about?"

"Nick. Joel said he was gay."

I laughed, which lightened nothing. I tried, "Joel was teasing you, Ma. It was his way of avoiding the topic of Nick and me as a possible couple."

"Is he bisexual?"

"Not bisexual. Not homosexual. Heterosexual."

"Are you sure?"

"Quite sure."

"When did this start?"

First day I saw him, I thought. "It's new. Since Christmas."

She tore a paper towel from the nearby roll and wiped her eyes.

I said, "Please tell me you're not crying over this."

"I'm not . . . not really."

"I still don't understand what you'd find upsetting, unless it's your lying son."

She finally turned away from the sink and faced me. "I knew this time would come — big goings-on in the family . . ." She pointed every which way — me, Nick, the police. "And even though I'm furious with your father, we're still your parents. When something goes wrong, my first impulse is to pick up the phone and call him. But I don't make that call, which means he's won."

I said, "Is that a reference to terrorists — that if you don't go about your normal business then Dad the adulterer wins? Because I don't really see the parallel. You can certainly call

Daddy. He'd probably be relieved you were talking to him." And while I had her at close range, I whispered, "Did you get the stuff?"

"Affirmative," she whispered.

I patted her purse. "Safe and sound?"

"In the zippered compartment where I keep my pills."

I heard footsteps on the cellar steps — Nick's. "There's an army of them downstairs — a photographer, a videographer, a guy taking notes on every single thing said or done."

"I asked about that," said my mother. "They videotape everything in case it goes to trial. Even up here, on their way in. The whole house."

"Not upstairs?" I asked.

"Just their path from the porch to here and down there," she said.

"Which reminds me," Nick said. "Mission accomplished?"

Not as happily conspiratorial as before, she said, "Yes. Found it."

"Good work."

"I never said I wanted to drive around town with it in my possession."

I translated her frosty tone for him. "Mom did a little snooping upstairs. She noticed your room looked unoccupied."

"And that's not cool?" he asked.

She didn't answer except to say, "I'd hardly call it snooping."

"Did you see anything downstairs?" I asked him. "Do we know any more?"

"They're ripping up the plywood. They knew there would be a cement subfloor underneath it, and there is."

"Is there any chance it's money buried down there?" my mother asked. "Or jewelry, or papers of some kind?"

I said, "The warrant said 'blood.' You can't go to court and get a warrant to search for bloodstains if you're really looking for buried treasure."

"Why don't you go back down?" my mother asked Nick.

I said, "My turn." I took the stairs even more carefully than usual, hand over hand on the railing. The usually dimly lit cellar was now illuminated by spotlights that looked movie set–ish and, indeed, a whole crew was bustling around. Brian, seated and supervising from the bottom step, rose to let me pass.

I asked if I could talk to him for a minute.

"How about when we finish up here?"

I asked, "Can you tell me whose blood you're looking for?"

"No."

"No you don't know yet, or no you can't tell me?"

"Faith? How would we know? We need to test it and find a relative or most likely exhume a body or bodies to even make a match."

"Exhume . . . like here?"

"No. From their graves. If they were buried, that is."

"Ugh. Exhuming a dead body always struck me as the creepiest thing imaginable, and the creepiest job! The poor guy who has to open the coffin —"

"That would be me," said a heretofore silent member of what Brian was calling the unit.

I said, "Oh, sorry. I'm sure you're used to it." The two were methodically crowbarring their way under and across my plywood floor. I asked, "Wouldn't there be a logical place to find blood? I mean, if someone died falling downstairs, wouldn't they have bled here?" I pointed to my own feet, a yard from the bottom of the stairs.

"Depends," Brian said. "Rick over there" — the man waved — "is a blood-splatter expert . . . Guys, it's five forty-five. Sean has basketball tonight, and I can't miss another game."

Excuse me. *Blood-splatter expert?* Was that not a phrase that stopped any conversation cold? "If you find blood, then what?" I asked. "Are you looking for one person's blood or several persons'?"

"Faith! Could we just leave it that someone might've died here, *not* accidentally?"

I said, "Okay, fine." I watched for a minute or two. More patches being photographed and videographed. Samples being bagged and tagged. I asked if they'd found something.

"Maybe."

I said, "In big cities, or at least on cop shows *about* big cities, they use a chemical that shows blood even after it's washed away. They can tell if a washing machine was used to cover up the murderer's bloody clothes. Even when the cycle is finished."

"Is that right?" Brian asked. "Imagine that." He made a little show of tiptoeing to my washing machine, lifting its lid, and peering in. "Just as I thought," he said. "Let's read her her rights."

His partners laughed. I said, "Very droll. Are you going to fix my floor when this is all done?"

"We'll submit your request to the district attorney," Brian said.

I addressed the videographer, in case a future jury would be weighing in on my guilt by real estate association. "I just bought this house four months ago. I wasn't even born when the previous owner might've killed someone."

Brian said, "Very nice. Did everybody hear that?"

Nods.

"It's almost six," Brian repeated. "Let's call it a day." And to me: "I'm sure I don't have to ask you not to disturb anything. Don't even go near it."

"Who'd want to after knowing what I know?" I said.

"Ten, fifteen more minutes and we're done," one of the men said.

I asked if they could drive away without attracting any more attention than they already had. And would it violate protocol if they left through the bulkhead door instead of the scandal-inducing way they came in?

34

Care to Share?

MY BROTHER FORWARDED our mother's follow-up e-mail: **WHY DID YOU TELL ME THAT FAITH'S ROOMMATE IS GAY BECAUSE HE'S NOT IN THE LEAST!!! I SUPPOSE IT WAS YOUR IDEA OF A JOKE, CAN YOU DO DINNER THIS WEEK? LUV, MOM.**

She also left a message on my father's cell phone, no details, just "Call me. It's about Faith" — alarming him and resulting in a 7:45 a.m. fact-check. Was I okay? Joel? The house, the car, the job?

Even though his call woke me, I answered with a lilt in my voice, rather coyly, Nick asleep next to me, "I'm fine, Dad. *More* than fine . . ."

Wouldn't anyone, especially a relieved father, say, "You sound unusually happy, honey. Tell me more." But his only follow-up was a return to a stickier "You weren't so fine when I last saw you."

I slipped out of bed with my phone, grabbed my bathrobe,

and crossed the hall to what was now our spare bedroom. "Would that be the lunch where you told me you were in mad love, would be shacking up with a much younger woman and her two brats?" I demanded.

"Sarcasm noted . . . But I gather you're okay?"

"I'm very okay! My basement, on the other hand, was apparently the scene of a murder or two, which may have been the reason for Mom's news bulletin."

"When? Since you closed?"

"No! The previous owner."

"Murdered?"

"Not the victim — the perp! She had a couple of husbands who died in falls down the cellar steps."

"*Husbands,* plural? No doubt naming her the beneficiary on their life insurance policies. You know what my reaction is to *fell* down the stairs? No, they didn't."

"That's exactly what Nick said. She pushed them."

"Remind me who Nick is."

"You know who Nick is! He's in my department — Major Gifts — my officemate. And since November he's been my housemate. Things changed on Christmas Eve, which I'm sure is the other thing Mom wanted to discuss."

"He's moved out?"

"No, just the opposite! We're now . . . a couple."

No congratulations issued forth, no mazel tov. "Your mother's message didn't sound like she had happy news to announce," he said.

"I know. She'll come around."

He asked if she had grounds for her objection other than the obvious one.

Not Jewish, he meant. "She's confused. Joel didn't help matters by telling her that Nick was gay to get her off the scent."

"What scent?"

"I think Joel was picking something up between Nick and me that I wasn't even acknowledging yet, so when Mom was quizzing him about my new roommate, Joel thought it was the fastest way to get the subject dropped."

Poor Faith, I was hearing in his silence. Poor, born-yesterday, clueless Faith. "Can I tell you what my feeling is when a man is thought to be gay? Almost always, where there's smoke there's fire."

"But Joel was teasing. It's a complete fabrication."

"Does he know the man?"

I vowed at that moment never to tell anyone about Joel's little joke, since the word *gay* seemed to hijack any conversation and distract any listener from the lovely news that Faith Frankel was now half of a couple. "All of that is beside the point. I was thinking you might be happy for me. Or at least be relieved that Mom wasn't calling you about me in an intensive care unit."

"Are you in love?" he asked.

This was the reconstructed Henry, the sensitive man with the new emotive vocabulary and throbbing nerve endings.

"I might be."

"Care to share with your old dad?"

I did not. I said, um, not at this juncture. It was still early in the relationship. Don't want to jinx anything. "How's Trixie?" I asked instead.

"Tracy."

"Didn't I say Tracy? No matter. Is she still the love of your life?"

"I can't tell whether you're being facetious."

"Kind of."

"The answer would be it's a love I never knew I was capable of."

Oh, dear. I said, "I'm not used to hearing stuff like that from you."

"Am I supposed to talk like the person I was before? Like a dead man? Like an insurance agent? I can't believe any of it; I can't believe Tracy shares these feelings. Do you know we go to services every Friday night, and I thank God for putting her in my path?"

What does a daughter, not given to similar confessions and pronouncements, say? I made some noises that sounded empathetic. And admitting to myself that only someone's worst enemy or ex-wife would begrudge him his miracle, I said, "Well, good for you. And good for your art, no doubt."

"It's fueling me! Chagall is so . . . so magical! Each painting has a narrative. The more I do this, the more I feel as if I'm channeling him."

"Dad? You're sounding New Agey. Nothing wrong with that. Just a little weird coming from you."

"I'm evolving."

"From what to what?" — asked too reflexively before I considered the treacly answer I'd have to endure.

"From a man with a frozen heart, at least in the sense of love given and love received, to what I've —"

"Who said you had a frozen heart? Tracy? She's saved you from us?"

"I didn't say that, Faith. And just so you know, this is me digging deeper, me unlocking feelings and, yes, potency I never knew I was capable of."

Oh, God. It was sounding familiar, and I realized why. If Henry Frankel was channeling anyone, it was annoyingly sensitive, self-involved, ex-nothing Stuart Levine.

"I'm your daughter! I've known you a lot longer than Tracy has. I never felt unloved. I always thought you were a good father, maybe even a great father, present circumstances not-withstanding. And as for 'love received'? You never noticed that Mom loved you, or your kids did? And your loyal clients, not to mention your adoring administrative assistants? And what about your parents? Bessie and Abe would turn over in their graves if they heard you say you were unloved."

After his melancholy sigh, I heard, "When I talk about love, Faith, I'm talking about passion."

"I got that! I thought you called to check if I was alive, but we haven't strayed too far off the topic of the new you."

"I'm sorry! It's just so overwhelming. And it isn't so much about me as my defending Tracy."

Did I hate my father at that moment? I said, "So sorry. I'll let you get back to your little miracle. As for Nancy Frankel, my mother and your wife, call her back. I'm sure she's sitting by the phone."

"I will."

"When?"

"As soon as I get to my studio."

"I thought you have a place to paint in Tracy's mansion."

"There you go again. It's not a mansion. Yes, I do. But I meant my studio on Gainsborough. You know I kept that, of course? And Tracy doesn't necessarily have to hear me raise my voice with your mother. Our last conversation was adversarial. I just want to say that if the shoe was on the other foot, and your mother had found *her* soul mate I'd be genuinely happy for her."

"You'd be relieved! You left her and found potency and passion, so why shouldn't she?"

"Faith," he said. "We have a lot to work on, you and I."

I said again, "Call Mom. All she wants to tell you is that the police are occupying my basement and I'm having sex."

"He's a good man, this Nick? A good partner? A mensch? Because you want to pick someone with whom you could have an amicable divorce."

"Now there's a goal."

"I do love you," he whispered. "Tracy's two girls . . . well, they remind me every day of what a reasonable child you were."

"Nice to hear," I said. *Trouble in paradise,* I thought.

35

·᷒᷒ᡈᠸᠵᡖᠵᠶᠦᠦ·

Codes of Conduct

N ICK AND I CONSIDERED taking the offensive and informing Human Resources that a new day had dawned. We'd quote the sentence in the ECD sexual harassment manual prohibiting romantic relationships between a manager and employee — so clearly *not* the case between equals.

But HR was staffed by gossips; word would get around, codes of conduct might be baselessly cited, and we'd have Reggie's smirking to contend with. So we stuck with our usual office collegiality, which required us to be our own two-person acting troupe, fund-raising in tandem without touching, still driving to work in separate cars, teasing each other within Reggie's earshot about imaginary social lives.

We found this endlessly amusing, which gave the most routine, gray, subfreezing days some added color. We did eat lunch together more often, our brown bags packed that morning, side by side in various states of undress, at our speckled Formica counter. Sometimes our sandwiches and snacks matched;

sometimes our knees touched under the cafeteria table. Did anyone notice? Let them.

And then came the trustees' retreat in the Berkshires. The whole Development team, minus me, packed up for the last weekend in January. I drew the short straw for the stated reason that my specialty was long-distance epistolary fund-raising, but everyone knew the real reason was to save the school money. Reggie and Nick could share a room at the conference center, whereas female me would, theoretically, need a single.

Back on campus, assigned to hold down the Development fort as if that carried the most prestige, I was in close touch with Nick. He'd text or call between meetings and after hours. If roommate Reggie was present, Nick would say, "Um, can't talk," or "Not a good time," and I'd say, "Got it. Reggie's there."

"Exactly."

Due to the frequency of these cryptic "can't talks," followed by Nick's too-long disappearances, allegedly to fill their ice bucket or find a newspaper, Reggie grew suspicious. Finally, Reggie asked, "Okay, dude. Who is she?"

What followed was reported to me by Nick upon his return, over my welcome-home lamb stew and mashed potatoes. He'd told Reggie the truth for this reason: our playacting was one thing, but lying when asked a very direct question struck him as unnecessary, cheap, even disloyal to me. He did not want to dissemble about what now constituted "us." So when Reggie asked, "Who is she?" Nick said, "I think you can guess."

"Did he?"

"Sort of."

When I pressed him, Nick said, "I swear it was in a kind of awe, and . . . and . . . definitely a thumbs-up — 'Not *Frankel?*'"

"And you said . . ."

"'Of course it's Frankel!'"

"Then . . . ?"

"He's such an asshole! Okay — he asked who made the first move and . . . how *is* she?"

"How am I *what?*"

"In the sack."

"No!"

"Yes! So I said, 'You know, Reg, even between us guys, that's a pretty throwback question, and you realize it constitutes sexual harassment because you're my manager.' Of course, that didn't shut him up. I believe the next question was 'Are you going to sell one of the cars. If so, which one? Any chance the VW Golf?'"

First I laughed, then asked the recurrent rhetorical question, "How the hell did he get to be head of a department?"

"QB1. Have you forgotten that?"

Impossible to forget. Reggie's office was a shrine to his varsity glory days, a whole console table devoted to trophies and framed photos. His Everton diploma, double matted in the school colors, hung above it, and in a clear Lucite box, Windexed at the first sign of a fingerprint, the sacred pigskin that scored some career-making touchdown.

"Now what?" I asked. "Now that he knows about us?"

"I told him I didn't want to hear about this at work. No leering. No stupid jokes. We were professionals. At least you and I are."

"Did you ask him not to tell anyone else?"

"Good luck with that."

"Everyone knows?"

"You can picture it, in a coffee line, to whoever was listening, 'Nick here has some news.' Or 'Nice going, lover boy.'

It saved him from making intelligent conversation with the trustees."

That prompted me to ask about certain board members, the few who wrote *me* thank-you notes for my big Hepworth score. I also brought up one of our favorite topics. "How was Dickenson?" — understood to mean how much did our headmaster drink before, during, and after the dinners.

"Under control. He sure can hold it . . ." Then: "Sometimes I wonder if he has any idea what a fool he hired as head of Development."

"Any rumblings about that at meetings?"

"Not from Dickenson, but from a couple of trustees. They asked me about Reggie after he gave a particularly lame department report. No one explicitly questioned his competence, but the gist was definitely *Is your boss this goofy on the job or just while public speaking?*"

"Were you honest?"

"Kind of. Each time I said, 'I'd be guilty of departmental disloyalty if I answered that truthfully.'"

Late, almost midnight, after the welcome-home celebration had gone horizontal, we were side by side in my slightly warmer, south-facing bedroom. Nick's eyes were closed, and his breathing had taken on the rhythm of sleep. Propped on my side, quite sure he was out cold and deaf to my question, I whispered, "What did you say when Reggie asked if I was good in the sack?"

His eyes didn't open but he smiled. "I said, 'Some things are too sacred to speak of aloud.'"

"No, you didn't."

He sat up, brought to life as if reliving the weekend's aggravation. "Okay, I didn't. I was pissed. I said, 'Did you really just ask me how my girlfriend is in the sack? Because Faith and I are your employees, and the school specifically bars . . .'" followed by more words, more sentences, more indignation.

But I didn't absorb the rest and didn't need to. My powers of concentration waned after hearing him use the lovely, unambiguous *girlfriend*.

36

Dead or Alive?

CLEARLY I WAS in a confessional mode, which happens when a person is drinking coffee with three police officers at her own kitchen table. Having taken a mental health day, I found myself confiding to the female among them that the possible homicide under investigation wasn't the only creepy thing associated with my house.

"Go on," said Detective Dolan.

I told them I'd been having nightmares about something I'd found in the attic, in a cradle, in an otherwise empty photo album — all at a pace that prompted Detective Dolan to suggest I go straight to the meat of it.

I said, "Sure. Sorry. Inside the album were pictures of twins, newborns. Girls, I think. On the bottom of the Polaroids, handwritten, it said, 'Born' such and such a date. 'Taken' such and such a date — a week later. I mean, why would two babies die on the same day, exactly a week after their birth? Doesn't that strike you as suspicious?"

"And who takes pictures of dead babies?" Sergeant Hennessy asked.

Officer Oskowski said, "People do that now. It's supposed to help later . . . like they were real persons, not just fetuses who didn't make it."

"What year was this?" Dolan asked.

"1956."

"Were there even neonatal ICUs?" he asked his partners.

"They had incubators, certainly," said Oskowski, mother of four, she added, one a preemie.

"My parents combed the death records and the obituaries, but didn't come up with anything," I told them.

"Then they didn't die," said Hennessy, the blood-spatter expert.

"Or . . . they died, but she never told anyone because she killed them and who gets death certificates for *that?* Certainly not the perp!"

"Whoa," said Dolan.

"Want to see the photos? They're right on the bookshelf . . ."

"I wouldn't mind," said Oskowski.

I retrieved the photos from their new resting place, a white envelope between the pages of my thesaurus. I handed them to her first, pleased to see she was taking my suspicions seriously enough to put her latex gloves back on.

"Creepy, all right," said Oskowski, passing them on.

"You're sure they're not just some random photos of someone else's babies?" Dolan asked. "And what about the handwriting? Do you have anything of the previous owner's to compare against these?"

I said, "They were taken here. No question." I gestured toward my gold-flecked Formica. "And you can just see the bottom of my cabinet above their whatchamacallits."

"Car cribs," said Oskowski. "The forerunner to car seats. And what makes you think they're not just asleep?"

"The sign? Not their names, nothing. Just 'Taken,' meaning by God or Jesus or whoever takes babies."

"If you knew the stuff we see," said Dolan, "you wouldn't think this was so weird."

"We know something about babies who die at home," said Hennessy. "We send a coroner. And then the undertaker comes. They leave in bags. Not in snowsuits."

This was a very good point. Dead or alive, these babies were dressed in matching snowsuits of indeterminate pastels.

"Spiffy ones. New," Dolan said.

"But couldn't you imagine a mother crazed with grief, thinking it's cold out, who'd put her babies in snowsuits?" I asked.

"Especially a fine, kindhearted citizen like Anna Lavoie," said Dolan.

"Why write 'Taken'?" asked Oskowski. "Why not 'Died' or 'Passed' or 'Slipped the surly bonds of earth' on that day?"

Dolan said, leaning back in the kitchen chair, arms crossed, "Want my theory?"

"Yes, I do, Detective," I said.

"Because they weren't dead. They're alive in these pictures. They're" — air quotes — "*taken* because she gave 'em away. She put them in an orphanage or in foster care, or sent them to an adoption agency. They were taken by a social worker."

"People had to know she was pregnant," I said. "You can hide one bump under a big coat, but with twins in there? She'd have been huge."

"Maybe the state took them away," said Hennessy. "Maybe someone reported she was loony tunes."

"But who'd rather say, 'My babies died,' instead of 'I couldn't take care of them'?"

"Anna Lavoie, sociopath, maybe," said Dolan.

"I say they're asleep," said Hennessy.

"Me, too, one hundred percent," said Oskowski.

I asked for another look. "Too bad the photos aren't in color so we can see if their little faces are pink," I said.

"Pink?" said Detective Dolan. "Look again."

"Café au lait is more like it," said Hennessy.

"They were born in 1956," said Oskowski. "Big scandal — raising babies who'd be walking advertisements for your affair —"

"With a black man who wasn't your husband," Hennessy said.

"They're starting to look more like they're sleeping than dead," I said.

Officer Oskowski said, "See that? On this one the nostrils are dilated as if taking a breath. And that's a little drool. Car cribs and snowsuits? These babies were going somewhere."

"You didn't notice that they looked a little . . . dusky?" Dolan asked me.

"I had a hard time looking at them at all. I thought — well, you know . . . death makes you a little bluish."

"And by the way?" said Dolan. "It's not against the law to give your children up for adoption."

"As long as you didn't murder them first," I said.

"They're probably out there somewhere," said Hennessy.

"Needle in a haystack," said Dolan.

"Do you know any biracial twins? Half something? Around sixty years old?" I asked.

The two men laughed, and Oskowski translated: "Flattering that you think we know the entire population of Everton."

"Besides," said Hennessy. "They'd stand out like bumps on a log in this town. You can bet she had them adopted several towns away."

"Wouldn't it be nice to know they were put up for adoption and they went to a happy home and had a nice life —"

"Forget it, Pollyanna," said Dolan. "You don't go churning

something like this up. Even if you found one of these twins, she'd probably know nothing. She may not even know she was adopted or had a twin. Or a white mother. And doesn't the fact there were no recorded deaths tell the tale?"

"I wasn't going to put up a billboard. I was just thinking that social media could help. I do know their date of birth."

"No offense," said Hennessy, "but it's none of your business."

"Let's say you got lucky on Facebook" — and with that, Dolan discharged a disdainful ha! "What then? Go after a court-ordered DNA test? It's a nonstarter. Forget about it, Nancy Drew."

"I wouldn't take it that far. I'm not going to fly to Maui to get a DNA sample from the daughter. Or exhume Mrs. Lavoie's body —"

"Exhume?" he repeated. "Did you say exhume?"

What had I missed? Weren't we discussing Mrs. Lavoie, presumptive mother of unaccounted-for twins? "Mrs. Lavoie," I said. "Anna Lavoie? The deceased multiwidowed possible felon?"

Detective Dolan was now the one who looked perplexed. He said, "Anna Lavoie is in a semiprivate room at ManorCare. Why would we be investigating the possible murders of a dead woman's husbands unless the suspected killer was alive?"

Off balance, groping for anything, I said, "Because . . . I don't know . . . you leave no stone unturned?"

"On TV, maybe. A rumpled retired cop who rights wrongs just for fun?"

"She didn't die here? Upstairs in my guest room?" I whispered. "She didn't die at all?"

"She's in and out of it. Faking the non compos mentis is what I think," said Dolan.

"Her roommate backs that up," said Hennessy. "They play canasta most afternoons."

"You've been visiting Mrs. Lavoie? Talking to her?" I asked.

"Trying to."

"How old is she now?" I managed.

"Ninety? Ninety-one maybe. She lies about that."

"Can you arrest a ninety-one-year-old?" I asked Detective Dolan.

He snapped his fingers. "Like *that*," he said.

37

·ᴖᴖ·

I Waste No Time Getting
Over There

THE PLACE WAS ONE STORY, neither sprawling nor appealing. A floor plan was framed in the lobby, an arrow pointing to an area designated SIGN IN.

"I'm here to see Mrs. Anna Lavoie," I told the woman — Jacqui, according to her name tag — who was dressed in pink scrubs patterned with shooting stars. I wrote my name on the sign-in sheet, and in the column labeled RELATIONSHIP I wrote *Buyer*.

"Room 111-B, the side closest to the window." She checked a chart, and said, "She should be back there in a few minutes. Beauty shop this morning."

"How *is* she?" I asked.

"We're not allowed . . . HIPAA laws."

"Can you say just something like . . . 'She can carry on a conversation' or 'She understands what's going on'?"

"Both. Believe me."

The door to 111 was open, but I knocked on the frame anyway. No one yelled permission to enter, so I did so on my own. The television was on, *The Price Is Right*, loud. A woman with only a few strands of white hair arranged over her otherwise bald head was watching from the closest bed.

I said, "Hello? Excuse me? Mrs. Lavoie?"

"She's over there." The woman gestured toward the empty half of the room. "You can sit."

I didn't immediately; I said I was told she'd be back soon, asked her how long she'd shared a room with Mrs. Lavoie.

"Since I got here."

"Months? Weeks?"

"Six weeks. A couple of broken bones in my foot. And the emphysema."

"Can I ask you a question about Mrs. Lavoie?"

"Are you a social worker?"

"No. Just, um . . . director of Stewardship . . . Is she, what's the right term . . . with it?"

"You mean does she have all her marbles? Most of the time."

I introduced myself, learned her name was Ruthie, and asked, "Is she a nice roommate? Or does she strike you as someone who'd hurt people when she was out in the world?"

"Hurt how? Their feelings?"

"Well, yes. That too, I guess."

"She's not what I'd call a people person. She has her moments." Her voice didn't lower its volume when she said, "She likes to win. Take it from me. And if it means cheating . . ." She added a sage nod.

"Jacqui at the desk said Mrs. Lavoie was having her hair done."

"She does that every week. I'm only here till my foot heals. The turkey broke some bones. It was only a breast, but it was frozen."

"Do you know if Mrs. Lavoie is more or less here for the duration?"

"She's not going anywhere! She tells me she's eighty-five, but she's more like ninety."

I said, "No harm in a little white lie like that, I suppose."

It was then that a tall, smiling, tattooed man with a shaved head wheeled the ancient, unsmiling, perfectly coiffed Mrs. Anna Lavoie into room III. If I had any question about her wits, it was answered by her sharp "Who's this?"

The man said, "We heard you had a guest. Isn't that nice?"

Mrs. Lavoie was dressed in the manner of a head librarian, in skirt, blouse, and jacket. There was a triple strand of pearly beads around her neck, and a rhinestone Scottie on her lapel.

"What's she gaping at?" Mrs. Lavoie snarled.

I said, "You're . . . you're . . . dressed so elegantly."

The helper explained, "We like our residents to dress, not to stay in their pj's and robes. Right, ladies?"

"Not me," said Ruthie. "I'm one of the invalids."

"Only temporary!" he said. "Anna? Where you wanna be now?"

"There." She pointed to the sole chair on her side of the room.

He said, "How about if you stay in this chair for now, and your guest sits in the visitor's chair? You call me when you need a lift."

"Do I know you?" Mrs. Lavoie asked me.

I didn't answer until she'd been wheeled in place, the brake hit, and the helper had drawn the curtain that divided the room.

I said, "I live in 10 Turpentine Lane. I bought the house from your daughter, Theresa."

"You bought it from *me*," she snapped.

"My understanding was . . ." I refrained from saying *that you were dead*, so I finished with "that you were possibly comatose."

"Who told you that?"

Who *had* told me that? Tammy the real estate agent? Mrs. Strenger next door? Theresa herself? I said, "It was my mistake. I misunderstood whatever they told me about your . . . reason for selling."

"Did they tell you not to buy it? That it's a deathtrap?"

"Not before the closing . . ."

"I lost three husbands there. One from pneumonia. And the other two . . . they had accidents."

I expressed my insincere condolences then asked the nature of the accidents.

"They fell."

"By any chance, down the cellar stairs?"

"I didn't push them," she announced. "But God works in mysterious ways."

"How so?"

"I didn't believe in divorce. Then they died. Things happen. I couldn't stand it anymore."

"Do you mean that you *did* take matters into your own hands?"

"I don't know what you're talking about. Raymond had pneumonia. He was my daughter's father. He died in that house." She looked down to the wheelchair's footrest. "They make us wear sneakers," she said. "They think we won't slip and break a hip."

"Then you remarried, I understand."

"I suppose so."

"Then you were widowed two more times. You told me that yourself just now."

"Mistakes, both of them."

"The accidents, you mean?"

"No. Getting married to people I didn't know very long."

"And when you got to know them, you weren't happy?"

"They wanted to go to bed with me," she said.

I heard a snicker from Ruthie's side of the room. I said, "But isn't that what all husbands want?"

"I told them when we married there would be none of that."

Oh, dear. What now? "Did they both die falling down the stairs?" I asked.

"Sure. They were very steep. The second one went to the hospital."

"And died there?"

Her expression did not convey *Tragically, yes,* but quite clearly *Took him long enough.*

Keep in mind I am hearing this from a ninety-plus-year-old woman wearing a tweed suit and crepe de chine blouse. I had not come to play detective about the conjugal, marital aspect of her criminal past. I'd brought with me both photographs of her possible twin baby daughters. Having hit her in a confessional mode, I took the Polaroids from my pocketbook. "Who are these babies?" I asked.

She reached for the photos, but I held on to them. "No, just look," I said.

After hardly a glance, she said, "I don't know."

"Is it possible these are your babies? Did you give birth to twins in December of 1956?"

"I don't know. Did I?"

"I think you did. And I think their father might have been . . . well, now we say person of color, but back then, maybe you'd have referred to him as colored."

"Oh," she said. And stopped there. She turned her face rather resolutely toward the window.

"I didn't mean there was anything wrong with that . . ."

The overhead TV went silent. I said, "These pictures were taken in your kitchen. I recognize the counter. Possibly you had these twins, and for some good reason, maybe you were under pressure, social pressure, and possibly between husbands at the time, you gave them up for adoption."

"No, I didn't," she said. "I wouldn't give my own flesh and blood away."

Ruthie called over. "She visits."

I stood and stuck my head through an opening in the dividing curtain. "*Who* visits her?"

"The colored girl."

I returned to my chair, and asked, "Did you hear what Ruthie said? Colored girl? Who is she?"

"My friend."

"Really? What's her name?"

"How do I know?"

"You said she was your friend."

Ruthie called over. "Jeannette."

"Jeannette?" I asked Mrs. Lavoie.

"If she says so."

"Does the other one have a name?"

"There's only one."

I asked Mrs. Lavoie again, "Did you have twins you gave up for adoption?"

"What's it to you?"

"I just need to know they didn't die under my roof."

"I didn't kill anyone," she said, "especially not them."

I asked Ruthie if this Jeannette might be around sixty years old.

"That sounds right. She takes the bus here."

"Is the girl who visits you one of the twins?" I persisted.

Still nothing.

I said, "Tell me what you did with the twins, and I'll leave."

"Someone else wanted them," she said.

"Who?"

"His mother."

"Whose mother?"

"Joseph's."

"Was Joseph the babies' father?"

No answer.

I said, "Is Joseph still alive?"

She shook her head.

"What did he look like?"

A sudden smile. "Handsome."

"Handsome like . . . Clark Gable? Gregory Peck? JFK?"

"No. Not them."

"Like who?"

She whispered, "Harry Belafonte."

Now she was looking through the handbag in her lap. I had the paranoid notion, surely inspired by *Masterpiece Mystery,* that she'd extract a petite pearl-handled gun and shoot me. What she brought forth was a roll of wintergreen Life Savers, took one, offered none.

"Just tell me that Jeannette and her twin sister are the babies in these pictures and no one hurt them." I made a fast mental inventory of my worries, and added, "And that they're asleep, and the word *taken* meant it was the day they went to live with Joseph's mother."

Ruthie called over. "They fight when they're here, in case you were thinking it was all lovey-dovey."

I asked Mrs. Lavoie, "Is that true? You and your daughter have words?"

She didn't argue with "daughter," but she didn't confirm that, either. What she said was "She doesn't come by bus. She drives."

I tried one more time. "Did Joseph's mother adopt the babies?"

"No."

"But she raised them?"

"Someone did."

I was now, finally, as annoyed as one can get with an ancient, wheelchair-bound, uncooperative witness. I said, "You know every one of these answers! And I can find out. The front desk keeps a sign-in sheet. They'll tell me their names."

"What are you, a detective?" she asked.

"I could be! And maybe I'll get a commendation, a civilian commendation for solving the Turpentine Lane murders."

"I don't know what you're talking about."

"Your husbands, the two you pushed down the stairs."

"They fell," she said. "Both of them were drunk . . . they were drinkers."

"What a coincidence."

"I called an ambulance. The police came —"

"Who are, as we speak, in my cellar looking for bloodstains. Someone squealed."

"I'm tired," said Mrs. Lavoie. "You have to leave."

"Why does Jeannette visit you? Is she trying to get the same answers I am?"

She half raised herself out of the wheelchair seat, and snarled, "I can have you removed."

"I've never met anyone like you," I railed. "Not in my entire life. It makes me sorry I bought your house."

"Poor you," she said, Life Saver clicking.

"You can still go to jail," I said.

"Ha!"

"You don't think so? They send old Nazis back where they came from even when they're ninety. And put them on trial even if they've lived quiet lives in a suburb of Chicago for, like, sixty years!"

"I don't think she was ever a Nazi," Ruthie volunteered.

"You're the crazy one," Mrs. Lavoie charged. "You're the one who's going to jail."

What did I think I was going to accomplish here? As I sat there wondering, she snatched both photos out of my distracted hand.

"They were pretty little things, weren't they?" she asked.

38

We're Done Here

I DROVE BACK TO TURPENTINE LANE and went straight downstairs to report every detail of Mrs. Lavoie's semi-confession. Detective Dolan said, awfully casually, "Yup. That's what I meant about her going in and out."

"I thought you meant in and out of consciousness, not back and forth between lies and the truth."

"She looks pretty good, doesn't she? Was she all dolled up with lipstick and rouge and everything?"

Rouge? Was he ninety, too? I said, "She threw me out. I upset her, asking about the twins. And she snatched the photos!"

He quipped, too jovially for the state I was in, "Should I arrest her?"

Ignoring that, I reported that her roommate spoke of a visitor named Jeannette who argues with her.

"Jeannette?" he repeated — rather sharply, I thought.

"Do you know a Jeannette who fits the bill?" I asked, thinking but not saying *Sixty years old, biracial, argumentative?*

Detective Dolan looked over to where Hennessy and Oskowski, presumably out of earshot, were inspecting my floor with what I now know was a black light. He motioned I should follow him in the opposite direction. By the washer and dryer, he said, "This is off the record. I'm not telling you this, and you're not hearing it, okay?" He checked his teammates again before answering. "The anonymous tip? About the cellar? Came from a Jeannette."

"How is that anonymous?"

"It was meant to be. She didn't give her name, but she had caller ID."

"Did it show her last name, too!"

"I can't say."

"Yes, you can."

I heard something that sounded like "Pepperstine" through his barely moving lips.

"Pepperstine?" I repeated.

"Pepperdine."

"Where was she calling from? Or just tell me the area code."

"This one," he said.

"So you've interviewed her?"

He mumbled some noncommittal syllables.

"Yes? No?"

"We spoke. By phone."

"So you didn't see her? You couldn't connect her with the babies in the pictures?"

"Yuh, like maybe if I was in a time warp, I could've. I didn't know about these mystery twins till you showed me the pictures."

Of course. That was only this morning, over donuts. "Mental health day," at first a lie, was beginning to describe my condition.

He said he had to get back to the station, to his office, to his paperwork.

"Wait! What made this Jeannette think that Mrs. Lavoie had thrown a couple of husbands down the stairs?"

"We don't know anything. And we certainly don't know if tipster Jeannette is nursing-home visitor Jeannette, do we?"

I said, "You're the one whose pupils dilated when I said her name. And you must know what's under my floor, and where this is going —"

"Okay. Calm down —"

"Because I could forever be associated with murders, like that Atlanta guy, who had nothing to do with the Olympic bombing, but for the rest of his life until he died before his time . . . and don't forget Lizzie Borden!"

Was Brian Dolan smiling? Had I jumped off the deep end? "Don't you have a job to go to?" he asked.

I asked if they were finished and — please — what was the harm in telling me, off the record, what the hell they'd found?

One looked at the other. Hennessy gave the nod to Oskowski. She said, "It *is* human blood."

"Whose?"

"Not Mrs. Lavoie's."

"So you got a DNA sample from her?"

No answer.

"Another search warrant?" I asked.

Hennessy said, "Maybe we asked ManorCare. Maybe they're not sticklers for protocol. Everyone likes to play detective."

"Their beautician . . . ," said Oskowski. "I happen to know her."

"Snip, snip," said Hennessy.

"Does this mean you won't be coming back?"

"We're done here," Hennessy said.

"What about fixing the floor?"

"Up to the district attorney. He'll probably compensate you."

Another turn in the continuing downward spiral of my unlucky domicile. I must've been wearing an expression that conveyed never-ending unwelcome complications because Officer Oskowski said, "I know this seems like a big job, part of your floor torn up, but it could've been much worse. We once found a body *under* the underfloor." She gestured around the cellar. "It's nice and clean down here. And dry, too. And otherwise? That nice man you live with? That looks like a good thing."

Hennessy groaned, but it was the indulgent kind that meant *See what happens when dames join the force?*

Nick wasn't at his desk — not unusual for someone who schooled himself on admission statistics, varsity scores, and the kind of campus news that played well while fund-raising. I texted that I'd come in to work after all and had a ton to tell him. He texted back: **meeting in Dickenson's office.**

I still had regurgitant worries about any conference taking place behind my back. **Everything okay?** I wrote, then very maturely didn't send.

I waited, made some overdue phone calls to stay-at-home alums I could reach during the day. Checked my supply of notecards and reordered. Wrote enthusiastically and sincerely to the scholarship funder whose recipient had been accepted early decision to Mount Holyoke. Nick returned looking . . . not unhappy, but without the spontaneous smile he tended to flash upon entering our office. "How'd it go?" I asked.

He closed the door then leaned against it.

"What? Tell me!"

Still in his overcoat and scarf, he dragged our visitor chair to my desk and sat down.

"How would you feel . . ."

"What? How would I feel about what?"

"It seems . . . I may become head of Development."

That was the raincloud overhead — this benign and marvelous thing, that nonchange of heart? "How would I feel? I'd be thrilled."

"It would mean, technically, that I'd be your boss."

There was a delay before my relieved brain grasped the likelihood of outer-office collateral damage. "And Reggie?"

"Out."

"Out altogether or demoted?" I whispered.

"Out on his ass."

"Yikes. Does he know?"

"Not yet. If I say yes, they'll tell him tomorrow."

"Why now? He's been an idiot from day one."

"He raises hardly anything. Apparently, they add up the numbers. And apparently, I do . . . very well."

I said, "I'm thinking you should sound a little happier."

His face, his shoulders, his slump — why so apologetic? Finally, he said, "Except you're the alum. You're the one who just scored the biggest get of the last year —"

"Wait a minute . . . you're not thinking that *I'm* thinking I deserve the promotion, are you? You're Major Gifts. I'm Stewardship. You have seniority. You came from Exeter. You're damn well saying yes and we're going to celebrate."

"I haven't made my mind up."

"You're accepting this! Who do you have to call? Dickenson? Can you e-mail him?"

"I told him I wanted to talk with you first —"

"Fine! You just did!"

"I had to tell them about us. So now they have to think it over — the propriety of it."

"No, they don't," I said. "You want propriety? Here it is. If we were boss and underling and we were doing what we're doing? Okay, that's against the rules. But coworkers, equals? Fine. Eventually, one of us gets promoted. That's life. Do I need to do HR's work for them?"

"Why didn't I say that to Dickenson?" he asked.

"Because you were blindsided. And Reggie out on his ass? That probably shook you a little, too, loyal team member that you are."

Well, almost. We both smiled guilty smiles because we never tired of ridiculing Reggie. "I know they want me to take it," he conceded. "The idea came from the board —"

"Which saw Reggie in action at the retreat, right? And they probably had an emergency meeting by Skype or whatever, and said, 'Why do we have a clown heading up Development when that intelligent Nicholas Franconi is his underling? What are we? The Topsy-Turvy Emperor of China?'"

When that didn't seem to register, I said, "Isaac Bashevis Singer? His book about the emperor who forces his subjects to do the opposite of what is true and good? It was our rabbi's favorite launching point for his sermons."

"*Hmmm*. Can't say the same . . ."

"One more thing. If they withdraw the offer due to romantic complications, we'll lie. Or I'll do something else."

"No way."

"Maybe this is a wake-up call. Do I want to write thank-you notes for the rest of my life? What kind of job is that for a college graduate with a major in English literature and a minor in French?"

"You're not quitting! What kind of wifey, old-school plan is that?"

"This might be the Fates knocking on my door, saying, 'Okay, we got you back to Everton, and according to our plan, you met Nick. But he'll still be there when you come home at night' — Right? That's not an overreach, is it? — 'but is there something more meaningful out there? Can't the kids on scholarship write their own thank-you letters, for Chrissake? Think about it, Faith.'"

"You're not quitting, and I'm telling Dickenson, 'Frankel is not a factor because this thing — us — started when we were equals, coworkers, housemates." At long last, a smile. "What we do in the privacy of our home has no bearing on our job performance at Everton Country Day unless you count the occasional feel I cop in the privacy of our office."

"Bravo," I said. "Now go over there right now and accept the offer."

Finally on his feet, he gave his scarf a swashbuckling toss, and said, "Here goes."

By the time he returned, I'd looked at the Everton Country Day job listings. There I'd discovered an opening — its five lines in red, indicating *Need you yesterday* — for a teacher of English in the middle school, for which I was, at least on paper, marginally qualified.

39

Good Try, Though

A WEEK HAD PASSED without any forward motion on what I was calling — inaccurately, but in homage to Nancy Drew — the Mystery of the 99 Steps. I phoned Brian Dolan and told him that I'd Googled "search warrants good for how long?" and discovered they were *not* for an indefinite amount of time.

He wasn't impressed. "We had your verbal consent for our return visits," he said. "Good try, though."

"I just want my house back. I want to stop thinking about what might have gone on here."

Was that an exasperated sigh I heard? "Can I give you a little advice?" he asked.

I could hardly say no.

"You're too worked up over this. In the great scheme of things, we were underfoot for two, two and a half days."

"Maybe true. But there's the emotional side of it — the creepiness, living in a house that was a murder site — and don't give me 'alleged.'"

"Ages ago."

"Then why is there a whole website called DiedintheHouse .com if such a thing rolled off people's backs? Not to mention the pragmatic side of it. How will I ever unload such a property?"

"We'll be in touch," he said.

At 5:45 p.m. that same day, I was the first one home, so why was my back door ajar? I carefully opened it to observe *not* the likeliest of visitors, my mother, but Anna Lavoie, dressed impeccably in a gray twinset, pearls, and pleated skirt, at my stove, heating water in my tea kettle.

I considering running for my life, or at least jumping back into my car, locking the doors, and calling 911, but I didn't want to leave her to burn down my house. When I called her name, she didn't startle or turn around.

I moved closer, switched on the overhead light, and switched off the burner with a snap. "What are you doing here?" I asked. "Who let you in? This isn't your house anymore."

"Then why do I have a key if I don't live here?"

"I bought it fair and square from your daughter who, I understood, had power of attorney."

When that appeared to give her pause, I said, "I'm calling her right now. She'll tell you." It took a bit of scrolling to find the Maui daughter's number on my phone while at the same time keeping my eye on my intruder. Reaching only Theresa Tindle's cheery outgoing message, I rattled off, none too calmly, "This is Faith Frankel. Your mother is in my kitchen on Turpentine Lane. She thinks she still owns it. She let herself in with a key, which you apparently failed to collect. Call me immediately. This is no joke."

Mrs. Lavoie was listening, her disapproval visible. "Frankel?" she asked. "Are you Jewish?"

I said yes I was Jewish; what does that have to do —

"That proves it," she said.

"Proves what?"

"That you don't own this house. I wouldn't have sold it to Jewish people."

I said, "It's bad enough that you trespassed, but you have the nerve to stand here in my own kitchen and insult me?"

A back-and-forth ensued over the words *trespassed* and *my kitchen*. Luckily, the phone rang. It wasn't the daughter calling me in record time, but Nick from his car. Did I need anything, because he'd be passing the market —

"Nick! Mrs. Lavoie is here. I'm home. I found her in the house! She thinks she still owns it!"

"Call 911," he said, "and I'm not kidding."

I told him to come straight home, to forget the market, and please stay on the line in case she tried anything.

"Who was that?" Mrs. Lavoie asked.

"My boyfriend. He'll be here in a minute. And he's big."

"Is he Jewish, too?"

I said, "Do you know how ignorant you sound?"

"*Is* he?"

"He happens to be Catholic."

"I used to be Catholic. I gave it up after I confessed some things the priest didn't like." She shook her head. "Didn't like one bit."

Because she was standing in front of our butcher-block knife holder, I asked her to move away from the counter.

"I will if you get me the paperwork."

I said, "First of all, you're in no position to be negotiating with me. And second, I'm not leaving you alone."

I heard Nick's car screech into the driveway. I said, "That's my boyfriend, and he's not happy about your being here."

"I hate men," she said. "I never saw the point."

Was this my fact-finding opportunity? "What about Joseph?" I asked. "Did you hate him?"

"Joseph? Who told you about him?"

"You did. You told me he looked like Harry Belafonte."

"I want you to leave," she said.

"And you had babies with him, didn't you?"

"I was too old to have babies! I'd already gone through the change. How could I have babies?"

"Twin girls," I said. "Jeannette and her sister. You saw the photos! In fact, you snatched them."

Nick flung open the back door, briefcase in one hand, hockey stick in the other.

"This is Nick," I said. "He's here to make sure you don't try anything foolish."

"Why, hello, Nick," she said. "Your girlfriend didn't tell me what a nice-looking fella she had."

"We're calling ManorCare," he said. "They probably have a search party out looking for you."

"I'm through with that place. They won't miss me."

He said, "You have no right to be here. You sold this house and you have to leave."

"No, *you* do."

I said, "I think you're bluffing. I think you know perfectly well that you're trespassing, but you still had the key and thought what's the harm in trying."

"I have no place to go. You're no better than my daughter."

I pointed out that breaking into someone's home wouldn't look good on her rap sheet, which was already a disgrace. And to further indict, I told Nick, "Before you got here, she said she'd never have sold the house to me if she'd known I was a Jew!"

"I was kidding!" said Mrs. Lavoie. "Besides, Jews don't live in this part of town. They live by the temple and the golf course."

I said to Nick, "We're not driving her back to ManorCare. Let the police deal with her." I turned to Mrs. Lavoie. "You can't stay here. Do you remember Detective Dolan? He visited you in the nursing home."

"Don't talk to me like I'm a rattlebrain."

"Watch her," I told Nick. "I'm going to get the title and show her who owns this house."

"Did I sign those papers?" she demanded.

"It doesn't matter," I said, though not one bit sure if that was true.

By this time, I had Brian Dolan on the phone. "Don't let her go," he was saying. "Keep her there. We're on our way. Be careful!"

When I returned to the kitchen, Nick appeared to be guarding the cellar door.

"Did she try something?" I asked.

"Only that she wanted to show me the cellar."

"Well, that settles it, doesn't it?"

Nick asked, "Mrs. Lavoie? What did you want to show me downstairs —"

"She didn't want to show you anything!" I yelled. "She wanted to push you down the stairs! That's her MO. And I'd be next!"

Mrs. Lavoie asked, "Doesn't anyone here have a sense of humor? I was kidding."

I told her we had very acute senses of humor and, by the way, what twice-widowed woman whose husbands died falling down these very stairs would ever go near them? The jig was up!

Mrs. Lavoie tsk-tsk'd through my rant, then announced that I was awfully touchy.

Nick said, "The police will drive you back to ManorCare."

"Heartless, the both of you," she muttered.

I said, "I'm sorry if your daughter sold your house without your permission, but according to lawyers for all sides, it was completely kosher."

"Kosher!" she repeated. "I told you you were Jewish."

I pointed to her daughter's name on the contract. "See? Signed, witnessed, and paid in full. By *me*."

"She *would* do that. She's the one who put me in that loony bin."

Past politeness, I snapped, "You're lucky it wasn't a state penitentiary."

"I wasn't home when those men fell if that's what you're hinting at. How do you push someone when you're not even home?"

I said, "Why did I ask? As if you were going to tell me the truth." I looked at my watch. The police station was no more than a ten-minute drive to Turpentine Lane, faster with a siren on.

"What do you do for a living?" Mrs. Lavoie asked Nick.

He said, "I work in an office."

Mrs. Lavoie asked, "Is that how you met her," tilting her disapproving head in my direction.

"That's private," he said.

"You had a lot of husbands. How did you meet *them?*" I asked.

"I forget," she said.

"When it's convenient, I'm noticing," said Nick.

"Probably at church," I said.

"Or temple?" Nick added.

"I know you're the kidder now," she said.

We heard an approaching siren then saw lights flashing. Within seconds, Brian Dolan and another officer were in my kitchen saying, "Ma'am? We're police officers. Put your hands on top of your head."

"Might this be a little overkill?" Nick asked. "She's ninety."

"Ninety and very lucky that her roommate is still breathing!" Brian snapped, searching her rather delicately before handcuffing her.

"Roommate?" I repeated. "Is she okay? Was it her emphysema?"

"What it *was*," he answered, "was a pillow over her face."

"*Ruthie?*" I asked Mrs. Lavoie. "You tried to kill *Ruthie?*"

"Who's Ruthie?" said the accused.

If Those Walls Could Talk

I FOLLOWED UP. Ruthie was in the hospital but okay. Brian told me they hadn't put Mrs. Lavoie in a cell, just sat her on a chair in the booking room where she was charged with attempted murder. "We were hoping someone would make bail," he said. "No one wants a ninety-year-old woman prisoner."

"How much bail?"

"Half a million."

"Has anyone paid?"

"We contacted the daughter in Hawaii ... so far, nothing wired."

I asked where Mrs. Lavoie was now.

"The county jail. In senior citizen isolation. It's kind and friendly. She's safe there."

The polite thing to say was "That's a relief."

Detective work needed to find Jeannette Pepperdine? Zero. As soon as Brian Dolan had spoken the phase "caller ID" with respect to their tipster, I knew she had a listed number and began compiling questions that might serve as my overture.

I rang the Pepperdine home and got one of those overly ambitious outgoing messages asking for name, time, the reason for the call, my phone number, and the best time I could be reached. I got as far as "I wanted to tell you that Anna Lavoie is no longer at ManorCare, but has been moved —" when a stern female voice broke in asking, "Who is this?"

I said, "I'm Faith Frankel. I live on Turpentine Lane, number 10, which once belonged to Anna Lavoie."

"My caller ID says Everton Country Day."

"Because I'm at work —"

"This isn't a good time," she said.

I said, "I'll be quick! It concerns the house I bought from a daughter of hers."

There was silence, and then only "How did you get my number?"

"It's listed." And without elaborating, I plunged in with "I found Polaroid photos in my attic, of baby girl twins, photographed in my kitchen."

More silence.

"May I ask if you were born on December 15, 1956?"

Still nothing until "Did I win something?"

"No. I'm trying to find those babies, to make sure they weren't victims of infanticide."

"Why?"

Why? Was she a sociopath, too? "Because it's my home. I'd like to know if infant twins born on that date left my house dead or alive."

I heard a clipped "Alive."

"Is your sister . . . still with us?"

"She lives in Texas with what she calls her partner."

I knew not to ask for clarification or offer congratulations. I said, "Thank you. Is it too big a leap to conclude that Anna Lavoie was your birth mother?"

When she didn't answer, I asked, "You still there?"

"Her name is on our birth certificate. Does that answer your question?"

"But you were adopted? And you went to good people?"

"We were never adopted. Our paternal grandmother took us. When she passed, the state put Josephine and me in separate homes."

I whispered, "Happy homes?"

"What do *you* think?" she asked.

I mailed her a thank-you note, offering what every good development officer keeps up her sleeve: an invitation to lunch. It took a follow-up call, at which time she said, "I hope we'll keep it social."

My answer was "Have you been to Bistro Voiture?" It was Everton's grandest restaurant, recently opened on the site of what had been a Chrysler dealership.

When she hesitated, I said, "Lunch or dinner, your choice."

"Thank you. I accept, though I still don't understand your interest."

An overactive imagination and buyer's regret came to mind, but instead I said, "Just intellectual curiosity. It's a puzzle. I think you could provide a missing piece or two."

"Friday night, six p.m.," she said. It wasn't a question.

I brought Nick, skilled in asking probing questions in charming fashion. Googling Jeannette had turned up nothing under "images," and I was eager to see what Anna and the King of Calypso look-alike had produced. She was already seated when we arrived. First, second, and third impressions: stunning, stylish, formidable. Her eyes were an unexpected pale green, striking against the mochaccino of her skin. Her dress was black, long sleeved, of a wool that suggested cashmere. And the scarf around her neck was arranged and knotted in ways I considered advanced. Her hair was black, just a cap of it, with hints of silver.

When we shook hands — her fingernails a deep maroon, mine suddenly feeling naked — she said, not happily, "I didn't know there would be two of you."

"I'm the boyfriend," said Nick. "I was curious to see how a showroom can turn into a restaurant."

I said to her, "I should've asked if *you* wanted to bring a guest."

"I'm widowed, and I don't keep company with anyone if that's what you mean."

So far every response indicated that all of my conversational gambits were mildly insulting. "Shall we start with a cocktail?" I asked, expecting her to sniff, *I don't drink*.

As a bow-tied waiter asked our water preferences and took our drink orders (martini, Manhattan, mojito), I pondered how one asks a stranger about the circumstances leading up to her conception. So I didn't; instead, I asked what she did, professionally speaking.

"Until this past June 30, I was in charge of the employee lunch program at John Hancock."

"How wonderful," I said.

"Faith's dad was in insurance, too," said Nick.

"Frankel Home and Life," I added.

"I had nothing to do with insurance," she said. "They could have been a manufacturer of cuckoo clocks as far as my interaction with that side of things went. I made sure their employees had good choices in the cafeteria and the executive dining room."

"Lots of fish and green leafy vegetables, I bet," said Nick.

I laughed, which caused Mrs. Pepperdine to stare at me as if merriment over antioxidants was highly inappropriate.

"Speaking of food . . . ," said Nick, as our roadster-shaped menus arrived. "I hope you're hungry."

"I'm allergic to shellfish," she answered.

I said, to be companionable, "I don't eat pork."

Nick was first to announce his choices: the chicken cordoba and the salade imperial.

Mrs. Pepperdine — I'd mentally switched to the formal nomenclature — remained tight-lipped until the waiter asked, "And, ma'am . . . ?"

"The corn chowder, please," which was followed by nothing except our insistence that she order an entrée.

As if very much against her will, she said, "I'll have the rib eye, well done."

Nick now delivered the prompt I'd planted on the drive over. "Faith? Do you have questions for our guest?"

I said, "I do." And to Mrs. Pepperdine: "You're probably wondering why I wanted to talk to you about Anna Lavoie."

"No, I'm not. You said there was a puzzle with some missing pieces. Apparently, I'm one of them."

Where to start? Maybe with the affair that led up to her life on earth? "I hope this isn't too starry-eyed of me, but I got the impression that Anna and your father's relationship was a love match."

"Love? Who told you that fairy tale? Lust, more like it!"

"Lust of the unwanted variety?" I whispered.

"As a matter of fact, it was. She seduced him."

Oh, God. Could I even picture tweedy, twinsetted Anna Lavoie as a lusty young woman?

Nick said, "Well, this is interesting."

"He was very handsome — a handsome, strapping man. She pursued him. She made suggestive comments every time he entered the room. And one day, one night actually, she had her way with him. *She* was the seducer! This was the 1950s. He would not have crossed that line."

Why pussyfoot around now? There would be no winning her over, no softening of the woman who'd turned her own mother over to the police. "How did you know who seduced whom?" I asked.

"How did I *know?* I knew because Anna Lavoie, when I finally met her, bragged about it."

A thought alien to everything I'd observed about Mrs. Lavoie entered my head — that she did have at least one kind bone in her body — and made me ask, "Is it possible that she didn't want to speak ill of your father, to paint him as the aggressor, so she took the blame?"

"No! She relished the telling! She loved presenting her younger self as fast and loose! It was very clear. She was proud of being a hussy!"

"Where did all of this take place?" Nick asked.

"She had an office in the Manning Building on Castle Street."

"Doing what kind of work?" Nick asked.

"She kept the books for a few small companies. Today you'd call her a freelance bookkeeper."

"And your father had an office there, too?" I asked.

"No. He cleaned them."

I must have looked disappointed because Nick said, "Faith was hoping you'd say Mrs. Lavoie worked at the next desk or did the books for *his* company."

"He could've been an accountant! In today's world he'd have owned his own business, and it would've had its own book-keeper."

"And that night, that one encounter . . . left her pregnant?"

"I can't say."

"Because?"

"Because she implied that there were many occasions."

"You'd think he'd have reported her," I said. "Tell his boss that he couldn't clean a certain office because the tenant sexually harassed him."

"Who'd believe that? Are you aware of history? And this was before sexual harassment had a name."

Nick said, "You must've gotten to know your father pretty well if you heard the backstory."

"I saw him once in a blue moon."

"Even though you were living with his mother?" Nick asked.

"He was married," she said. "And his wife wasn't someone to put up with any foolishness."

"Didn't his wife wonder why her mother-in-law was raising twins?" I asked.

"And one of them was named Josephine?" said Nick.

"She'd fostered children before us. It didn't raise any eyebrows."

The waiter was back with our drinks. What to toast fifteen minutes into an awkward, sullen conversation? "Cheers," said Nick.

Frowning, Mrs. Pepperdine joined in our clinking of glasses. What now? Nick helped out with "Your grandmother couldn't have been a big fan of Mrs. Lavoie's."

"She hated her; well, hated the idea of her. And was afraid she'd come collect us — which was hardly realistic. Could anyone have been more selfish? Letting two babies be wards of the state? 'It was easier,' she told me! Easier than what? Signing adoption papers?"

I asked how old she and her sister were when their grandmother died.

"Fourteen! And unfortunately, we were big strong girls, and we looked it."

"Unfortunately?" I asked.

"Both of us went to families who needed help. Josie to a family with a bunch of kids, and I was sent to a cucumber farmer in Hatfield."

"He grew only cucumbers?" Nick asked.

"For pickles. To pickle companies. The whole crop, except what he sold at his farm stand."

I sat not so patiently through their discussion of what size cucumbers became what pickles. Half sour, full sour, Kosher dill, gherkins, bread and butter. I tried to signal to Nick *Who gives a fuck?*

Our soup and salads came. We ate and made small talk that provided a break from my interrogation, learning she had one grandchild and one on the way. Though he'd never smoked, Mr. Pepperdine had died of lung cancer. She moved to her current apartment six months after his passing against the advice of the bossy friends who said she shouldn't make any changes for a year.

When the appetizer dishes were cleared, I asked if she'd ever been to 10 Turpentine.

She said, "No, why would I?" adding, "If only those walls could talk."

To ask or not to ask? I did. I plunged in with "How did you know that two of Mrs. Lavoie's three husbands died in tumbles down the cellar steps?"

"She told me she was very unlucky in the marriage department. I asked if they'd carried life insurance. She had the nerve to smile."

"Nothing surprises me anymore," I said.

Nick asked, "Did Faith tell you that Mrs. Lavoie is in jail for attempted murder, for an entirely new crime?"

Mrs. Pepperdine dabbed her mouth with her pink linen napkin. It didn't hide the fact that we'd finally made her smile.

It Never Snows in Maui

D ID I OWN my house or not? By meal's end, I felt as if every question Mrs. Pepperdine asked, and every look she bestowed, suggested that I shouldn't get too comfortable in any one of my five unprepossessing rooms.

The minute we got home, despite the hour, I called my lawyer and left a worried message. Was she sure that Theresa Tindle, apparently neither a beneficiary nor the executrix of her mother's estate due to her mother's being quite alive, had the right to sell me my house? We had a title search, correct? Wouldn't that have told the tale?

After a few more hours of my wondering aloud who'd be suing me and how much it would cost, Nick asked, "Why not call Theresa? It's only afternoon in Hawaii. Ask her outright. Did she or did she not have the right to sell you this house?"

Theresa answered on the first ring, and after I'd identified myself once, twice, she said, "Can you speak up? The TV's on."

Wasn't turning the damn thing off the polite thing to do? But then I heard a male voice talking in a professional manner about weather. Very bad weather. He was a meteorologist, predicting more snow, saying next that the barometric pressure was dropping and the snow would start around midnight, that the mayor had already canceled school, all schools, all day tomorrow and the next day, too.

That was *our* weather, our prediction: eight to ten inches' worth. And I knew that sonorous voice. I left the bed with phone in hand, turned on the TV across the hall, flipped through the local channels on mute until the veteran steady-Eddie Boston weatherman Micky Medina was mouthing the exact words I was hearing through my phone.

I said, "Theresa . . . um. I have the same TV station on."

Had she heard me? Did that register as the accusation I intended it to be?

"Channel seven here," she said, all innocence, followed by silence — from her and her TV.

Nick had left the bed and was now standing next to me, looking puzzled. I held up one finger. *Watch me; Perry Mason in action.*

I said to Theresa, "I was originally calling with a question about ownership of my house; whether you sold it to me free and clear, i.e., did you have power of attorney? But now I have another question . . ." For drama, for the audience at my side, I waited a beat before asking, "Where *are* you?"

"You mean this minute?"

I said, "Yes, I mean this minute."

"In my bedroom."

"Where? What state?"

"Hawaii! Like always. Oh . . . were you wondering because of my area code? I never changed my cell phone number."

I'd given no previous thought to her Massachusetts area code, never questioned it since Nick's was still 603 and mine the old 917.

"You're sticking to your Maui story?" I asked.

"Are you calling me a liar?"

Oh, that — the first refuge of double-talkers I have had the misfortune to challenge. "Either you're mistaken, or they're predicting a blizzard in Maui."

She said, "I don't know what you're talking about. It never snows in Maui."

"Well, that's funny because you're getting a nor'easter."

"Haven't you ever heard of satellite dishes?" she asked.

I smothered my cell in my armpit to muffle my asking Nick, "Can you get a Boston TV station in Maui with a satellite dish?"

"Doubt it," he said.

Next she was asking, "Why would I lie about where I live?"

I chose to say as psychiatrically as my unnerved brain allowed, "I think, if Anna Lavoie were my mother, and she was being well looked after in a nursing home — or more recently in a county jail — I might pretend to live on an island in the Pacific, too far away to be her emergency contact."

When she didn't confirm or deny that, I took a leap, and asked, "Are you in Boston right now?"

"No, I am not in Boston."

I said, "Maybe not in Boston proper, but I think you're in its viewing area, watching channel seven."

I expected her to hang up. She didn't. In rather dignified fashion, she said, "I do have power of attorney. It was my right to sell you your house. I certainly didn't want it! You own it, and my mother knows it. I forgot to take the key away from her. I'm surprised she showed up at the old house. I never expected her to leave ManorCare. Well, I do, eventually . . . in a box."

Who says such a thing about her own mother? Well, now I knew: the same daughter who pretended to live five time zones away.

It wasn't like me to hang up without some kind of good-bye, no matter how frigid. I decided against "You're as crazy as a loon, just like your mother." And also against "Welcome home," since she probably never left.

The right valedictory came to mind. It would be well deserved and quite possibly news. "My boyfriend and I just returned from dinner with your half sister," I told her.

42

Neither the Time nor the Place

I WAS FIRST RUNNER-UP, or so they told me, for the middle school teaching job. I could hardly complain since the winning candidate coached two sports to my none and had master's degrees in both American literature and education.

Nick's promotion went through, with the proviso he relocate to the administration building, arguably a more logical place for money to be raised, down the hall from Financial Aid. I stayed put in Sheffield Hall — HR's unsubtle solution to our intradepartmental romance.

The school's official announcement stated that Reggie had tendered his resignation, and lest the grateful community forget, his records for touchdown passes and yards rushed were unbroken.

He must've known that we understood he'd been deposed, but we pretended otherwise. "Irons in the fire," he promised, adding that it was Pope Benedict's resignation that had been his inspiration.

"Really?" I asked. "The pope's?"

He explained that the pope's stepping down made him realize that even someone in a high position, like a department head or the Holy Father, could move on and explore other options.

Nick and I indulged this; we even invited him to join us for a farewell dinner, which he accepted. I asked if there was someone, anyone, he'd like to bring.

"A date, you mean?"

"Maybe someone you've been seeing for a while and would feel comfortable, given the situation."

Nick said, "Let me translate: Faith is asking if you have a girlfriend."

For the first time ever, in a discussion of his private life, Reggie spared me the usual bluster. "I wish I did," he said, "especially at a time like this."

Nick said, with a sweep of his arm toward the window overlooking campus, "You're a free man. You can ask out anyone now."

"Any ideas?" Reggie asked, after what appeared to be a mental survey of eligibles.

"What about Ronnie what's-her-name in Financial Aid?" I asked. "She's at the gym every morning. You could just casually show up at the same time —"

"Except I won't be able to use the gym after I leave. And she's engaged."

I asked him if he knew Tammy McManus, the real estate agent. She was divorced now. About the right age.

"Can't," he said. "Her ex was a running back for Everton when I was QB1. I mean, jayvee, but still."

"Man of honor, you are," said Nick.

"You don't need to bring anyone," I backtracked.

Reggie said, "You don't have to do this. It's not like we ever went out to dinner before."

He was right; Nick and I even dodged him in the lunchroom. I said, "Only because you were the department head, Reg. If we'd invited you to dinner, you might've thought we were brownnosing. I realize now that was silly. You're not the kind of guy who'd think we had ulterior motives," I spun.

Nick added, "And you don't have to bring a date this time. There'll be other opportunities. Right, Faith?"

"Plenty," I lied.

"You have girlfriends, right?" Reggie asked me. "Any eligible bachelorettes who might like to meet Reggie O'Sullivan?"

"Umm. Just not off the top of my head. I'll definitely give it some thought."

He always called me Frankel, but this time he said, "I really appreciate it, Faith. I know you think I can be an asshole, and maybe I'm not the first guy you'd set up with a friend, but I'm a good guy when you get to know me."

But all things occupational and social were on hold because it was the snowiest February on record. Classes were canceled, with the campus increasingly unreachable each time another foot of snow fell. We'd see the sun for a day between blizzards, then down came another wallop, cars and hydrants and back-yard furniture buried, icicles dangling two stories down. I checked daily on my mother, whether she had power and food. And when had Joel last plowed her driveway?

"Just once, after the first storm."

"Do you need him to come back?"

I thought she was going to say yes, please, at the same time expressing disappointment with his unreliability and blue-collar career choice. Instead, she gushed, "What a winter! *Everyone* needs him every other day! And you know he gets more to sand the same driveway? Was this not the best year ever to invest in a plow?" Her voice went conspiratorial. "He finally got some help, a dispatcher. Do you know who she is?"

"Who *who* is?"

"The girl who answers his phone. Any leads?"

I did know who she was because I'd asked. It was Leslie, the ex-sister-in-law of Stuart. "No one I've met," I said.

"Are you telling me everything you know?"

"Of course not."

"A lot of mothers would resent that. But I get how a sister and brother might keep some secrets from their mother. It's normal, I'm sure."

"What secrets do you think I'm keeping from you?"

"Maybe things that would hurt my feelings?"

I said, "Her name is Leslie and she's mailing out invoices for him. Would that hurt your feelings?"

"I meant things you might be protecting *me* from."

She meant my father and his adulterous life. I told her I had nothing to report because he and I didn't talk.

"We e-mail, you know."

I said, "Ma, shouldn't you be communicating through your lawyer?"

Ignoring that, she asked, "Have you met her?"

"Leslie?"

"No, the woman who gives your father what I never could."

"I haven't. Nor do I want to." I walked to the kitchen window. Nick was sweeping the roof of his car with our kitchen broom. "Would you believe it's snowing again?" I asked her.

"One thing, hon — a favor?"

I expected, thanks to my change of subject, that her request would involve sidewalks or gutters or fresh milk. But what she said was "I want you to meet this woman."

"To what end? What could I tell you that wouldn't be painful?"

In chummier fashion than I expected, she explained, "Usually, when a husband cheats, the wife knows the other woman — either she lives next door or works in the same office. But I know nothing! Maybe you could snap a picture."

"But if I tell Dad I want to meet Tracy, it'll look as if I'm giving them my blessing."

"Who said anything about giving them your blessing? You could size her up without being cordial. I've seen you do that — remember Stuart's mothers? Bring Nick. Didn't he go through a divorce with his parents?"

"No. His mother died."

"Same thing," she said.

"Come next Saturday," my father had said, after conferring with Tracy. We were on our way, Nick driving and I with the street and house number in hand. But how could it be this big brick columned and porticoed one with so many cars in the driveway and more spilling out onto the street? We parked as close as the overflow allowed, wondering if we had the wrong night. I called my father's cell phone and he answered. "Did you say 38 Wingate Terrace? We're here, but there seems to be a party going on."

The massive oak front door opened, exposing a two-story atrium with a live ficus tree straining toward the skylight and wall-size tapestries above champagne-colored marble tiles. "You made it!" a woman cried. She was wearing an outfit that was all at once pants and tunic, black and white, opaque across personal places and translucent elsewhere, with rhinestone — or were they diamond? — earrings nearly grazing her shoulders.

I said, "I'm Faith. Henry's daughter. And this is Nicholas Franconi."

"I know who you are! Come in! Caesar! Take their coats! Did you bring shoes? Never mind, just take off your boots. You won't be the only ones in stocking feet!"

Who was Caesar, and was he appraising my business-casual turtleneck and skirt? And who were these people milling about in the room beyond, all dressed up and holding blue drinks? Our greeter hadn't introduced herself, but it was clear this was our hostess — auburn haired, coral lipped, not even forty, and stunning by anyone's standards: Tracy.

"Darling!" she called toward the crowd at the bar. "Faith and her friend are here!" And to us, "The bartender designed a special drink just for tonight!"

"The occasion being . . . ?" asked Nick, unwinding his scarf as Caesar waited with outstretched arms.

"A preopening, prerepresentation. Meet the artist in his milieu. And, of course, meet . . . you two."

I said, "I had no idea. I hope you didn't . . ." *Hope she didn't what? Worry that we'd be baffled and underdressed?*

"Darling!" she called again.

And trotting toward us was my father, in a dark suit and a red silk handkerchief in his breast pocket. He kissed me and shook Nick's hand. I said, "I didn't realize we were invited to a party."

"I hope you don't mind," Tracy said. "The caterer was already hired, and the invitations had already gone out when you wrote." She leaned sideways and bumped shoulders with my father. "Some people I know are better at painting than keeping their social engagements straight."

"We could have rescheduled," I said.

Nick asked, "Are these people friends of yours — by which I mean do they know the situation?"

I appreciated that blunt question with its suggestion that a visit to the home of Public Enemy Number One was fraught enough without a pack of sequined art patrons looking on. Tracy seemed puzzled, but not for long. She smiled, then leaned in to confide, "They absolutely know that your father's creations are copies. Of course! We're proud of the 'faux,' aren't we? We don't hide it. We celebrate it!"

"Faux as in f-a-u-x," my father explained. "Is that apparent? It's obvious when written, but I'm not convinced it works when spoken."

I said, "Alliteration is always good."

"And who doesn't want their very own custom Chagall?" Tracy asked, her eyes now scanning the crowd.

I said, "I think when Nick referred to the 'situation' he was asking whether your guests know I'm Henry Frankel's daughter and this is our first meeting."

"We'll talk, I promise," she said. "But first I need to find the caterer." With a pat to my forearm, she strode away.

My father said, "She's not happy with the flow of canapés. The trays aren't leaving the kitchen fast enough."

"Glad she has her priorities straight," I said.

"Please," he said. "Not now."

"Do you even *know* these people?"

"I've met some of them. The rest are friends of friends, supposedly collectors. A couple are dealers."

"A drink?" Nick asked me. "Mr. Frankel? You all set?"

My father answered by raising his highball glass.

"Fine. Be right back."

"Nice fellow," my father said, once Nick had left.

"He is. I thought that's what this night was supposed to be about. I'd meet Tracy and you'd meet Nick."

"Plenty of time for that."

Did he mean plenty of time before we left or plenty of time over the course of our lives? I didn't ask, because a woman who looked too much like Tracy to be anything but her sister was trying to get my father's attention, shouting "Hank!" in our direction.

"Is that woman addressing you?" I asked.

"Be right there," he told her, and to me, "She's Tracy's sister. I think this one's Stephanie."

"She's calling you Hank."

"Tracy started that. She likes it better than Henry."

"Hank Frankel? That's ridiculous."

"We need you!" Stephanie yelled.

"Give us a minute," I called to her. "I'm his estranged daughter."

"That wasn't necessary," my father scolded. "Now I'll have to explain that we're not estranged and that was your idea of a joke."

Nick was back, holding two martini glasses. "Am I interrupting something?" he asked.

"Not at all," my father said. "I've been summoned. You'll excuse me?"

"Just tell me one thing. Are you enjoying this?" I asked.

"It's part of the job," he said. "The schmoozing, the networking."

"I didn't mean that. I meant the big picture — living in apparent nouveau-riche luxury with a woman young enough —"

I stopped myself. I was brought up better than that. I was a guest in this woman's home. Plus, Nick was looking reproachful.

"This isn't the time or the place," my father said. "I'll be back as soon as I see what Stephanie wants."

What could I say besides okay, fine, go pitch your wares?

Nick was also managing a glass plate on which sat two mini pigs in a blanket and two deviled eggs. "Don't worry," he said. "I've been told it's *glatt* kosher."

It was my first laugh since we'd crossed the Newton town line.

The caterer had brought a roasted chicken stuffed with prunes for the small family dinner that followed the party. As soon as we two couples were seated in a room tromp l'oeiled to resemble a gazebo, ivy enclosing us, Nick asked how the evening had gone saleswise.

"These things take time," my father said.

"Believe me, I'll follow up," said Tracy.

Nick said, "It's like in fund-raising: we plant the seeds, then we water them, tend them, and hope they bear fruit." He winked at me. Reggie's favorite simile.

"For whom do you fund-raise?" Tracy asked.

Wait. Tracy didn't know where we worked? I must have started stabbing my chicken breast in a newly aggressive manner because she rushed in with "It's for a school, right? A boarding school?" And to Nick, "This came after your walk across the country? Do I have the right sequence?"

"Wrong guy," he said.

Tracy shot an accusatory look at my father.

"That was an ex-fiancé, you might recall," he said.

"We work for a private day school," I said. "Everton Country Day. I'm head of Stewardship, and Nick was just promoted to director of Development." And to prove that I was a less self-absorbed human being than she, I asked how old her daughters were, their names, and, come to think of it, where were they this evening?

"Chloe, thirteen, and Alexis, almost ten. They're with their father, skiing."

I said, "Now I remember — it was the older one's bat mitzvah that brought you and my dad into . . . contact."

"I don't think I know how you discovered Mr. Frankel's work," said Nick.

Tracy beamed. "I was at a restaurant on Beacon Hill, and I noticed they had a Matisse on the wall — not a print, but an oil painting. I called our server over, pointed, and said, 'That Matisse? Do you know who did it?' She said, 'I'll ask.' And before we left, she came back with the manager's business card with your father's name and phone number written on the back with just the word *artist*."

"So you called?"

"The next day! I told him how I'd been blown away by the brushwork, and asked him if he copied *any* Impressionists or just certain favorites, certain subjects. He said, 'Give me a for instance,' and I said, 'Marc Chagall,' and one thing led to another, especially when I mentioned that Chloe, even at twelve, was an art lover and an upcoming bat mitzvah."

My father must have sensed that I wasn't appreciating the pride and relish with which their storybook meeting was being narrated. He took over with a dismissive "So she came to my studio and we tossed around some ideas, and she left with a very rough sketch."

"Were you married at the time?" I asked Tracy.

"Separated."

"I don't think we need to rehash all the wheres and whens," my father said.

"Let me take some ownership of this," said Tracy. "Your father was all business, all artist, literally splattered with paint.

He was not the kind of man who flirts with a would-be patron, especially someone like me."

"Someone like you?" I repeated.

"A young, married, reasonably attractive Jewish woman, mother of two. And a lawyer."

"He knew that?" Nick asked.

"It came up in our first conversation."

My father explained, "She thinks her law degree prevents someone from taking advantage of her — in case they think she won't read the fine print."

"Of course," said Nick.

"The point I want to get across is that your father was effectively an innocent bystander. I was the one who made the first, second, and third moves. I look back and I think — it's crazy! Who can explain it, who can tell you why, as the song says."

I said, "Funny, isn't it — the double standard?"

"How do you mean?"

"Where we come from, what you described would be sexual harassment."

She laughed. *Wasn't Faith delightful!*

"But something took hold, obviously," said Nick.

Tracy's answer was a kiss blown in my red-faced father's direction.

"I'm curious," Nick said, "as to why you'd keep trying if you were getting rebuffed."

"Rebuffed? I wouldn't go that far. It was more . . . Henry? Can you explain?"

"I'd rather not," he said. "I think Faith has heard enough." I was starting to wonder where the Emily Dickinson–quoting, teary-eyed, besotted lover boy of the previous month was.

Tracy continued. "He was acting so noble that instead of making me walk away it became a challenge —"

I believe this was the juncture at which I threw my napkin back on the table and rose to my full height. "Really? Must I hear how you came on to my married father, who presumably fought the good fight until you — what? — ripped off your clothes and took matters into your own hands?"

Did she protest or apologize? No. Her smile said, *How did you know the rest of our adorable story?*

"Dad?" I asked. "Can I talk to you?"

Out of range, I said, "This is who you chose — someone so fucking *confident,* so proud of seducing you that she doesn't know when she's sticking a knife in a daughter's heart? I can't do this."

"What do I tell her?" he whimpered.

"Tell her that two cocktails made me woozy and we'd better call it a night. Or tell her I hate her."

All he could say was that those cocktails were named Blue Angels in tribute to the original Chagall he copied.

Just in time, Nick appeared with my purse. He shook my dad's hand. "Thanks, Mr. Frankel. Really. Our door is always open. And" — with a nod back to the table — "good luck."

Until that moment, I hadn't known what I'd report back to my mother. But as we turned away, my father's mumbled answer was exactly what I'd bring home. "I'll need it," he said.

43

Overall Frankel Anxiety

Trust me, he's miserable," Nick said on the drive home. "Miserable and filled with regret."

I asked whether he meant misery over the night's double booking and my related meltdown? Or because he'd broken my mother's heart? Or simply because he was with Tracy?

"Keep in mind I was meeting him for the first time, but I'd say he's a man who's in deeper than he wants to be."

I felt a surge of optimism. Would "being in too deep" imply a need to crawl out of such a misguided hole and back to my mother?

Mind reader that he often was, Nick said, "I'm not saying he wants out. Maybe he knows how ridiculous he'd look if he changed his mind after putting everyone through this for what? A fling?"

"Why couldn't he have kept his flings to himself?"

"Flings? Plural?"

"I'm thinking so, more and more."

"Maybe he got what he deserved," Nick said, followed by an

excellent impression of Tracy's breathless self-reverence: "Initially, your father didn't want me, despite my brains and beauty, so the next visit I took matters into my own mouth — whoops, I mean hands — and well . . . Hank, do you want to take it from there?"

"Pretty damn close!" I said. "You'd think she was bragging to girlfriends while they're side by side, getting their mani-pedis."

"Ha! Faith Frankel's unkindest cut: mani-pedis!"

I said, "He needs an exit strategy!"

"How about out the front door and into his car? They're not married. Those aren't his kids. He's been there how long? Two, three months?"

"*If* that! And he needs to take back his art. I don't mean the actual pictures; I mean the concept, art for art's sake, the freedom to copy whatever painting he wants to without someone saying, 'We need you to make the boy a girl and change the donkey to a Chihuahua.'"

After a few miles in silence, I said, "I should write him, don't you think?"

"As long as it's not asking his forgiveness for finding his girlfriend's company unbearable."

"I wasn't going to apologize. I was going to offer him sanctuary."

"Now don't take this the wrong way, but consider this angle. Here's a guy who's getting on — How old is he? Sixty-five? — and suddenly this rather attractive, some might say hot, woman throws herself at you. Do you walk away because she's obnoxious and bossy?"

"Do you think she's hot?" I asked, careful to sound as if it were merely intellectual curiosity.

"I think most people would say — Tracy included — that she is quite attractive."

Was it snowing again or was it just the latest powder acting like a squall? I turned on the radio, which for weeks had been tuned to the local station that was our best bet for a forecast. We heard that snow was indeed expected in the early morning hours.

Nick said, "Go, Joel."

I said, "On one hand, I'm happy for him. But next winter, who knows? It could be a drought."

Nick said, "One of the things I love about you is your doomsday outlook based on affection for whoever's at risk."

Was that a declaration of love or a figure of speech? I could hardly ask for clarification, especially because Nick had returned to the topic of plowing. Why was I worried? "If he collects all the money he's owed, he'll be fine," he said.

I told him Joel was getting extra money from the city to move snow around. "There's no place to put it! He's cleaning up, figuratively and literally. And he seems to have a girlfriend." I might have made a more convincing case for my brother's professional and personal prospects if my voice hadn't gone shaky.

"Sorry," I said. "It's just the night. That horrible woman. My mother alone. Joel's livelihood depending on precipitation."

"Just overall Frankel anxiety? Not anything else?"

I knew what he meant by "anything else." Us, Nick and Faith. For a second I thought of asking if he'd like to marry me, but, really, who does that in a car?

There was still a catch in my voice when I said, "I've never been happier."

Nick laughed. "I can tell."

How to package the Tracy debacle to my mother? I texted her, **I'm beat. We'll speak in the a.m. Long story. PS: did *not* like the woman.**

I called Joel, prepared to tell all . . . *dying* to tell all. I knew from the way he answered — brightly, with a never-used "Hi, sis" — that he was signaling to a guest that the female caller was a relative, not a ladylove.

"I'm guessing Leslie's there?"

"Correct."

"Do you want to call me back?"

"No. What's up?"

"I had dinner with Dad tonight, well, a partial dinner. And I met Tracy."

I feared he was going to say, *You traitor*, but he asked, "Was I supposed to go to that?"

"No! I didn't even ask you. When would you have been able to get away? Like, April."

"So how was it? Are we one big happily fractured family?"

"No! It's worse than before. He'll probably never speak to me again after I pretty much stormed out."

"Of where?"

"Tracy's big house."

I could hear Leslie in the background, obviously up-to-date on our father's adultery, asking, "What was she like?"

I said, "If she means Tracy — she was stunning and inappropriate. She regaled me with the details on how she seduced Dad."

"Are you *kidding* me?" — at which point he repeated my words to Leslie.

"I think it was supposed to make me feel better that she was the aggressor and he resisted."

"And Dad? Is he catching on?"

"Nick thinks he might stick it out because . . . you know."

"The sex?"

"Pretty much. A guy, sixty-five . . . in his wildest dreams . . .

along those lines. But Nick also thinks he's miserable and filled with regret. So which thing wins?"

"You probably don't want me to answer that."

"Maybe you could visit? Scope it out man to man?"

"Leslie's been saying the same thing."

I told him there was another reason for my call because there was more snow in the forecast. "Nick and I want to pay you for the plowing and shoveling. No more comps."

He laughed. "You mean could you please plow my driveway?"

"Bye," I said. "Love you."

Nick told me over breakfast that the last thing I mumbled before drifting off to sleep that night was "I think I'm going to like Leslie."

I tried to be circumspect with my mother. After all, if my father married Tracy, she'd be my stepmother, and if there were future family occasions, especially of the joyous kind, wouldn't I want the atmosphere *not* to be poisonous? I might have let slip some of the adjectives I meant to stifle, such as "domineering," "insensitive," and "hypersexual," but I was careful to balance those with compliments about her decor.

Her first question was "Does he seem happy?"

"On a scale of one to ten? I'd give it a four."

"And would you put it at four for Tracy, too?"

"She'd probably give herself an eight-point-five. But this is very unscientific." I advised her to tread lightly, to repeat none of that to Dad. "On the other hand, if he writes you about last night's visit, would you forward those e-mails to me?"

"He asked me not to show it to you."

"How about reading it to me?"

"Faith, let's make a deal. You won't ask to read every e-mail your father sends, and I won't quiz you about Tracy. Deal?"

I said, "That's a lousy deal. He's my father. Tracy is the common enemy. She's renamed him Hank."

"If there's something I think you should see, I'll forward it."

"Did he say anything about Nick?"

"He said he thought Nick was a mensch."

"And I was a brat? And we left in a big huff?"

"You're not tricking me into any more information swapping" — quickly followed by "Oops."

"Oops what?" I asked.

"Photos. Can we make an exception to our deal? I assume you took one of Tracy?"

I had, as she'd requested. But the two I'd snapped showed Tracy looking young, Titian haired, laughing, and happy — even better and taller than in person — so much so that I'd deleted it.

I said, "Oh, darn. I forgot."

"Is it Nick?" she asked. "Your new lack of focus?"

"It depends. Are you going to fight me on that?"

"Why would I? Is anything sacred? I married a Jewish man from a Jewish home, and where am I now? Alone."

"You're not alone."

"You know what I mean. My husband left me for a trophy paramour who thinks he's an artistic brand instead of an artist."

"Hank Frankel," I said, "walking cliché."

"Who's sorry now?" she asked.

44

❀

Is That a Yes?

ADDING TO THE CURSES visited upon 10 Turpentine Lane, I would count the sudden appearance of Brooke. Was she surveilling the house? At least on this Friday it seemed that way, since our doorbell rang approximately five minutes after we pulled in the driveway.

It took me a few seconds to grasp who this was on my porch in high-heeled boots and a fur coat made of something white and sheepdog shaggy. I heard no hello, no apology for dropping in unannounced. "Is Nick home?" she asked.

I said, "Hi, Brooke. I'm the doorman, Faith. We met at your party" — in a tone meant to remind her of her past unpleasantness.

"I need to speak to Nick," she said.

I left her on the porch, in a show of no greater hospitality than what I'd extend to a purveyor of religious brochures. Nick was reading the sports page splayed on the kitchen table, so involved in March Madness that he hadn't taken his coat off yet.

"You have a visitor on the porch," I said. "It's Brooke. I'll go up-stairs."

Why didn't he yell to me when the coast was clear? I came down after hearing the door slam shut and a car roar off. "What did she want?" I asked.

She wanted him. She'd changed her mind and was rescinding the marriage ultimatum. Any timetable, any venue, any kind of ring, even none, would be okay. Could they try again without any pressure or deadlines?

"And your answer was . . . ?"

"I think you can guess."

No, I couldn't. I was afraid to guess, because bad news — especially lately — simply flew in the window in the form of uni-formed policemen, brazen women, and the undead. He went back behind his newspaper, feet crossed on the coffee table, leaving me uninformed and paralyzed. And worse, he was hum-ming.

"Nick?"

He lowered the page and smiled.

"Not funny!" I cried.

"You earned it — ye of little Faith."

I plopped down next to him. "So, did you say, 'Sorry, Brooke, that ship has sailed'? And for good measure, 'Even though it's only been a few months since I've been with Faith . . . when the right one comes along —'"

"Pretty close."

I motioned, coachlike. *More please.*

"I told her everything had changed. She asked when, and I said, 'Oh, about a week after I moved in.'"

"Did *I* know that?"

"You should. You started it."

He liked to say that. It referred to my appearance at the breakfast table, on Christmas morning, scantily clad — a standing joke. Faith as wanton woman. I didn't mind one bit.

Stuart called, asking to speak to Nick, apparently soon after Brooke returned to their apartment. I said, "Can I take a message?"

"How about you forward me to his cell?"

"I don't know how to, and wouldn't if I could. Case closed."

"I'll just say it then. Brooke poured her heart out to him. It took days for her to work up the courage and lay it all out on the line. He sent her away without even a hug."

"Stuart? How old are you?"

"You know how old I am."

"Is that what you learned from your aborted mission across the country wearing a sign that said FREE HUGS? That a hug means anything? Because everyone hugs now. It's the new hello and good-bye and the new handshake. Meaningless! Is that what you were going to scold Nick about? Because I'm going to save you the indignity of being laughed at."

"I don't know who you are anymore," he said. "And it makes me so sad."

"Tell it to your memoir," I said. "How's that coming?"

"I'm working on it now, full-time."

I knew what that meant. No more job.

I said, "Well, good luck with everything. I'll give Nick your message."

"Brooke needs a roommate," he said. "I'm moving out."

"To where?"

There was a long enough pause that I guessed the answer. "Back in with your mom and Rebecca?"

"My mom's Rebecca. You mean Iona."

"Okay, Iona. Is that a yes?"

"Temporarily. Until the baby's born."

I had a panicked few seconds thinking Brooke was pregnant with Nick's baby until I remembered Stuart's insemination contribution. "What happens then?" I asked.

"I'll be watching the baby when the moms go back to work — in exchange for room and board."

"What do you know about babies?"

"A lot, by the time he's born. They have books, and I'm watching YouTube videos. We're having a boy. That's the whole idea: role modeling, a male influence, which I hope doesn't sound like gender stereotyping."

"You'd be the last person I'd accuse of gender stereotyping."

"It was their idea. Well, Rebecca's idea: first to consider me as the sperm donor and then as their governor."

I coughed out, "Governor?"

"That's the masculine form of governess. I think it has more dignity than *manny*."

"Will this little boy know you're his father? Is he going to call you Daddy?"

"To be negotiated. Besides, don't babies take several months before they start talking?"

"Oh, brother."

"Where did you say Nick had gone?"

"Nowhere. But I'll tell him that it was unforgivable that he didn't give Brooke a hug before she stormed out" — which produced a snicker from Nick, now stretched out on the couch and listening to every word.

"Also, if he knows anyone who needs a place to crash," Stuart continued. "Well, more than that. Someone who could take my place at Brooke's."

I told him I was surprised Brooke would want to stay in Everton without a real job and — not to be unkind — any friends.

He told me I was sounding judgmental. Brooke considered online retailing very much a real job. "As for friends, she's in a book group. And she considers Nick a friend even if it's officially over."

I said, "It's been officially over long before today."

"You'd know that, of course, being an expert on 'officially over,' as if there's no continuum. No second chances."

I knew what he meant: our breakup. I didn't acknowledge that, hating to admit I once tolerated him and wore his mangy red thread around my finger.

Stuart said, "Let's face it. Brooke needs a man."

"Other than you, I take it."

"I offered. But we both get that our values are incompatible. Maybe you know someone?"

"Seriously? Who are the two least likely people in all of Everton and possibly the wide world to find Brooke a man? What could I say to recommend her to anyone?"

"That she has a two-bedroom apartment, a car —"

"Plus a nasty streak and no manners. I can't believe you even asked."

"You guys work outside the home. You interact with people. I don't know why you'd feel like it's a weird request."

"Because Nick is her ex-boyfriend and because she's never been anything but rude to me. How's that?"

"You'd be doing me a favor. She can't make the whole rent herself. It's kinda up to me to find my replacement. Apparently, I signed something."

"Is that so? You 'signed something.' Would that be a quaint document known as a lease?"

"I guess so."

Just to get him off the phone, I said, "Okay. I'll think about it. But it's a big ask: to find Brooke a date-slash-roommate. Even if I knew someone . . . oh, never mind. It's never going to happen."

"You *do* know someone. Who is it? Your brother? A friend of your brother's?"

"No one. Forget it."

"Give me his name and I'll make it happen."

Whom did I know who was downsizing, single, male, deserving of Brooke, and vice versa? Not Reggie O'Sullivan. I swear I didn't mean to speak that name.

45

Poor Chagall

AFTER ONLY ONE VAGUE hint by me, my wonderful brother drove to Newton on a snow-free Saturday morning in late March, rang Tracy's bell, told the pre-teen who answered that he needed to speak to Henry Frankel.

"He's busy," said the little girl, later determined to be Alexis.

"Which way?" my brother asked, taking the first step into the foyer.

"Hank!" the little girl yelled. "Come quick!"

"What is it *now?*" my father answered.

"A stranger!"

"I'm not a stranger," Joel said. "See the truck in the driveway? Frankel Towing and Plowing? Frankel. Like Henry."

"If you don't go away, I'm calling 911," and with that, she brandished a sequined pink phone.

"Don't be such a twit," said Joel. "I'm his son. He's coming home for a visit."

How did I learn of the rescue/intervention? A three-word text from my mother on Sunday morning: **Joel got Daddy.** After just two tries, I had my hard-to-reach brother on the phone, but only because Leslie was good enough to answer when she saw my caller ID. "I'll put him on," she said, adding, "Quite the day."

Joel reported, "I didn't make up some excuse. I told him he was coming with me."

"Did you say permanently? Or did he think it was going to be, like, dinner with us?"

"He knew. He took his white-noise machine and as much as he could stuff in one suitcase."

"Where was Tracy during this commotion?"

"Not home. Shopping with the other kid."

"So you charged into the kitchen?"

"He came out into the — what do you call that thing? It had a tree in it."

"Atrium."

"He came out, and said, 'Joel! What are you doing here?' I said, 'Not exactly the welcome I was hoping for. Want to go for a ride in my truck?'"

"He said he couldn't leave because the kid would be alone. 'Where's your mother?' I asked her. 'Can you call her?' I was being extra nice because she looked like she was going to start bawling."

"And was Dad reassuring her that you were his son and she shouldn't be afraid?"

"No! Did I mention Leslie was with me? I figured some sensitivity might come in handy. By this time, Dad was upstairs, grabbing more than I expected him to come back with. Leslie asked, 'What's your name, honey? . . . Alexis? This is Joel Frankel. Henry is his daddy. He hasn't seen him in weeks. I bet you miss your dad, too.'"

"Kinda brilliant," I told him.

"She's right here," he said, "so I can't pay her too many compliments." I heard Leslie's laugh.

Six days later we were three Frankels across — father, son, daughter — in the cab of Joel's truck, returning to Wingate Terrace to reclaim his artwork. We'd called in advance. Tracy said she would be present, along with her brother, also a lawyer — a big guy, in case our father had some notion about taking *Blue Mitzvah*.

"Who does she think I am?" Dad asked us. "A shmuck who'd steal a painting that she commissioned and paid for?"

"As if you'd want a portrait of her little brat," I said.

"Zoe had her moments, but she was basically a good kid."

"Isn't her name Chloe?" I asked.

My father shrugged. He was looking out the window, commenting every so often on the height of the snow drifts or denigrating the occasional lane-changing drivers.

Today's return to Newton was the first time I was seeing him since Tracy's dinner party had gone so wrong. "Where did you think Joel would be taking you?" I asked him.

"Home. Your mother and I were in touch."

"E-mailing, I heard."

"And talking."

"And how's that going?"

"*Mezza mezza*. Relief, then some anger bubbles up. But I deserve it. I'm sure my children agree."

I did agree, but we were on a mission to the enemy camp. What if he was welcomed back with kindness and forgiveness, leading to a change of heart? I reached for his closest hand, and said, "Remember in the first *Godfather* movie? When Michael Corleone sees that beautiful Sicilian girl for the first time and he's thunderstruck? That's what happened to you."

My father said, "No, it didn't."

I gave Joel a nudge. *Pay attention. We're getting to the crux of this ugly matter.*

"She was relentless," Dad said. "I was living alone. She loved my work. I let my guard down."

"And that turned out to be what? Disappointing? Not the key to happiness?" I prompted.

"Do you know she offered to sit for me? To be my model? Where do you think that led? Did you ever see *The Nude Above Vitebsk*? She thought that would be her ticket in. I let it be! I didn't know her or what I was getting into!"

I almost left it there, but I couldn't help myself. "When Joel and I had lunch with you, and you were telling us about Tracy, you were reciting poetry. And so deeply in love that you didn't touch your frittata."

"I wish I could take it all back."

"You have," said Joel. "You're back with Mom."

When Dad didn't answer, I said, "You *are* back together, right? You're not staying at your studio?"

"I'll paint there. Your mother and I are taking it one day at a time. Or maybe one argument at a time."

"How about couples counseling? That couldn't hurt," I said.

Joel said, "Maybe Mom needs to punish you for a while. Maybe she's in the driver's seat and enjoying it."

Dad looked not happy but resigned, possibly hopeful, like a man accepting the terms of his parole.

❧

Tracy's brother answered the front door, dressed expensively for the gym, and greeted us with "We were expecting Hank, not an entourage."

I said, "Well, he wasn't expecting anyone here to lend a hand. And his name isn't Hank."

My father said, "I'm here for my belongings."

"And his car," I said.

"Do you have proof of ownership for that car?" the brother had the nerve to ask.

I said, "This is offensive! He's not stealing anything. He's taking what belongs to him. We're here to get the rest of his clothes and his paintings —"

"Where's Tracy?" Joel asked.

"My sister is up in her room."

"I'd like to meet her," said Joel. He'd warned me of this in advance, that he needed to see who had bewitched our father, had disrespected our mother, and disrobed in front of a stranger, uninvited.

"What's the point?" my father asked Joel.

"Closure," I said. "Like when the victim's family visits the prison to meet the murderer."

"I resent that," said Tracy's brother.

"Don't you think she'd want to supervise the deacquisitioning?" I asked.

"Right," said Joel. "In case we jack the silver."

The brother said, "Just get on with it."

My father pointed to the eggplant-purple room straight ahead, site of the ill-fated party. "I'm taking everything that your sister didn't commission."

"I don't know how I can even look at them now," a voice said — Tracy's — from the curving stairway.

I said, needlessly, "Joel, this is Tracy."

"I'm the son," he said. "We'll be out of your way as soon as we load the truck."

Tracy said, "Hank? Can we talk? In private?"

All eyes shifted to my father, the once-champion salesman, never at a loss for words. But all he managed was "I'd rather not."

"Whose idea was this?" she yelled at Joel and me. "You think he's going to be happy living in Podunk, painting whatever he feels like when the mood strikes him?"

"Oh, wouldn't that be a crime," I yelled back. "Painting whatever he wants to — art instead of business! Not Chagalls customized for every Jewish festival!"

"I've told you I'm sorry, Trace," my father said. "I've explained as best I could . . ."

"His clothes are where?" asked Joel.

"And my camel overcoat?"

"I gave everything to Fernanda," said Tracy.

"You *what?*" said my father.

"Clothes and shoes. Fernanda has three sons and a husband. And what doesn't fit them she sends to Ecuador. How did I know you were coming back?"

"Passive aggression," I said. "Very nice."

"I just want the paintings," my father said.

"You're lucky I didn't give those away, too," she said, still preaching from midstairway. "I was *this* close to copyrighting your Chagalls," she said. "They were *my* idea. *My* brainchild."

That did it. That knocked our tongue-tied, now-furious father out of his stupor. "You want them? You want to give them away? You think anyone besides you wants a fake Chagall. Poor Chagall! I should visit his grave and apologize!"

Joel said, "C'mon, Dad. We'll take that big dark one. Faith, you get the smaller ones, and we're outta here in two trips."

"They have names!" Tracy shouted. "I worked hard on those titles."

Tracy's brother said, "Just go. Take your paintings and leave."

"Your father loved me!" Tracy shouted. "Everything was fine until you came to our opening."

With a red painting in hand — *Bride with Rooster* — I backtracked to the bottom of the stairs. "It's *my* fault? How do you figure that?"

"Asking me questions — your boyfriend did — about how we met, how we became a couple. It came out sounding so cheap. So aggressive. And overly sexualized. It vilified me! And embarrassed your father!"

"If you think it's my fault, be my guest. I've known Henry Frankel my entire life, and so has my brother —"

"Faith," my dad said. "Don't bother."

"Is this ... this desertion because you feel sorry for her?" Tracy yelled.

"Sorry for *me?*" I asked.

Joel said, "Not you. Mom. Let's get out of here." He and my father were inching toward the front door, father and son shouldering Dad's largest and gloomiest painting, a triptych — peasants, Cossacks, a rabbi. Once outside, we wrapped the panels in blankets brought just for that purpose.

When I said, "This one might be my favorite," Dad told me they'd hoped it would be purchased by a synagogue or hang in the offices of a Jewish philanthropy. Tracy had named it, in happier times, *Fleeing the Pogrom.*

46

Why So Touchy?

On our way to work, from the passenger's seat, reading aloud from his phone, Nick asked, "What's this? Brooke wants me to thank you for playing Cupid."

I said, "It's probably an old text referring to Stuart — back when he moved in with her."

"No. It just came. For, quote unquote, playing Cupid? That's not some random phrase. Did you set her up with someone?"

Oh, God, I had; I'd spoken the name Reggie O'Sullivan, an involuntary utterance after Stuart's attempted matchmaking. I said, "When Stuart asked if I knew any single guys, Reggie's name slipped out. I was fresh off a conversation with him, his last day at work — remember? Answered forlornly how he didn't have a girlfriend? Then I forgot about it in all the excitement of kidnapping my father."

By this time, we'd reached campus and were parked in the reserved spot that had come with Nick's promotion. I switched off the ignition, and asked, "Are you sure Brooke wasn't being sarcastic? As in *Gee, thanks, Faith, for fixing me up with the douchi-est guy you know.*"

Nick handed me his phone. "Be my guest. Ask her." I typed **Faith here. Nick gave me your message so just wondering if you were being ironic or sincere.**

The dotted gray cloud told me she was composing a reply. Soon it appeared. **Sincere.**

You're seeing each other? I wrote back.

Her answer was a winking emoji. "It's true," I told Nick. "She wasn't being sarcastic."

"It's asinine," he said. "Ridiculous." But clearly not delivered in the good-humored way in which he most often disparaged our old boss.

After work, in our kitchen, salad greens being rinsed, the radio was on, a local anchor reporting from Red Sox spring training. I said, "Spring! I wish." Then, feeling the need to fill the void, I continued, "One year my father took Joel and me to spring training. Dad caught a foul ball and told the player that *I'd* caught it, so sign it to me. Now I think that Dad was easy with the white lies. Imagine if I'd known then what was ahead."

"His affair, you mean."

"Everything. Who could have predicted that fiasco? Tracy! Talk about an unlikely couple." And thinking of my brother living with Stuart's ex-sister-in-law, and the unmentionable Brooke and Reggie, I added, "A lot of that going around."

Nick was standing by the cupboard, one hand on the stack of plates, suddenly motionless. "Is that how you see us: 'unlikely'?"

"Not in a bad way. I mean, yes, we were both involved with other people when we started working together, so it wasn't the likeliest hookup."

"Hookup, really? Like Reggie and Brooke — *that* match made in heaven?"

"Those two again? Don't be ridiculous. There's no comparison." But I couldn't leave it at that. I had to throw out, "Why so touchy? What is it about my accidental matchmaking that annoys you so much? Is it Reggie with Brooke? Or *anyone* with Brooke?"

"I don't deserve that," he said. "I'm not the one with the Brooke hang-up."

We'd never before exchanged a single harsh word. "Would that be a crime, to feel insecure about the previous live-in girlfriend — correction, *hot* live-in girlfriend — who came knocking on our door wanting you back? I wouldn't call that a hangup. I'd call it normal girlfriend anxiety."

I looked up to gauge his reaction, expecting to hear more words I'd have to worry about. But he was smiling.

"You're smiling," I said.

"I could be."

"Then we're not having a fight?"

"If this is your idea of a fight, then you were raised in the most civilized home in America."

Was that true? I said, "I think you're right, up to my father's artistic period."

"I know I'm right." He gestured around the kitchen. "Haven't you noticed what we have here? It's calm. It's easy. It's pretty great."

"Do you mean us?"

"As opposed to the ancient linoleum and sixty-amp service? Yes, us."

"In that case, whew."

He asked if I'd tortured the salad long enough. I stuck a finger

in the bowl for a vinaigrette assessment. "Needs a little lemon,"
I said. "I think there's one in the right-hand crisper."

"Sure," he said. "Coming up."

Relief was making me brave. "Watch out for the elephant in
the room," I called.

That stopped him, just as I'd intended it to.

I said, "I'm going to make a declaration. Here it comes . . . not
to scare you, not that you have to answer, but I've been meaning
to tell you that I really love you."

It took a few long seconds before I heard an unsatisfactory
"Thank you."

That had inspired nothing except a change of subject. He
said, "You know, I'm not really in the mood for salad and —
what else was it going to be?"

"Cabbage soup."

"That should keep. How about if we go out?"

I said sure. Okay. The soup would be better tomorrow.

"I'm thinking La Grotta."

We were going, at this awkward juncture, to a restaurant?
Common wisdom reminded me that breakups are supposed to
be less messy when delivered in public. "Isn't it something we
can discuss here?" I managed to ask.

Later he told me I'd turned pale and looked so worried that
he had to spill the beans.

He said no, not here. No way. Who did I think I was dealing
with — a man who got down on his knee in the crappy kitchen
of the murder site we called home? Or my partner in crime and
life and second chances, Nicholas Paul Franconi?

47

News

NICK AND I DIDN'T rush into announcing what we were rather coyly calling "our understanding." He did phone his father, too far away to meddle or spill the beans. Mr. Franconi wasn't thrilled about the Jewish part. But Nick, winking at me, said yes, sure, we'd go to pre-Cana conferences; sure, we'd raise the children Catholic. Locally, we chose my brother to tell first, the family member least likely to ask questions about insurance beneficiaries, florists, caterers, and who'd officiate at our mixed marriage.

We disguised the invitation, said it was time I met Leslie and for Joel to have more than a passing acquaintance with Nick. How about dropping by for a drink? Saturday night? Six, six thirty, so it doesn't interfere with your evening plans?

Which explains why he took the "dropping by" so casually that he showed up with not only Leslie — tall, dark hair artfully twisted, in jeans and boots and a sweater that was surely not purchased in Everton — but also his buddy Brian Dolan and Mrs. Brian Dolan. All four were on their way to a movie, Joel explained. He thought, having heard that Brian had set up shop here, that I'd be pleased to see him off duty, too.

After securing two more glasses from the kitchen and pouring the champagne, Nick cleared his throat in hammy fashion, and said, "First, welcome, everyone. Leslie, very nice to meet you. Faith and I think you've been an excellent influence on Joel, who now answers his phone and returns messages at least fifty percent of the time."

Leslie raised her glass and gave a little bow.

"And welcome, Brian and Patty. Patty, I don't know if Brian's told you that our basement has become his second home. Sure, the neighbors think Faith and I are under house arrest, but we hold our heads high nonetheless" — apparently a cue for Brian to ask, "Did the chief call you?"

I said no. Was there news about the bloodstains?

"Bloodstains? Do I know about this?" Leslie asked Joel.

"Ancient history," he told her. "The previous owner probably killed a couple of her husbands here."

"Allegedly," said Brian.

Shop talk inspired Joel to announce, "I'm on the police department's tow list as of this week."

Nick said, "Wow. Quite the get. Was that bid out?"

Brian said, "No. We maintain a list and we call them in order."

Patty Dolan asked, "Is that what we're celebrating?"

Finally, the needed segue! I slipped my arm around Nick's waist. "Want to take this one?"

"Ladies and gentlemen," he began. "We've gathered you here tonight — well, not exactly Brian and Patty, but you're totally welcome — to tell you that the most wonderful woman I've ever shared an office with . . . has asked me to marry her!"

"I did not! You asked *me*."

He said, "I did, didn't I!"

"At La Grotta," I told them. "But not officially until dessert."

"She made a scene."

"I cried. The people at the next table asked if I was okay."

Nick said, "I told them, 'I just asked her to marry me. I think this is how she says yes.' They sent two glasses of champagne over. It turned out that he was an alum."

"Of course he was," said Joel. "By the way, Nick, I called it."

"No, you didn't," I said. "You only predicted that it wouldn't stay platonic."

"It was never platonic," said Nick. "Or was that my overactive imagination?"

"So it's official?" Patty Dolan asked.

I said, "Yes, and you're the first to know."

Hugs and high-fives were exchanged. Patty took my left hand for a quick survey then dropped it quickly. I said, "He's not allowed to buy me a ring due to previous bad associations with that custom."

"How long have you known each other?" Leslie asked.

I asked Nick, "When did I start at ECD? Two years ago? Eighteen months?"

"It'll be two years on September 30," he said.

I kissed him for that, for an anniversary date I didn't know he'd been observing.

"I fell first," Nick said. "But we were waylaid by complications."

"On both sides," I said.

"Isn't there always?" said Leslie. "And as a former relative by marriage of the dick who was one of those complications, I'd say the best man won."

"What higher compliment than that?" said Nick.

"Have you told Mom and Dad?" Joel asked.

"Not yet. Soon. This was our trial run."

Brian said, "I feel a little funny. Like we crashed your engagement party."

"Nonsense," said Nick. "You're our forensic family."

"Let me take pictures," said Patty. "At least we can do that much. The family portrait won't have to be a selfie."

"In front of the fireplace would be good," I said.

Leslie said, "Just you three, really, Faith and Nick and Joel," steering me by the shoulders between the two men.

I waited for Joel to agree, surely remembering photos documenting life with his short-term ex-wife. Instead, he said, "No, Les. You're in the picture if it's okay with the bride and groom."

"Of course."

Nick said, "How did it get this far that I'm marrying a Frankel and I've only met Joel in the driveway?"

"A hundred and ten inches of snow," said Joel. "There's your answer."

"Say 'whiskey,'" Patty directed, then snapped away.

Nick said, thankfully with a grin, "So, Joel, I understand you told your mother I was gay."

"Look how well that worked out," Joel said. "It was kind of brilliant of me."

"And entirely fictional," I added for the Dolans' benefit. "It was Joel being cute."

"He *is* very cute, isn't he?" said Leslie.

"Can you see why I wanted her in the picture?" Joel asked.

"So do we," I said.

"Have you set a date?" Patty asked.

Nick said, "Not that I know of. Have we?"

I said, "I might let my parents weigh in on that."

"Hullo, ice sculpture and prime rib," said Joel. "Are there any châteaus around that rent out their ballrooms?"

"There's always right here, under our outlaw roof," said Nick. "On Halloween. We'll invite Mrs. Lavoie and Theresa."

I said, "I'm going to make a toast now."

The group went silent. "Nick?" I said. "I should probably save this for our wedding, but in case we elope — and there's no one there to hear it except some strangers at city hall enlisted as witnesses — let me say this now: I look back and I picture that former person — me — sharing an office with you, my secret crush . . . if anyone had told me then that we would live together, that we'd food shop and cook and drive to work in one car, let alone kiss . . . let alone share a bed. And now this! Engaged . . . well, I never would've believed her, that former me. I pinch myself every day."

Nick said so softly, so heretofore un-Nick-like, that we all leaned closer, "Me, too, kid." Then: "In that office, watching you blot the sentences you'd written with your fountain pen. And eat cheese sandwiches you brought in a wax-paper bag. I thought it was obvious. I thought you could tell. I thought we'd be sent to Human Resources jail."

"Now you kiss," said Leslie.

Was it Nick or I who asked Brian before he left, "Anything new on the case?"

He grimaced. "I didn't think this was the time or the place to talk business —"

Nick said, "What better place than this?"

"It will probably be in the *Echo* tomorrow."

What did I expect to hear that didn't fit our happy occasion? That Anna Lavoie was going free?

"It was Theresa Tindle," Brian said.

It took a few long seconds for that to register.

"The daughter," he said.

"What about her?" I asked.

"Arrested."

Theresa "Terry" Tindle, lately not of Maui, if ever. "Why? What for?"

"Manslaughter."

"Of?" asked Nick.

Brian cocked his head toward the kitchen and beyond.

"The daughter did it?" I whispered. "How do you know?"

"Not from the batty mother, I assume," said Nick.

"The sister came to us," he said.

What sister? Jeannette, of course — chronic tipster, the sibling Theresa had never known until I made the match.

Brian said, "I'm only telling you because it's going to be in the paper tomorrow."

"Is she in jail?"

"Out. On bail."

"She must've been a kid when she did it," I said.

"Not a kid under the law. Sixteen. And was sent away. She pushed the first stepfather, and her mother apparently thought it was such a good idea, and easy — if a kid could do it — *whammo*. Good-bye, husband number three."

I asked if Mrs. Lavoie had been rearrested — if there was such a thing.

"She's already in custody. Don't forget she's ninety-one. Just had a birthday . . ."

"What about the blood? All that crime-scene investigation in my still-torn-up basement."

"We know the blood was from males. Head injuries bleed a lot. But no match and no likelihood of a match."

"I take it you didn't exhume either body?" I asked.

"No need. Couldn't anyway. Both men were very conveniently cremated."

"And how did Jeannette piece this together?" Nick asked.

"She didn't have to piece it together. Tindle confided in her. And if you thought it was a confession, unburdening herself, forget it. She was bragging! *You hated my mother? I hated her worse! I did her this big favor, made it look like an accident, and what thanks did I get? She sent me away to a home for bad girls, so you and I, sis — neither one of us had it so great.*"

"So now I know who I bought my house from: a teenage murderess."

Leslie said, "But if you hadn't bought this house, you and Nick might never have become housemates, let alone objects of each other's affections."

Nick said, "Oh, I think we would have, regardless."

I said, "Ten Turpentine Lane's best work."

Patty asked, "Think you'll stay here?"

I said, "Murder times two? By four hands? I could sell tickets to this place."

"Let's change the subject," said Brian. "Too much shop talk."

"It's our turn to toast the happy couple," said Patty.

"*L'chaim,* right?" her husband asked.

48

Nancy Knows

I T WAS JEANNETTE PEPPERDINE who called to tell me that Mrs. Lavoie had died. What did one say to the unwanted birth daughter of an alleged criminal and sociopath? Consolation would sound hollow. I asked Mrs. Pepperdine how she was taking it.

"I'm taking it by functioning as the next of kin, making the arrangements."

"Not Theresa?"

"She has an ankle bracelet, if that's what it's called. She can't leave her apartment."

"How did you hear that Anna died?"

"The warden called her lawyer. Somehow, from some list of contacts, it trickled down to me. An officer came to my home."

"That's nice. Like police on TV do."

"Nothing is nice about this," she said.

I asked what Mrs. Lavoie died of.

"Probably old age. She went to sleep and didn't wake up."

"No autopsy? Wouldn't that be the usual protocol when someone dies in prison?"

"How and why would *I* know what prison protocol is?"

"Sorry. Of course you wouldn't. Well . . . thank you for letting me know."

"There's something at O'Donnell's Funeral Home on South Main at eleven a.m. tomorrow."

"A funeral?"

"A service, we're calling it."

"Not at a church?"

"I tried. I called Sacred Heart and Saint Stephen's. No one returned my calls. Apparently priests read the newspaper."

I said I'd try to attend, but it was a work day. I'd have to ask the head of my department.

Next to me in bed, Nick said, "Go. It could be fascinating. I'll hold down the fort. But I can think of an obvious plus-one for this occasion."

I called my mother. "Delighted," she said. "We'll make a day of it."

She was dressed for a celebrity's funeral in an Ascot-worthy black hat and a black suit with a lavender silk rose pinned to her lapel.

"Dad didn't want to come?" I asked.

"He's painting."

"Here?"

"At the studio, night and day. Or so he says."

"'So he says'? That doesn't sound very friendly."

She shrugged. "He thinks all he had to do was come home. He says that if you look at all the years we've been together his time with Tracy was just a grain of sand passing through the hourglass of life."

"*Dad* said that?"

"It's from some song. I said, 'Henry, it's me. I'd prefer if you didn't wax poetic.'"

There was no man or woman of the cloth presiding. The first person to speak was the warden of the county jail where Mrs. Lavoie had spent her final months. He was red faced, chubby, barely contained in a suit and tie. He said, "Welcome friends, family, neighbors. I was asked by Anna Lavoie's family to say a few words — not only was Mrs. L. in my Golden Age unit, but from what they tell me, I knew her at her most . . . cooperative. And a sharp cookie! Oh, boy, was she ever. She had visitors, too, not just her lawyer. And she taught some fellow inmates to crochet. Because she had a cell to herself, by which I don't mean she was in solitary, she got to decorate it the way she wanted. Was she happy? She wasn't miserable. I guess all that's left to say is rest in peace, Mrs. L., no trial to worry about now. You made a nice dent in paying your debt to society." He checked a sheet of paper on the podium. "Okay. Next you'll hear from Mrs. Jeannette Pepperdine. Thank you."

Jeannette, in a not-particularly-somber paisley dress, began, "I didn't know Anna Lavoie for most of my life. She gave birth to my twin sister, Josephine, and me after what she liked to call a liaison with our birth father. For obvious reasons, we were her big secret. She didn't raise us, didn't want to, but something wouldn't let her give us up entirely. I think I have a better appreciation of that now. We were able to talk about it for the first time on my last visit. I can't absolve her of her sins or pardon her crimes, but I *can* say" — she turned to the coffin — "I don't think growing up under your care and under your roof would have been right or godly for any of us. Ironically, you did what

was best for Josie and me." She turned to Theresa in the front
row, seated next to plainclothed Brian Dolan. "I'd like to take
this opportunity to speak to my half sister . . . Theresa? I know
you're furious with me, but I had to tell the authorities what you
told me about your role in your stepfathers' so-called accidents.
I have to sleep at night. And maybe, with the truth finally out,
you can, too."

"Thanks so much," Terry hissed. "I didn't kill anybody. I was
exaggerating. I was *joking!*"

"Then you'll plead innocent," said Jeannette. "And you'll have
your day in court."

"I was a kid!" Terry yelled.

"I'm sorry. I did what I thought was right —"

"Fuck *you!*"

Who was in charge here? Wasn't anyone going to referee? My
mother stood up. "I've heard enough. This is a memorial service
no matter what skeletons are in your closets. There's a time and
a place for everything," which prompted the funeral director
to announce from the back of the half-empty room that burial
would be at Holy Sepulcher on Route 27, exactly eight-tenths of
a mile after the traffic light on Upper Hope.

"Who's going to show up for *that?*" my mother whispered.

"Not us," I said.

Why would I be surprised that a reporter would attend Anna
Lavoie's funeral? I'd noticed the scruffy young man in a cordu-
roy jacket scribbling furiously, but why was he walking in my
direction?

He wasn't. He wanted the ID of the woman who'd called for
an end to the sisters' shouting match. Name and relation to the
deceased?

"Nancy Frankel. No relation. Someone had to speak up. I

thought their behavior was disgraceful, and you can quote me on that."

"You must've known Anna Lavoie if you came to her funeral," he said.

"I'm here simply because my daughter asked me to accompany her."

"And that's you?" he asked me. "Name?"

"Faith."

"Faith what?"

"She bought the deceased's house," my mother supplied.

"Knowingly?" he asked me.

I said I didn't understand the question.

"Did you know people died there under suspicious circumstances when you bought it?"

I said, "No comment. I don't need my name in the paper. And I surely don't need my address in there."

"It's *been* in," my mother said. "As the scene of the crimes. Did you *not* read the front-page story when the Tindle daughter was arrested?"

"Above the fold," said the reporter.

I said I'd missed the write-up; I'd learned of Terry Tindle's arrest last weekend straight from Detective Dolan.

My mother waited until we were in the car. After clicking her seat belt into place and as she checked her lipstick in the visor mirror, she asked, "When did Detective Dolan fill you in? Maybe the other night when he came over to your house with Joel, amid the celebration?"

Uh-oh. "Celebration?" I repeated, despite knowing exactly what I was being accused of.

"The little party celebrating your upcoming *wedding*."

"Is that what Joel told you? That we had a party?"

"He thought I knew — me being the woman who gave birth

to and raised you. Leslie was shushing him in the background after he divulged the big secret."

"Mom, it wasn't because —"

"Is it true? Are you and Nick getting married?"

"Please let me explain. Telling Joel was a dry run. The real announcement is coming . . . I wanted to tell you and Dad over a proper lunch or dinner, which is where we're headed" — something I didn't know myself until this second — "to the hotel dining room. I wanted it to be ceremonial, with tablecloths and flowers, not just a drop-by visit or a phone call. I wanted to do it right. You know why? Because of this quite amazing thing that's happened. Because of Nick. I didn't want to just pick up the phone —"

"It's not about Nick," she said.

"It's *only* about Nick, thank you." I started the car. "So do we go to lunch or would you rather start your boycott now?"

"We go to lunch. There won't be a boycott." She reached over and gave my hand an apologetic squeeze. We were the last car left in the parking lot; the negligible procession of mourners had pulled away, so I did, too.

"Do you know where you'll hold the ceremony?" she asked, after several minutes of silence. "Or the reception?"

"We haven't discussed that. I think the *when* should come before the *where*."

"I'm not asking church versus temple versus city hall. I'm thinking 'mother of the bride.' How can I get a dress until I know the where *and* the when?"

I said, "Well, I can't get a dress until I know my mother's on board."

I made a quick call to Nick while my mother was inspecting the ladies' room. "My mother knows. Joel told her. I'm at the

Everton Arms, taking her for a fancy lunch, pretending it was my plan all along."

"Good move. Take your time. Even better: tell her it was my idea."

Ten minutes later, along with our salads, two beribboned glasses of champagne arrived. "Compliments of the future groom," said our waiter.

"I heartily approve," my mother told him. "It took some adjusting, but you know what's important? He's a real mensch. And he loves my daughter."

"Hear, hear," I said. We clinked glasses. "And to you and Daddy . . . to better days ahead."

She didn't take a second sip. She put her glass down and said, "I might as well tell you now. It's over."

"Of course it is! I knew it was over from the minute we packed up his brushes and drove away from her house. Actually, from the minute I met that awful woman."

"Not Tracy. I was referring to your father and me."

"*Over?* When he's just returned? I thought it was what you wanted — you were so miserable when he left."

"My life changed. I developed a routine. I swim three mornings a week. I'm in a book group. Dinner can be one lamb chop, or scrambled eggs, or a bag of potato chips. I'm content. Everything on the DVR playlist is mine."

"But that's all so . . . nothing. You can still have all of that."

"That may be true, but I saw who your father really was. I didn't like it then, and I don't like it now."

"Now? When did you decide this?"

"Actually, today. At the funeral, as the whole dysfunctional scene played out. Here was a woman who had to be miserable in her marriages, but she couldn't admit it, couldn't hire a lawyer, couldn't file for divorce, couldn't leave. She wanted out, so she killed them. What kind of life is that even if she wasn't caught for fifty years? And she didn't want to keep her black babies for fear of what people would say, but she couldn't cut that thread, either. So I sat there and I asked myself, *What do you want, Nancy? Henry or no Henry? The insurance salesman turned Romeo turned Hank?* Suddenly, it was crystal clear."

"But, Ma — there's a middle ground between staying married and pushing your husband down the stairs."

"Correct. You ask him to leave."

"So Anna Lavoie is your reverse role model? She died in prison so you don't have to? And what's stopping you from swimming three mornings a week and having potato chips for dinner with a husband around?"

"Please, Faithy. Your father will be fine. He might even be relieved. We'll stay friends. We'll dance at your wedding. And you know who else inspired me? You! Wedding bells ahead! That's my second epiphany of the day. Because you're so happy, I can do this."

Rolls arrived, capturing too much of my attention to please my mother.

"Faith! That was me looking for a confirmation. I was hoping to hear *You're right, Mom. I've never been happier.* Can you do that for me? I mean if it's true."

"Of course it's true. Ridiculously true."

"I knew that. If it weren't for the Catholic part . . . Well, never mind. I'm on board. I'm fully embracing my role."

"Good," I said. "I think."

"Mother of the bride. MOB . . . finally! I'll be fabulous at that, don't you think? It's just what I needed right now. So thank you." She asked what time I had to get back to work.

"No time," I said. "I'm sleeping with the boss, remember?"

She smiled. "In that case, do you want to peek into the ball-room after dessert?"

No, I did not. Nor did I want to taste test the red velvet and the lemon poppy seed and the banana layer cake with coconut drizzle that she was ordering with an eye toward a future dessert table. Had I thought about attendants? Flowers? Colors?

Not yet. Not once. But she was looking so engaged and so professionally fulfilled that when she exclaimed, "Violets in mason jars! Low-key and very you!" what else could I say but "Perfect!"

49

"Dearest Nick..."

THERESA'S MANSLAUGHTER TRIAL required a change of venue. How was it possible that every potential jury member polled had either read about the case in the *Echo*, had gone to the same high school as the defendant, or had a parent at ManorCare? My mother said she would represent the family at the future trial and could probably get Aunt Elaine to keep her company. She fully understood that I had more pressing, personal things to think about.

Our dogged reporter kept the story alive. He asked if I'd like to write my own so-called mood piece, sharing with readers the experience of living in a house where people had died, some at the hands of previous residents. I said, "Really? You'd like that?" Five minutes later I sent it. **Old bungalow on newly congested street. 2 bdrms, 2 cellar floors, cement & plywood (needs work). Original kitchen. Steep stairs. Interesting history. Best offer.**

The reporter called right back. "Is this supposed to be a joke?"

I said, "I'm not sure."

The *Echo* ran it, with a picture of me filched from the Everton Country Day website, explaining in parentheses that this had been my response to a request for a first-person account of owning an alleged crime scene. "Note: not intended to be a classified ad."

Nevertheless, I heard from Tammy McManus, real estate agent. May she show the house if a serious buyer came along? Some people — not saying they had the healthiest of motives — love the idea of a murder site. Sick or not, how about Saturday morning, eleven a.m.?

I told her I'd have to think about it. But please know this going forward: if anyone is going to make an offer on a house that's not for sale, they'd better make it worth my while. This house has gravitas now. It's got heat. I'd want real money for it.

Nick asked, "Was that what I think it was? A buyer?"

"An agent, doing some wishful thinking."

Two days later, an out-of-town couple visited. It was not customary to have the current occupants present, but we were doing Tammy a favor, and I was curious to see who'd want to buy a notorious deathtrap. Sweet, wide-eyed, with crosses on chains around both of their necks, Betty and Mike Morelli were the answer. They seemed oddly unconcerned about the crimes. Their tour wasn't a thorough one. It was as if their minds had been made up before crossing the threshold, before seeing the rooms or flushing the toilet. I found myself indulging in some negative salesmanship. Had they known about the unsavory things that had be*fallen* previous owners? — earning a frown from Tammy.

"We do," said her husband.

"And that's okay with you?"

The woman said, "We'd take very good care of your house.

We'd probably update the kitchen. But we'd honor its landmark status and its history."

"We're going to make an offer as soon as we know that it's actually for sale," said Mr. Morelli.

"My fiancé and I will decide," I told them. "And if so, we'll put our heads together to come up with an asking price."

"We'll have the right of first refusal?" the wife asked.

"You bet," said Tammy.

After they left, I said, "They struck me as a little woo-woo. I was expecting more . . . I don't know, people who wanted to monetize the place. Sell tickets. Give virtual tours. But I got the opposite impression: that there was an unnatural calm about them."

"Do we care?" Nick asked. "I mean, is there any sentimental value after owning this place for six months?"

I said, "I refuse to answer that question on the grounds that the sentimental value is standing right in front of me."

My hunch was correct. Mrs. Morelli was otherworldly all right. She made her living communicating with the dead.

"What if she's a charlatan?" I asked Nick.

"Perfect, when you think about it," he said.

"Should we put it on the market for real? To see if there might be others out there? A bidding war?"

"Bird in the hand," he said.

We asked them on their victory visit, "Why Everton?"

"She had a dream," explained her husband. "And no one, especially me, ignores Betty's dreams."

"You dreamed about this house?" Nick asked.

"Not exactly," said Mrs. Morelli. "I dreamed I was trying to get paint off my hands — it was oil based — and I was using turpentine, which was very odd because I hadn't been doing any painting and don't own any turpentine. I could even smell it in the dream! So I Googled 'turpentine' as soon as I woke up. And almost every link came up with this address."

Tammy was smiling at them, as if this were as logical as their having skimmed the MLS listings.

"Clearly preordained," said Nick.

"Where were you living when you had this life-altering dream?" I asked.

"Long Island," she said. "But Mike is originally from Worcester."

We told them we had much to do before we could close, because we were getting married in June.

"See?" Mrs. Morelli asked her husband.

"See what?" I asked.

"A lucky house. You two know that already, though, I bet. That carved pineapple on the newel post? That clinched it for us, too."

In June the campus was in full bloom and free of students. The nonsectarian, nondenominational chapel would accommodate our small guest list. To perform the ceremony, we enlisted a judge, married to a woman in my mother's book group, conveniently Jewish. The school's chaplain knew a priest who wasn't too sensitive about blessing mixed marriages and those not held in a proper church, so we asked him to semipreside.

My mother never abandoned the cause. She'd been reading *Brides, Town & Country Weddings, Martha Stewart Weddings* and TheKnot.com. She applied online ("Do you know a bride whose mother's wedding dress needs a makeover?" read the summons) to a reality show devoted to exactly that, repurposing frightful hand-me-downs even though I'd already bought a perfectly beautiful dress off the rack from a sample sale.

We invited no one from the faculty or staff who'd ever sent an unkind word in my direction during the Hepworth crisis. That left a few hockey team members from the faculty; most administrative assistants; the basketball, football, and water polo coaches; and the dining-hall director.

The wedding was going to be short, sweet, dignified, scripted. Until Nick's father, a gray-haired, stocky, shorter version of his son, rose from the front row, took the microphone, making me nervous when he exchanged what might have been a conspiratorial nod with the priest. But then he drew a piece of blue stationery from his inside jacket pocket. He claimed — and we had no proof otherwise to dispute this — that Nick's mother had left this letter to be read at her son's posthumous wedding. "Posthumous for her," he corrected.

He got no further than "Dearest Nick" when the tears came. His wife, Nick's stepmother of only three years, leading with a hanky, left her seat and took over. She prefaced her reading by saying, "I didn't know Susan. But she had lovely taste in everything. And she is a hard act to follow, which I mean in the nicest way possible. On a personal note, I'm grateful to Nicholas myself because he was the one who bugged Paul to go to our class reunion. Soon after, not *too* soon, he asked me out to a show."

She began. Nick's mother, we heard, predicted this would be read on a sunny day — probably not in a church but on a beach. She hoped his father would be there, alive and well. She knew Nick would be standing next to someone who was kind, who was smart, who felt she was the luckiest woman on earth. "Tell her that you were an easy child. You were kind and funny, even as a baby. Tell her that you invited every child in your class to your birthday parties in first, second, and third grades so no one's feelings would be hurt. Do you remember you were class president in fourth grade? And won an art prize in seventh? I hope you're still drawing." The letter ended: "Your father and I had only one child, and we always knew we hit the jackpot. Lucky, lucky us. Be happy. Make her happy. Love always and forever, Mom."

Nick left my side to hug his father and kiss Janet. And then, being Nick, said, "My mother failed to mention that I ran for reelection in fifth grade and lost to Jamie Adler."

We needed that. The air changed. Our short, solemn event was transformed into an open-mike wedding. I joined Nick to say, "Most of you know I do this for a living. No, not the bridal part. Hardly! I mean the letter-writing part, all day long. Mr. Franconi never could have known that a letter from Nick's mother could be such a perfect gift. Every word ... so true. Well, not the beach. But thank you."

In mauve lace, my mother confirmed that Nick had indeed found the wished-for bride foretold in his mother's letter — kind, highly intelligent, a salutatorian, a daughter par excellence. My father read a Shakespearean sonnet he'd brought along, just in case the opportunity arose.

Even my brother spoke. "No one's happier than I am. Faith used to call me every other friggin' day because of one catastrophe or another — she was losing her job, she needed a piece of furniture moved from one side of a room to another. 'Where do I get my tires aligned?' Now she never calls except to check on my love life." He grinned. "Update on that topic available from Miss Leslie Stern at the reception ... so, Nick, I owe ya."

Nick was last. He'd written and illustrated a timeline, interposing our personal, emotional, and professional lives with our domestic history. He'd started with the 1906 certificate of occupancy for 10 Turpentine Lane. Then, born 1926, Anna née Dunne, later Tindle, Tomaszewski, and Lavoie. Mingled with dates of the crimes and scandals were our own birthdays, our starting dates at Everton Country Day, the Friday in November when he moved in. His delivery? Deadpan. "Christmas Day, a mere six months ago," he continued. "Faith comes down to breakfast in a negligee" — which caused the priest to cough. Nick looked up from the flowchart, and said, "Three months ago, on March 22, I propose to Faith Rachel Frankel at La Grotta, the same place, the same table, where on the previous Christmas Eve eve, I'd found the courage to convey, though possibly not in words, that I was in love. And today, this lucky thirteenth day of June, we are married."

Then we were under the embroidered chupa that my mother had been saving for so long. From the video, I know that the judge married us, that an uncle gave a blessing in Hebrew, and the priest said a prayer. The recessional was Mendelssohn. There was lunch at the Everton Arms — salmon in parchment, fashionable cakes, too much champagne, and violets and sweet peas in mason jars.

There were presents and envelopes yet unopened; we had, on an easel for all to admire, a floating bride and groom in the manner of both Marc Chagall and Henry Frankel. The reception spilled out to the terrace, where random hotel diners joined the celebration. "Meet the new Mrs. Franconi," Nick said, as we danced past total strangers. "Don't you agree she's never looked lovelier," making me laugh each time.

I wouldn't have guessed that plain gold bands could be so beautiful. Engraved inside mine: not our initials or the date, but Latin words that translated to *Now I know what love is*.

And all day, just as Nick's mother had promised, writing to us in the future, there was nothing but uninterrupted sun.

Acknowledgments

My deep thanks to: Mameve Medwed and Stacy Schiff, trusted, steadfast first readers and dear friends; Suzanne Gluck, perfect agent personified; Lauren Wein, editor from heaven; Jonathan Greenberg of Sotheby's New York for advice in all matters artistic; James Mulligan, Commissioner, Rockport, Massachusetts, Police Department, for his gracious consultations; Dr. Perri Klass, for providing medical answers; Matt Jacobs, whose faux Chagall, which he painted for the movie set of *Romeo and Juliet in Yiddish*, inspired my character's specialty. And to Eve Annenberg, its star, for that tip.

Q&A with Elinor Lipman

Faith, your narrator, lives at Ten Turpentine Lane, a small, somewhat unappetizing bungalow with a past. Did you know or live in such a place?

Not "live in" but knew. It was a dark, creepy house on my childhood street, in a thicket of overgrown *Fantasia*-like trees and shrubs and weeds — the whole thing looming large in my memory. The owner had been a reclusive widow, always dressed in a long, black, witchy dress, rarely seen. I used to cross the street rather than walk past her house and certainly never trick-or-treated there. Fast-forward forty-plus years and I found out that my best childhood friend had bought the house and had moved in. I was astonished. I was going to write an essay about visiting a house as an adult that had spooked me as a child, but then it struck me as not only a setting for a novel, but a character in the story.

How did you choose "Turpentine" for the name of the street?

By accident. It seemed just right, a nice strong noun — memorable, maybe a little amusing, even if toxic. And not even farfetched: It turns out there are many Turpentine streets (Rd., Cir., Ave., Trail) in the United States.

Faith works at a private school as Director of Stewardship. Is that a real job?

It is! It's the person who writes thank-you notes for a living for an institution. As soon as I heard that such a position really existed out in the world, I thought, "That's going into a novel, pronto." Of course "writing thank-you notes for a living" is an oversimplification, but it fit Faith's somewhat low self-esteem. "Donor relations" is probably what the job description says out there in the real world.

Is it giving too much away to ask about her dad's artistic pursuits?

No! It's one of my favorite plot lines. Spoiler alert: He's taken up painting in retirement, and his specialty is personalizing Chagalls. Weddings, anniversaries, bar and bat mitzvahs — there's always some angels or princesses or donkeys or brides or rabbis to be customized.

How did you come up with that?

An artist friend, Matt Jacobs, painted a fake Chagall for his wife's movie, *Romeo and Juliet in Yiddish*. I asked his permission to borrow that notion for the book. I've been fascinated with the idea of copying and copyists ever since I saw some beautifully done fake Magrittes decorating the walls of a New York restaurant (named Magritte) and was told they weren't prints but actually commissioned for the restaurant. They're not forgeries since they're not passing them off as the real thing. Homages, really. Quite often I fall in love with a painting and think *Hmmm. I wonder what a copy would cost? I'd love that Degas on my wall.*

As for the mission undertaken by Stuart the fiancé. You don't seem to be championing it.

Very true. I know I'm not being fair to people who walk across the country for a cause. But Stuart has no cause, just self-aggrandizement, phony slogans, and Facebook postings. I had a lot of fun with him, all at his expense.

Faith and her family are Jewish. Was that a choice that is central to the story, or could they have been anything?

The way their religion came about is almost embarrassing to admit, but it does illustrate the way I write, sentence by sentence. I don't outline or even know where the story is heading or how it will end. About halfway through, Faith's mother is commenting on a cheating husband. A Yiddish proverb that fit the situation came to mind: "You can't dance at two weddings with one *tuchas*." (*Tuchas* of course being the formal word for tush). Instantly, the family went from Franklin to Frankel. It turned out to be good for the story, creating some useful romantic tension. And with Chagall already in there, the characters seemed to be asking to convert.